UNDERGROUND MAN

UNDERGROUND MAN

a novel

Inspired by American entrepreneur James D. Jameson,
Polish publisher Grzegorz Boguta, and their friendship forged in history

Christina M. Murray

WOLF HOUSE PRESS
DEL MAR | CALIFORNIA

Underground Man: a novel

For information about this title or to order other books and/or electronic media, contact the publisher:

Wolf House Press
2010 Jimmy Durante Blvd., Ste. 205
Del Mar, CA 92014

ISBNs:
979-8-9903050-2-1 (hardcover)
979-8-9903050-3-8 (ebook)

Printed in the United States of America

Cover and Interior Design: Bill Greaves, Concept West

For freedom, solidarity, and those who sacrifice to uphold them.

ВИШГОРОД
Хотянівка
Осещина
Горенка
ПУЩА-ВОДИЦЯ
ШЕВЧЕНКА
ПРІОРКА
ОБОЛОНЬ
ВИГУРІВЩИНА-ТРОЄЩИНА
БЕРКОВЕЦЬ
Вишгородська
ЛІСОВИЙ М
Біличі
НИВКИ
Новобіличі
Сирець
Київ-Петрівка
БІЛИЧІ
СВЯТОШИН
Святошин
КИЇВ
Рубежівський
Борщагівка
Караваєві Дачі
Київ-Пасажирський
Київська Русанівка
Борщагівка
Софіївська Борщагівка
Алмаз
Протасів Яр
ПОЗНЯКИ
Київ-Волинський
Київ
ЖУЛЯНИ
ВИШНЕВЕ
Вишневе
Крюківщина
ТЕРЕМКИ
ОСОКОРКИ
КОРЧУВАТЕ
КИТАЇВ
Крюківщина
ПИРОГІВ
Гатне
Петро Кривоніс
Новосілки
о. Жуків
Тарасівка
Юрівка
Чабани
Хотів
Нове
Віта-Поштова
ЧАПАЄВКА
о. Козачий
Круглик
о. Ольгин
Лісники
Лісники
Малютинка
Кременище
Зайців
Іванковичі
Ходосівка
Мархалівка
Підгірці
Рославичі
Підгірці
Гвоздів
Креничі
Р 27
Р 31
М 07
Е373
М 05
Р 12
Е 95
М 04
Р 10 27
ДНІПРО

Prologue

The bag loomed, a dank cavern wafting a putrid, organic smell. Gustaw gagged and wrenched his neck away, smacking his skull into the concrete behind him. Instant throbbing echoed the sound of the impact, wetting his eyes. He growled at this foolish pain, self-inflicted and humiliating, like a clumsy hurt from childhood.

His left elbow bounced off the same cold wall and set another nerve shrieking. The "funny bone," his American friend James would have called it, though Gustaw found no humor in the sensation.

The coarse fabric passed the crown of his head. He wrenched his shoulders around and felt the balls pull in their sockets. His chair rocked a little, but a slicing burn from the rope was his only reward. His wrists remained twisted together in the small of his back.

The second man grabbed his upper arms and yanked him forward, steadying his torso. Gustaw's eyes closed instinctively as the bag holder shimmied the cloth down, ripping out hair, folding and scraping past his ears as he writhed.

In the movies, this process only took a moment, but Gustaw would make his captors work at it. He felt a careless wrist brush his right cheek and snapped his mouth toward it, chomping into soft flesh and holding on. A fist descended on the side of his head once, twice, before he let go, licking warm salt from his lower lip.

The bag man swore under his breath in Russian, as if he, rather than Gustaw, were the wronged party. But they had already won. With a quick downward thrust, the bottom of the bag hit the top of his head, enclosing him to his neck in its hot, damp ecosystem pungent with the stench of rotten onions and worse.

He stopped struggling then, breathing shallowly through gritted teeth to keep from retching. Something crusty scratched against his left eyebrow, suggesting that a prior occupant of the hood had failed that test.

His captors paused for a couple of heavy, rasping breaths before reaching under his armpits and hauling him to his feet.

"Get moving," hissed a soft voice as something small and hard rammed into his spine, shoving him to a stumbling lurch forward.

Grasping his elbows firmly, they half-guided, half-prodded him out of the room and down a hallway. A bell clanged, and the same clunky elevator from last night jolted them wildly to a stop on a lower floor.

"Walk," the louder one ordered, and a few meters later they were outside in the churning night air.

With each groping step forward, the ground shifted around his shoes. Gravel?

Thunk. His thigh banged into something unmoving, and he pitched forward with a yelp. Cursing his clumsiness, they jerked him upright before he could fall. Then they were both in front of him, dragging him onto a cold, flat surface. He heard one of the men jump down, and the platform shook with the shift in weight. A door slammed, an engine started, and the vehicle was moving him toward an unknown place and an unknown fate.

This was not how Gustaw had imagined this errand going. It should have been simple—a little cash to grease the skids of a deal they wouldn't care about anyway. Easy side money for people whose only interest was money, people who wouldn't even notice that he was also distracting them, buying time for the real plan to succeed. Perhaps he could still accomplish that much.

He lay face up with his torso half-turned onto his left arm and his hands still tied behind his back. His many hurts clamored, but he ignored them and began scissoring his legs slowly. His activity met no resistance, physical or verbal. So, he planted his feet and began scootching his body backward until he encountered a vertical obstruction that seemed flat enough to lean against. When he had elbowed and squirmed himself up to something like a sitting position, he began speaking.

"This is all a big misunderstanding," he said, breezily conversational.

"So you have said," was the dry response.

It was the smarter, soft-spoken one, who had seemed to be in charge throughout the hours of questioning. That must mean the big guy was in front driving, not back here keeping an eye on Gustaw to prevent his escape. How insulting!

He sighed inside the hood. Of course, they were right. He'd never manage to untie his bindings and break out of this moving vehicle, even if they had left him unguarded.

When these men looked at him, they didn't see a revolutionary hero who had helped defeat Communism and reshape the world it left behind. That's how James had always viewed him, despite the passage of time. But these brutish gangsters only saw the gray-haired grandpa with stiffening joints who blinked back at Gustaw from the mirror every day, and that guy was no threat to anyone.

Maybe the American's flattering vision had seeped too deeply into Gustaw's consciousness over the years, emboldening him to disregard the man in the mirror and impersonate that younger man again. Natalya would have said so—did say so, in fact: "I don't like the new government either, but you've done your part. Let the kids' generation sort it out," she'd grumbled. "You're embarrassing yourself with all these meetings—a child playing spy games, a discontented codger with a sports car."

But how could he look away when everything he had worked for was falling apart? Eventually, her spoken objections devolved into subtler protests—stomping feet, banging doors, and household objects deposited too brusquely on surfaces. Then domestic silence descended between them, and Gustaw was free to do as he pleased.

Their marital tension felt depressingly familiar, his third wife's disapproval echoing the first's frustration all those years ago, when they were both so young. Maybe that boy—the ambitious idealist filled with boundless energy, who had let his bride fend for herself and the kids while he and his friends struggled to remake Poland—had been the one playing spy games. It had worked, though, hadn't it? And weren't they all better off for it in the end?

Besides, this was no time to worry about whether his wife—current or former—might someday forgive him or be proud of him, let alone to wonder if she still loved him. And he certainly didn't have the luxury, bound and bruised in a fast-moving vehicle driven by gangsters, of asking himself whether he would ever see her again.

Gustaw could use some of his younger self's boundless energy now. He took a too-deep breath inside the hood and had to choke down the acid that rose in his throat. It had been a long night, but he wasn't done trying to engage with his captors. *I used to be good at this,* he reminded himself. And he still was, frankly, or he'd probably be safe at home in Warsaw.

Anyway, the stakes were too high to give up—or consider the personal cost. He and the Ukrainian kid had a plot to expose. He just hoped the kid's part of the plan was going better.

"Somehow you've gotten the wrong idea about me," he started again. "I came to you with a simple business proposition."

"You came as a spy," spat the other man. Even through the hood, his voice was louder than Gustaw had heard him speak before. "You've been chattering all night long about secret police and corporate lawyers and some company you claim to be starting, but you still haven't answered the one question I have grown very tired of asking: Who sent you to Ukraine?"

"No one sent me. I work only for myself," Gustaw insisted, probably for the fiftieth time, although it wasn't exactly true.

Technically, James had sent him, though not for this purpose. The well-heeled American would be astounded—but maybe a little impressed?—to see him now. It was Gustaw's final thought before a solid object slammed into his left temple, ending the conversation.

NOWE
MIASTO
STARE
MIASTO
Ogród
Zoologiczny
Park Praski
PRAGA PÓŁNOC
PRAG
WISŁA
MARIENSZTAT
POWIŚLE
ŚRÓDMIEŚCIE
UJAZDÓW
Stadion
Dziesięciolecia
Wybrzeże Gdańskie
Wybrzeże Helskie
Wybrzeże Szczecińskie
Wybrzeże Kościuszkowskie
most Śląsko-Dąbrowski
Trasa W-Z
most Syreny
most J. Poniatowskiego
al. Solidarności
Al. Jerozolimskie
Krakowskie Przedmieście
Nowy Świat
Marszałkowska
Al. Ujazdowskie
Al. Armii Ludowej
Al. Niepodległości
Wisłostrada
Czerniakowska
Targowa
Jagiellońska
Ząbkowska
Ratuszowa
Miodowa
Królewska
Świętokrzyska
Tamka
Solec
Książęca
Piękna
Koszykowa
Wilcza
Hoża
Krucza
Mokotowska
Emilii Plater
Ogród Saski
Pałac Kultury i Nauki
Teatr Narodowy
Uniwersytet Warszawski
Akademia Sztuk Pięknych
Akademia Muzyczna
Muz. Narodowe
Muz. Wojska Polskiego
Giełda
Politechnika Warszawska
Sejm i Senat
Park Ujazdowski
Zamek Ujazdowski
Ogród Botaniczny
Park
Pałac Łazienkowski
Park im. J. Piłsudskiego
Główny Urząd Statystyczny
CWKS "Legia"
Torwar
Warszawa Wileńska
Warszawa Stadion
Warszawa Powiśle
Warszawa Śródmieście
Dw. PKS
Targowisko
Bazar Różyckiego
Urząd Dzieln. Praga-Północ
Urząd Dzieln. Śródmieście
Pomnik Syreny
Pomnik Braterstwa Broni
Pomnik Powstania Warszawskiego
Pomnik Króla Jana III Sobieskiego
Grób Nieznanego Żołnierza
Kolumna Zygmunta III Wazy
pl. Zamkowy
pl. J. Piłsudskiego
pl. Trzech Krzyży
pl. Defilad
pl. Na Rozdrożu
rondo gen. de Gaulle'a
Filharmonia
Szpital Wojewódzki
Szpital Dziecięcy
Szpital Akademii Medycznej
Obserw. Astronom.
Stara Pomarańczarnia
Katedra Polskokatolicka

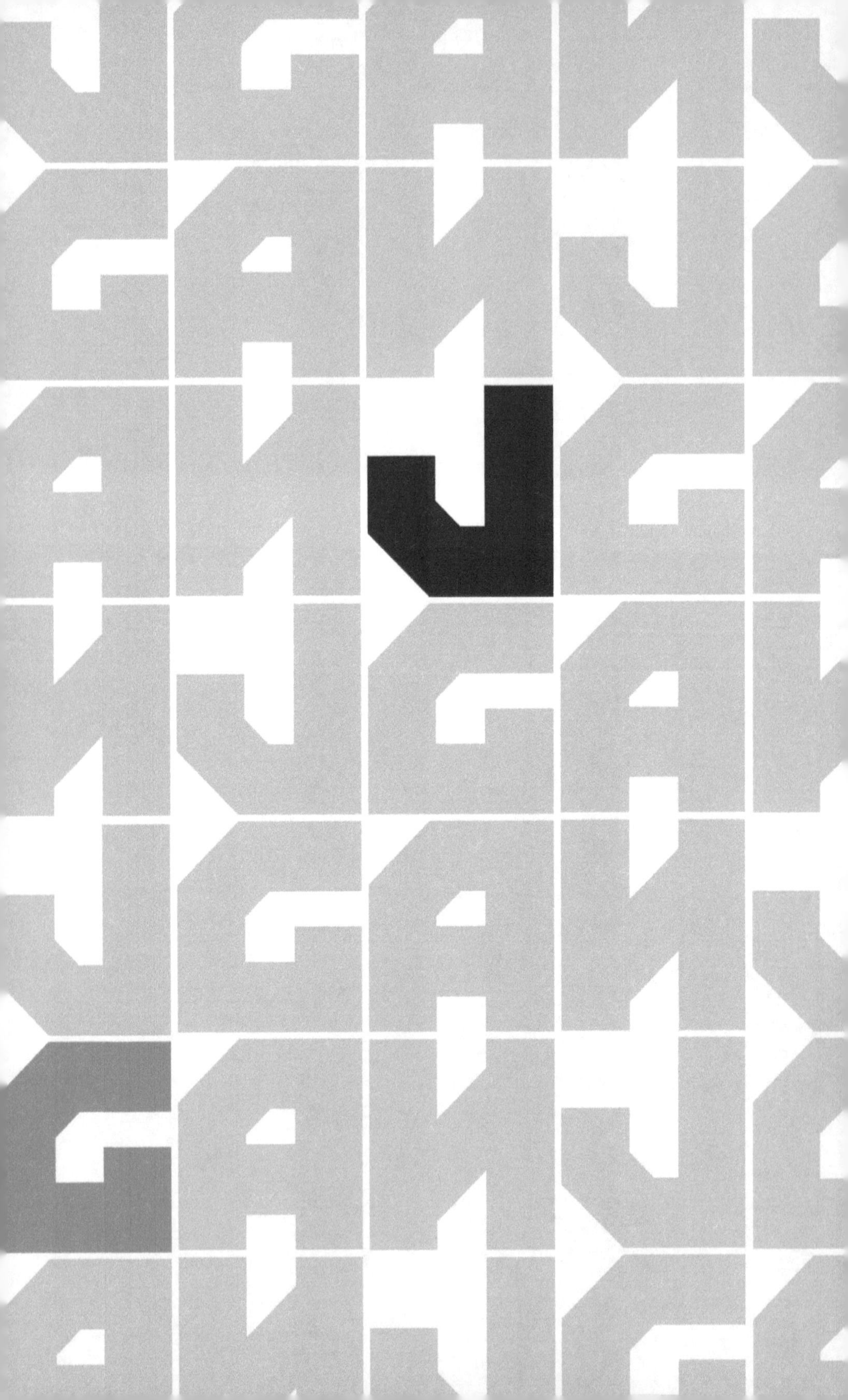

1

James

April 2016
Southern California

Gustaw Bogutsky missing in eastern Ukraine. Awaiting your instructions.

The message from his Polish publishing business showed clearly on his iPhone screen, but James Jensen couldn't help glancing toward the ficus tree in the corner of his office for an explanation, as if his old fax machine from twenty years ago would still be there spewing out answers.

"Missing from where?" James asked the indifferent, possibly artificial, potted plant. "What was he doing that far east?"

James had spent a good portion of the past five decades traveling. He had used conveyances as chic as private jets and yachts and as humble as a spitting camel or sputtering motorbike. He'd suffered through delays, detours, bad weather, overcrowding, and tragic accidents. He'd been lost, stranded, forced to turn around mid-course, and had to resort to bartering or even bribing his way to his destination. But he couldn't recall ever having been missing. The word evoked images of abducted children printed on milk cartons and flashing Amber Alerts on freeway marquees.

This was the twenty-first century, an interconnected, digital age. How could a sixty-three-year-old man with a smartphone, credit card, and all his faculties intact actually be lost? Even a political malcontent. Even in a war zone. Surely the world had evolved past all that?

And what could James possibly do about it?

This is troubling news, his right index finger poked out a reply. *Please advise as to last known location, travel itinerary, and meeting schedule.*

That should keep Warsaw busy, James thought. By the time the publishing executive compiled a proper report, James's old business associate would've wandered back from whatever impromptu tryst or tea party he'd stumbled into in Ukraine, and they'd all have a very sober discussion about keeping in touch with the office while on assignment. He nodded toward the ficus pot in satisfaction.

The techno-chimes of an incoming Skype call pulled his attention to the laptop computer on his desk. He swiveled his chair toward it. It was the head of the publishing house calling. Had Gustaw already returned? What time was it in Poland anyway?

"Ludmyla, what a surprise. It must be the middle of the night there."

"No one has heard from him for three days, James. No calls, no emails, no texts. He didn't check out of his hotel, board his train, or use his credit cards. The police searched the room. His wallet and luggage are still there."

"His passport?"

"That, too, I think," the publisher replied. "His wife is frantic, James. She wants to know what we're doing to find him."

"I'll bet she does," he muttered silently.

"What are the police saying at this point?" he asked aloud.

"I think they've done all they're planning to do—unless you want to offer a personal gratuity?"

James snorted at the delicacy of the euphemism. "Gustaw would love that, wouldn't he, being tracked down by corrupt cops? Though it would serve him right for disappearing like this. No, let's put that idea on hold for now. What about Marko at the publishing house in Kyiv? Ask him if any of his contacts can motivate the authorities to keep looking. Also, find out if they have private investigators in Ukraine. If we're going to have to pay someone to find him, I want to be above board about it."

"Of course."

"Please keep me updated, Ludmyla. And make sure you get some rest."

Not that James would be getting much sleep himself. Drifting off was one thing, but somewhere around 3 a.m. he knew he'd wake up to use the bathroom and spend the remaining hours until dawn staring at the ceiling imagining all the things that could've happened to Gustaw in eastern Ukraine. Because his subconscious, at least, understood that being a worldly, sophisticated man was no protection against all the terrible things in the news. Beheadings, hostage taking, assassination by radioactive poison. As well as the random risks of accident and injury—being aboard the wrong bus or airplane when it goes over an explosives-laden stretch of road or is intercepted by a wayward missile.

Gustaw understood those risks, too, arguably better than James could. Still, he had chosen to enter that conflict zone far from the Ukrainian publishing house James had sent him to monitor and even farther from his own country's much-lamented crises. Despite more than a quarter century of friendship and shared experiences, James couldn't imagine what drew him there.

Could something have gone wrong with Gustaw's errand in Ukraine, or was there another agenda at work? Clicking open his email on his laptop, he began rereading old messages from Gustaw looking for clues.

Six months earlier, Poland had elected a right-wing nationalist party called Law and Justice, providing a fertile subject for the friends' exchanges. The new government's platform—pandering to an overwhelmingly Catholic audience, preying on nativist fears about dark-skinned, Muslim migrants, and promising monthly stipends to families with young children—was anathema to the liberal, open society that Gustaw Bogutsky had championed since before the fall of the Soviet Union.

Between the two of them, James's old friend had not minced words. He had disparaged the naivete of his fellow voters and suggested that the election results showed the limits of democracy itself, where "uneducated fools" had the same say as thoughtful, well-informed citizens. His country's new leaders were "zealots," peddling a fictitious conspiracy that Russia had arranged a 2010 plane crash that killed the sitting Polish president, even though investigators in both countries had determined it was an accident. They were "xenophobes," vilifying today's Syrian War refugees while conveniently forgetting the times in history when fleeing Poles were welcomed in other countries. They were "historical revisionists," whitewashing all negativity or nuance from their portrayal of Poland's imagined heroic past.

And, once Law and Justice had trampled free society and turned public policy over to the bishops, Gustaw predicted bitterly, they would crash the national economy with their ill-conceived and unaffordable policies, wiping out decades of progress.

In one response to Gustaw's laments, James had suggested that perhaps these political developments were a temporary setback; the pendulum would swing the other way and a different party would be elected once the Polish people realized what they'd signed up for.

I wish I thought that were possible, was Gustaw's reply. *These idiots expect to be ruling Poland for the next 100 years, and despite all the horrible things they've done already, their supporters think they're doing a wonderful job.*

You would not believe the things you see on state-run television, which used to show independently reported, factual news programs. Now, after a demonstration where tens of thousands of people filled the streets, they take video of eight or ten stragglers off on the sidewalk and claim that no one came to march against them. It's the same bullshit the Communists used to do, but the young people don't remember any of this and think they can believe what they see.

James had hoped the trip to Kyiv would distract his friend from the bleak developments in Poland, at least for a few days. He never imagined that Gustaw would leave the Ukrainian capital, let alone travel into the conflict zone.

He shifted from his email to an internet browser and started reading about the war, as if a Wikipedia summary could tell him something he didn't already know about the simmering conflict between Ukrainian forces and Russia-backed separatists in the east of that country. The element of surprise had helped Russian invaders annex Crimea quickly in early 2014, seizing that strategic area in southern Ukraine and holding a sham referendum to legitimize the takeover. When Vladimir Putin sent Russian troops to do the same in the eastern Donbas region, however, Ukrainian military resistance stalled his expansion plans there. Territorial gains and losses since then had kept the two countries at a relative stalemate but not a bloodless one.

Clicking on a video link drew James down deserted alleys and up apartment towers with guys in camouflage crouched behind concrete walls, framed in shot-out windows, or ducking into snow-capped trenches, their automatic weapons pointed at an unseen enemy. The daylight scenes revealed gray swarms of smoke in the background, while the night shots exploded across the screen like dueling fireworks displays, balls of light chasing from left to right, then right to left in the blackness. *And that's where Gustaw is,* he thought, *somewhere in that mess?*

James couldn't understand a word of the video he was watching, but the soundtrack certainly brought back memories. Ordnance must've changed considerably in the decades since he was in college, but the *pit-pit-pit* of the smaller rifles and the echoing boom of the bombs falling just out of camera range called to mind the long-ago war he'd managed to avoid.

It was the luck of the draw—literally—that had kept James out of Vietnam. A high draft lottery number for his May birth date meant he wouldn't be conscripted to fight. Like most of his countrymen, he instead saw the conflict on a flickering screen in his living room, intermittently facing the greater horror as his less-fortunate classmates returned home in bandages or body bags. His cousin Greg died there toward the end of the war.

While much of his generation was deployed to Vietnam, James had married his childhood sweetheart Anna and taken his new bride to a more peaceful jungle. In Indonesia, he'd partnered with a retired Army general friend of his father, who loaned him $75,000 to buy into a new venture. Their business sold helicopters to the state-owned oil company of a regime eager to embrace the advantages of a capitalist economy.

The job was his introduction to the international entrepreneurship that would become the most exciting part of his business career.

He wasn't fighting actual battles in Indonesia, but the lessons James learned there—how to launch a business and build human capital in a developing economy—had helped the world move past socialism just as surely as U.S. military efforts during the Cold War. His investment in Eastern Europe was only the most prominent example.

Meaningful progress without violence. Maybe that's why he and Gustaw had hit it off so quickly all those years ago. The underground activist had fought successfully against Communism in Poland without ever picking up a gun. In defiance of official censorship, Gustaw instead published books and pamphlets advocating political and economic change. The unwavering pacifism of that work over more than a decade was a point of pride for the Pole.

How inexplicable, then, that Gustaw should now fall out of contact in the middle of a conflict zone. James still couldn't wrap his head around the word "missing."

One thing was becoming clearer, though, every time he unfolded his *Wall Street Journal* in the morning. This was not the world he and Gustaw thought they were building all those years ago, when the young American entrepreneur and the young Polish publisher first put their heads together to visualize the future of ideas in a Poland freshly freed from the shadow of Soviet Communism.

By 4 a.m. James was wide awake again, his mind racing. Slipping from the bedroom in his robe and slippers, he blew a kiss at his sleeping wife before shutting the door gently behind him.

He started toward the kitchen, nursing childhood memories of warm milk. Halfway there, he thought of the housekeeper in the adjoining room and changed his mind. He didn't want to wake her and invite questions about the cause of his sleeplessness. Besides, dairy didn't always sit as well these days as it had when he was a younger man.

Instead, he headed for his home office next to the garage. The dogs in their outdoor kennel might hear his approach and grow restless, but the human members of the household would be insulated from his pacing. A pod coffee maker there would suffice for his hot beverage.

As the single-source Ethiopian dark roast spurted into his mug, he squinted up at the "brag wall" of photos hung above the credenza, their gilded frames artfully arranged by Anna and the housekeeper. In its small, private way, the display showed a man moving through history, his decades of entrepreneurial effort punctuated with moments when he shook hands and brushed shoulders with political leaders and industry titans. Maybe his own name would not be immortalized for posterity, but these portraits proved that James *had* touched the live wire of key events: Russian President Boris Yeltsin soliciting Western investment in post-Soviet Russia; astronaut Neil Armstrong, the first man to walk on the moon, attending a gathering of aerospace notables; Li Lu, a student dissident who'd fled China and become a Wall Street banker after losing the 1989 battle for democracy there, immortalized at a weekend retreat for financiers.

The photograph that drew James's attention this morning showed a receiving line of suited men gathered for a champagne toast to celebrate the 1992 privatization of a state-owned publishing house in Warsaw: Polish Academic Publishing.

The company was just one of the many state-owned businesses returned to private ownership in the years after Communism in the Soviet bloc disintegrated, but his group's investment had come early in that process. At the time, few Western corporations wanted to gamble on Eastern Europe. So, James had cobbled together his own holding company of private citizens willing to pitch in a hundred thousand or two hundred thousand dollars each to help shepherd one Polish enterprise into the free market future. It was the West's duty, James had insisted as he courted wealthy donors for the effort. Those who understood how capitalism fostered prosperity should use their knowledge and resources to help the Polish economy recover from the ravages of centralized planning. Like-minded friends and colleagues were glad to participate.

In the photo, smiling American investors stood to one side, serious-looking Polish managers to the other, with the tall, blond James and compact, dark-haired Gustaw in the center, foam overflowing their fingers as they guided the bottle together toward the clustered flutes on the table in front of them.

He pulled the frame off the wall and scanned the faces. There was that high-strung bookkeeper, always bristling at James's questions about the accounts; and Jozef the chief editor, grumbling to himself in Polish when one of his projects wasn't approved. Rudolf, Gustaw's expatriate friend from Chicago, had seemed such an asset in the beginning, but he wound up being as entrenched in his ideas as any of the Poles who had never left their country.

Retirements and restructuring over the years meant that none of the Poles in the picture still worked at Polish Academic Publishing, but James was satisfied to realize that most of his investors were still onboard, still recognizing value in their venture all these years later. What he and Gustaw had built in the wake of that cork popping meant something—in jobs created, worthy books and journals printed, wealth built for investors, and knowledge disseminated to ordinary Poles.

Granted, they hadn't been able to publish everything Gustaw and Jozef would've liked, even in the days of fantastic profitability before the investment banks almost brought it all crashing down. But no business could afford every project, not the underground publishing company Gustaw had founded during Communism nor the state-owned version of Polish Academic Publishing that preceded James's investment. Priorities had to be established, financial constraints taken into account. Gustaw had understood that, in the end.

His friend was missing. That knowledge, existing only as rational information in James's mind until this moment, suddenly hit him square in the gut, and he had to gasp for air, his fingers trembling as he returned the photograph to its hook. His head gave a slight, involuntary shake, denying that such an absurdity was possible.

Surely the plucky Pole, who served up tea and philosophy with equal largesse in those late-night chats when James was in Warsaw, would not be taken down by some prosaic mishap? Not after weathering some of the worst dangers of the previous century unharmed.

With caffeine and panic swirling through him, the insomniac's illusion of alertness raised new, profound-seeming questions in James's mind. How, for instance, did anyone know that Gustaw had gone to eastern Ukraine when UkraineLaw, the company he was sent to visit, was in Kyiv? Technically, James had sent Gustaw there as a consultant for Polish Academic Publishing. Could the Polish publishing house know more about his itinerary than Ludmyla had let on?

James had no reason to imagine that anyone at Polish Academic Publishing was involved in Gustaw's disappearance. After all, they were the ones who told him about it. What better way to throw suspicion off themselves, though?

A few months ago, James had nearly fallen out of his chair when he learned that his beloved publishing company, reborn from the ashes of Communism to spread free thought, was writing a history textbook with no mention of Lech Walesa, Poland's first president after Communism. How was that even possible, let alone academically coherent?

James remembered well Walesa's heroic role as strike leader during the unrest of the 1970s, when Polish workers protested rising food prices. Like Gustaw, the anti-Communist labor movement leader had been imprisoned during martial law in the early 1980s. He emerged from prison as a powerful figurehead who became a household name worldwide. With the exception of the Pope at that time, John Paul II, there probably wasn't a single Pole known to more Americans than Walesa. And now, a few decades later, his own countrymen were trying to erase him from their past?

It stank of self-censorship to James. But whatever debate or misgivings management might've had were over long before he caught wind of this development, and they seemed alarmingly reconciled to its necessity. After all, Walesa had angered the country's new leaders by criticizing Law & Justice's intended "reforms" to Poland's highest court.

What other compromises might Polish Academic Publishing be willing to make with the current regime to better navigate the new nationalistic order? Would they help the government "deal with" a relentless old agitator who'd just come out of retirement?

No, of course they wouldn't. None of this made any sense. Gustaw was an adult—a private consultant, not an employee—and if he wanted to take a few days off by himself, it was no one's business but his own.

His wife, Natalya, missed him? That was between the two of them.

On his last few Warsaw visits, James had made an art form of ignoring the tension between his friend and his spouse—the chilly silences, caustic glances, and whispered arguments in the next room. But selective deafness only went so far, and Gustaw eventually opened up about their discontent.

"I'm not ready to sit in a rocking chair and play with the grandchildren," he had grumbled over beer one evening at a pub down the street from James's hotel. "Someday, sure, but not now, with Poland going to hell again. Young people don't realize what's at stake yet. By the time they figure it out, it will be too late. Natalya should understand; she saw it all before, too. Her own father had to leave the country back then. But now, if our life gets harder, she's just going to blame me for getting involved."

So maybe Gustaw's apparent disappearance was nothing more than an unannounced respite from having to explain himself at home. James could sympathize. His wife Anna was a unique blessing to his own wanderlust, allowing him more latitude for extended absences than most women would tolerate. He could not imagine being tied down to someone else's expectations without revolting eventually.

But what about that abandoned hotel room, all the luggage still inside? People walked away from their lives every day, right? James had observed Gustaw's recent frustration over events in Poland and in his personal life. Could his friend be one of those people?

How many times had Gustaw had the chance to do just that, though, and instead elected to stay? He could've left during Poland's martial law period in the early Eighties, when his Communist captors urged him to defect to the West, ridding their society of one more disruptive malcontent. After the Iron Curtain came down a decade later, Stanford University had offered him a research job in California. But he had chosen to remain and rebuild his country, tying his own future to its uncertain one. Surely Gustaw wouldn't abandon Poland now after all the progress of the intervening decades?

There was no excuse for delaying the call any longer. It was the middle of the day in Poland. James got himself a glass of water, just in case this turned into a long conversation, then picked up the landline on his desk and dialed Warsaw.

Natalya answered on the second ring. "James. Have they found him? Is he hurt? Tell me he's not dead!" Gustaw's wife did indeed sound frantic, and he had to admit that he had no news to share. Strange that she could imagine he would know something before she did.

"Where could he be?" she croaked in a raw half-whisper.

"I haven't spoken to him in a couple of weeks. Did he tell *you* he was going to leave Kyiv?"

"No."

Had he only imagined that fractional pause before she answered?

"And when were you expecting him home?"

"Friday. The early train. He asked me to meet him at the station so he wouldn't have to take a taxi when he was tired from the overnight trip. I had to rearrange my whole morning, but I was there waiting for him. I kept expecting him to call and say he'd overslept or gotten off at an earlier stop to buy a cup of tea and was late getting back onboard. Why wouldn't he call me? Something must have happened to him."

James had anticipated tears, but hearing them still made the muscles in his neck and shoulders bunch up in a spasm of helplessness.

"We don't know that, Natalya. Of course, I'm also concerned that you haven't heard from him, and I'll do everything I can to help find him. I promise."

Had he really said that, not two minutes into the call? He was no detective. Eastern Ukraine was a lawless, corrupt war zone. People disappeared from places like that all the time.

But James was the one who had sent Gustaw to Ukraine, never mind that he wound up in the wrong part of the country.

"I'm coming to Warsaw, Natalya," he announced in another snap decision. "Find out anything you can about his meetings before he left Poland. Maybe this has nothing to do with the Ukrainian publishing business."

He hung up the phone, already second-guessing himself. Gustaw would probably show up in Warsaw when James's flight was halfway over the Atlantic, making the whole endeavor a waste of time and expense. He hadn't even checked to see which meetings and appointments would have to be rescheduled to accommodate this impulsive journey.

His hand wavered over the phone receiver as he considered whether to call Natalya back and retract the offer. Then he imagined trying to concentrate on his normal activities while he waited for news, obsessively refreshing his email and jumping expectantly each time the phone rang. He banished the notion with a firm headshake and settled back into his chair.

Having committed to making the trip, James found he was eager to get to Poland as soon as possible. He fired off an email to put his assistant to work on the logistics, then headed back to the bedroom to start packing, noting the void in the abandoned rumple of bedsheets when he arrived. Anna was already up.

Travel was such a routine occurrence in his life that he barely thought through the preparations—clothes, toiletries, a laptop for reading and communication while he was away. He dug his passport and his Polish debit card out of the floor safe in his dressing room, along with a few hundred zlotys in cash left over from his last visit.

With the basics stowed in his leather duffle bag, he considered whether he might need any special gear. On other excursions he'd packed sporting goods—fishing rods, camping equipment, or hunting rifles that required weeks of applying for permission to take aboard planes. On those occasions, even when the unexpected happened—a helicopter crash, a flareup of his heart arrhythmia—he knew what type of adventure he was signing up for.

Now his mind flirted with wild scenarios for the days ahead. Would he need survival or first aid supplies? Surveillance equipment? Cash for bribes? Perhaps, he chuckled to himself, coming back to reality, he should pack a meerschaum pipe and deerstalker hat. Or an oversized magnifying glass? But he was not Sherlock Holmes.

In the end he added blue jeans, a pair of comfortable walking shoes, and a rain-resistant windbreaker to his bag. If Gustaw's colleagues in the Polish opposition were being monitored by the government, he might not want to be too conspicuous when he met with them. It was a strange thought after twenty-five years of open travel in Poland, but Gustaw's disappearance had him thinking cautiously.

Not cautiously enough, in Anna's opinion, which she expressed while standing on the sunporch wrapped in a towel and dripping from her morning swim.

"You're going to go talk to his anti-government friends to find out if he's missing because of whatever they were planning? What makes you think you won't end up missing, too?"

She put her hands on her hips in what the kids secretly called her "Angry Mom" pose.

"I'm going to Poland—not eastern Ukraine," James assured her. "That's where Gustaw was. The Polish government isn't going to start kidnapping American businessmen off the street. They want NATO troops and missiles protecting them from Russia, not an international incident."

He chuckled a little and could see Anna wrestling with whether to be offended. But she was fond of Gustaw, too.

"Just promise me you'll be careful," she said eventually.

He kissed her cheek. "Of course."

Standing in line at airport security, where the metal pin in his shoulder always earned him an extra-careful screening, James had time to ponder what he was walking into and how he might prepare for it.

He'd been following current events in Eastern Europe well enough; it was his responsibility as a major shareholder in a business there. And even before Law and Justice's surprising election victory in Poland, he'd monitored the rise of Viktor Orban's similarly nationalist government in neighboring Hungary. James's understanding of this trend was straightforward: international institutions such as the European Union, founded with such optimism years earlier, had not brought Europe's people the prosperity they'd expected. Now populist movements around the continent were demanding more autonomy for their countries in the belief that local control would deliver better results.

Once elected, however, nationalist governments had attacked competing domestic institutions—courts, media, and civil society groups—consolidating power in the name of their election mandate. The result was a sad loss of freedom for nations—and people like Gustaw—who had struggled and sacrificed to win it.

"New Europe." That's what they'd called Poland and Hungary a dozen years ago. Not the stodgy old Western Europeans with their squeamishness about invading a faraway place for its own good and everybody else's. Back then, the Eastern Europeans had been part of the "coalition of the willing"—those countries sophisticated enough to recognize the threat of rogue nations and leaders and brave enough to fight against them.

Now that refugees from one of those faraway places were invading them back, however, some countries that supported the U.S. invasion of Iraq in 2003 were not so willing to help manage the aftermath. As people from war-torn Syria overloaded lifeboats to cross the ocean to Europe, these nations threw up fences and camps to contain them.

James had expected things to evolve differently in the Middle East; a lot of people had. "You can't make an omelet without breaking some eggs," they'd told each other a handful of years ago, nodding sagely. U.S.-led wars in Afghanistan and Iraq had destabilized the Middle East in a good way, they argued, directly resulting in the Arab Spring protests then sweeping the region, which would surely bring political freedom to more people. But the intervening period had shown, with unresolved civil wars, the rise of the Islamic State, and the Syrian refugee crisis, that broken eggs are no guarantee of a hearty breakfast.

And now those Eastern European countries once billed as the modern, dynamic up-and-comers were leading the West again—this time in a turn toward nationalism.

James was a globalist—had been since he was a little boy listening to faraway places on the shortwave radio his dad gave him for Christmas one year. "Citizen of the world," he called himself, reveling in his freedom to stride across national boundaries, first through his travels and explorations, then later as a businessman and investor.

In exchange for his beneficial work, though, he expected room to maneuver and often resented the involvement (read: interference) of government bureaucrats with what he was trying to accomplish. Like when he was in his twenties and tried to ship inexpensive cantaloupe from California to Japan, where the melons sold for exorbitant sums, only to have it rot as it sat delayed in customs. The stench of decaying fruit often came to mind when he found himself snarled in red tape.

So, it was no surprise to him that the people of Poland and Hungary were frustrated with their European Union overseers in Brussels. He just couldn't understand that nationalist impulse to turn inward, away from the new experiences available to those who would embrace a wider, interconnected world. The populists weren't just rebelling against inefficient regulators trying to impose their one-size-fits-all solutions from the center, much like the Soviets had in their day. These formerly welcoming places were kicking back at the foreign investors who had bankrolled their emergence from socialism: people like James himself. It was disheartening to realize that so many in Poland had learned so little from their past.

From the airline's frequent flyer lounge, James phoned Matt Larson, an old college fraternity brother who'd gone on to a life as a neoconservative think tank analyst. James hadn't spoken to him much in recent years, but he'd heard colorful rumors. Matt had been tied to a host of international controversies, had the confidence of at least one European spy service, and wielded the influence to single-handedly topple world leaders—purportedly. James liked to imagine his old friend living such a life of intrigue, but he'd never asked. He didn't think Matt would admit to him if the stories were true.

Virulent anti-Communism had made Matt a champion of Polish freedom since before James's investment in the re-emerging nation. Even so, he had urged caution in doing business with people indoctrinated as socialists since childhood.

"It's not their fault, but that's how they were taught to think about things," he had said. "I'm sure a lot of them understand that Soviet domination hurt their country. They're ready to try something different now, but their embrace of capitalism might not be as permanent as you want to believe."

At the time, James had dismissed those concerns, though he had had occasion to reflect on them again when things got rocky at Polish Academic Publishing. Anyway, it was nice, then and now, to have an ally in engaging with the former Communist world.

"So, your underground hero has gone missing?" Matt boomed after James outlined the situation. "What did you say he was doing in eastern Ukraine?"

James hesitated for a moment before responding.

"I think he might have been interviewing a job candidate."

"In a war zone?"

"I never expected him to look there." James cringed at having to explain himself. "The truth is, our joint venture in Kyiv has been struggling for years. It's our local partner Marko. He's never been willing to adapt to digital technology. So, Gustaw was trying to find us a more forward-looking manager for a new venture. This is just between us, of course."

"Who would I tell, Jim?"

It was a question best left unanswered. Officially, Matt was a university professor and think tank analyst. Behind the scenes, who knew?

"What I'm afraid of is that the Polish secret police might have followed Gustaw to Ukraine," James said. "He's been pretty outspoken against the new government."

"And you think Law and Justice might see him as a real threat? They did win the election handily."

"All I know for sure is that he's missing," James conceded, refusing to entertain the broader question. How should he know what his friend is capable of these days—or how seriously the authorities might take his recent activities? "Do you think the Poles could be involved?"

"I suppose anything is possible," Matt mused, his deep, sonorous voice imbuing the platitude with gravitas. "The Soviet-era secret police were disbanded years ago, naturally, but Kaczynski, the real power behind the current leadership, has been in the game for a long time. He probably knows some people who know how things worked back in the day."

"What do *you* know about the situation in eastern Ukraine?"

"Well, the ceasefire seems like a farce—an excuse for so-called diplomats to stay at a fancy hotel at taxpayer expense while they negotiate another one. I wouldn't recommend traveling there."

"Is the Polish government active in the region?"

"They would have some presence in Ukraine, of course," Matt said, and James wasn't sure whether he was talking to the college professor or the spooks' spook. "It is a neighboring country, and there's a lot of migration to Poland. I'm not sure what clandestine resources they devote to the east. My sense is they're focused on domestic policy right now."

"Gutting their Supreme Court. Demanding that banks adjust the terms of home mortgages because the Polish currency has fallen in value." A dismayed Gustaw had kept him apprised of every new crack in the liberal, free market edifice.

"Child credits for working families. Outlawing abortion. It's a Catholic country, James, as were you last time I checked. Are you having second thoughts about your conversion?"

James suddenly remembered why he and Matt hadn't talked in a while. Clandestine mastermind or not, the man had a pedantic streak. If the discussion didn't circle around to the perils of the Iranian government—Matt's favorite bogeyman—it would almost certainly turn to how the Judeo-Christian traditions drove the evolution of human freedom.

Critical as Matt was of the mullahs in Tehran, secularism was a bridge too far for the neocon—the path that leads to political correctness, moral relativism, and other forms of cultural rot.

"Not at all," James insisted. "I'm just not comfortable with some of the new government's policies. I'm starting to wonder if it's still a good place to have an investment."

There was a brief silence.

"Well, I do hope you find your friend, fifth columnist though he might be," Matt said. "I'm sure you'll figure out the business part in due course. It seems to me, though, that if you're willing to set up shop in a den of corruption and civil war like Ukraine, then a few changes in Polish social policy shouldn't scare you away."

James had hoped Matt would soothe his misgivings, but his words felt like a dismissal.

"That's a fair point," James said, eager now to end the call. "I think my flight is starting to board. I'll let you know how things turn out."

"I'll be waiting for word."

Fifth columnist? Did Matt really think Gustaw was the one who had abandoned the coalition of Polish workers, intellectuals, and Catholic clergy who had united against Communism in the 1970s and 1980s? The free, open society the publisher had worked for all those years ago was the same one he was trying to preserve in Poland today.

2

James

Warsaw, Poland

Natalya collected James at the airport in a sobering echo of the many times Gustaw had played chauffeur to welcome him to Poland. Gustaw's wife looked pale, tired, and pessimistic, swaying slightly in low heels as she greeted him at the baggage claim. To his unspoken question, she shook her head once, a tight jerk left, then right to signal that there'd been no revelation of her husband's whereabouts during his flight.

He followed her toward the parking garage, his long strides failing to keep pace with the *clip-clip-clip* of her shoes on the concrete.

"To your hotel, then?" she proposed as they drove. Gustaw had always taken him directly to his lodging for some rest and a shower before they tackled the business of the publishing house.

From the beginning of their collaboration a quarter century earlier, the trek from Southern California to Eastern Europe had been an endurance test: two days by air, his 6'5" frame folded into an airplane seat before arriving gritty-toothed and groggy after a West European layover that was always a little too short for a decent nap. Even after he and Anna leased the flat in London and started booking first-class tickets, it was still a serious undertaking. Just into his forties at that time, he was discovering—through lower back pain, his first pair of reading glasses, the occasional lightning bolt of heartburn—that his body would not always be as resilient as it was at twenty-five. Now, the extra decades only added to his fatigue.

"Let's get some coffee and talk. I'd like to get started right away." James had splashed some water on his face, swallowed a heart pill, and changed his shirt in the airplane lavatory before they landed. That would have to do for now. "Gustaw told me he'd put together an informal think tank of sorts to talk about strategy for the next election. Do you know who was involved?"

She was facing forward, watching the road, so he couldn't say for sure that he saw her lips compress at the question. She answered matter-of-factly.

"I don't have an attendance list, but I probably know a lot of them. I could give you a few names to start with, and they can provide the rest. You think this group might know where Gustaw is?"

"I don't know any more than you do, Natalya." Nothing likely to be relevant, at least. "But if he had business in eastern Ukraine, he didn't tell me about it." That much was true. "Maybe one of them knows what he was doing there. That's all I was thinking."

"Or maybe his work with them somehow got him in trouble with the government here?"

She was sharp. He shouldn't underestimate that.

"Does that sound crazy to you?" he said.

"Yes, but so does Gustaw traveling to eastern Ukraine and disappearing."

"How did anyone know he'd gone there? Ludmyla didn't explain that to me."

"I don't know. I suppose maybe he told Marko or someone else at UkraineLaw before he left Kyiv?"

As the city passed by out the car window, James was comforted by the modern skyscrapers rising above blocky apartment buildings from the Communist era. The glass and steel towers gave visual confirmation that Warsaw had prospered over the decades since he had started traveling here.

"I'd like to buy you breakfast, if there's a place we can stop," James said, belatedly realizing that they had skirted the commercial center and were heading instead toward the Bogutsky home.

"Thank you, but I'm not very hungry. I have coffee at the house. I thought we'd just go there. I can cook some eggs and sausages for you, if you'd like."

"I hate to put you to the trouble." Or subject his arteries to the Polish interpretation of an American breakfast. He smiled graciously.

"You came a long way," Natalya insisted. "It's no trouble."

In the end he convinced her that a couple slices of toast would suffice, and they sat at the small Formica table in the kitchen while she poured strong coffee from a press into petite porcelain cups. In the close quarters, James could see where a few threads of gray had crept into her blonde hair, but the skin on her trembling hands was smooth as she served him. *Even younger women age over time,* he thought, then looked away quickly, pretending to examine the colorful bowls and platters displayed on the counter. Polish pottery had been a popular gift when he first began traveling here, and Anna and his sister-in-law had amassed quite a collection.

"We'd been arguing, you know," Natalya confessed with no warning, putting down the press and tucking her hands away in her lap.

"Oh?" He hoped his surprise sounded sincere. "I'm sorry to hear that. Every marriage has challenging periods, of course."

"I was so frustrated with all this activism of his," she volunteered, though he hadn't asked for details. "He was off to meetings, talking on the phone late at night. Last month he wanted to take money out of our savings to start printing leaflets against the government. 'It's the twenty-first century, not the French Revolution,' I told him. 'Why can't you start an online blog that doesn't cost anything?'" She shook her head. "It's as if he's trying to relive his youth. So, his party lost the election. I'm not crazy about Law and Justice either, but they didn't steal power. He's been talking about them like they're an invading army and he has to go back into the underground to stop them."

"From what he told me, he was trying to help put together a winning message for the next election," James said. "That doesn't sound like an unreasonable response. Was there more to it than that?"

"Maybe not. It just seemed so out-of-proportion to me. He's in his sixties. He should be thinking about retirement, not playing spy games."

"Is that what he's been doing?" James' tone was sharp.

She looked up, startled.

"If we're going to find him, Natalya, we need to have all our cards on the table. I sent him to Kyiv. He went east on his own. If you or his friends here know why, that might help us."

"I don't know why he went to the east. I only wonder if . . ." She shrugged, suddenly blinking back tears. "What if he left me, James? What if he disappeared on purpose? Do you think he could have done that?"

Gustaw *had* parted ways with two previous wives, the first by her choice, the second his, but not with a vanishing act.

"Do you?" James asked.

She shook her head. "That would be better than some of the things I've imagined, though."

"I understand, but we don't know anything yet. Let's contact some of his friends and see if they have any answers."

"What do you mean, 'missing,' Mr. Jensen?" The speaker was a distinguished (according to Natalya) newspaper columnist who spoke fluent English, so the question was hardly one of translation.

"He didn't return home as expected from a trip to Kyiv," James tried to clarify. "No one has spoken to him in several days."

"How many is 'several'?" chimed in another of the handful of people seated around the café table. James seemed to recall that this one was a university administrator. Or was she the engineer? Hopefully one of them was a dictionary editor, because they weren't going to make much progress if he had to redefine every sentence he spoke. Sighing, he started to count back the days from Ludmyla's first message.

"Last Wednesday," Natalya said. "He was due home on Friday, and I got an email a couple of days before about which train he would be taking."

"Did you actually speak to him, too, or was it just the email?" the administrator/engineer wanted to know.

"Only email. I replied to his message, but he didn't answer."

"Hmm." The questioner pursed her lips a bit, as if reflecting, but didn't say anything more.

"Was that unusual?" James asked Natalya. "That he didn't respond?"

"Not at all. I just figured he was busy. There was nothing he needed to respond to."

James watched the faces around the table as she spoke, but if any of the others were aware of tension in the marriage, he saw no sign of it.

Gustaw's like-minded compatriots had been remarkably accommodating of their request to meet, turning up for a same-day, mid-afternoon coffee gathering as if it were a normal occurrence. James had to plan such happenings weeks in advance, so seeing these people clear their schedules at a vague request from a colleague's wife was comforting. With friends like these, perhaps Gustaw would be okay somehow.

"As I was saying, we are concerned not to have heard from him for almost a week," James said. "I thought perhaps your work together had taken him out of Kyiv for some purpose we're not aware of."

The weathered faces glanced around at each other, suddenly serious and sober, but no one spoke up.

"Can you tell me anything about what you were planning?" he pressed. "Or what he'd been talking to you about lately?"

"I don't understand," said the columnist—was his name Simon? "Do you think something has happened to him or that he's simply gone somewhere without telling you?"

"We don't know," James said. "Our main concern, of course, is his safety, and we can't know that he's safe when no one seems to know where he is. Obviously, we'd like to learn that he's gone somewhere voluntarily, if any of you can tell us that."

In their silence, James looked around the crowded café, wondering if the venue had been a mistake. Perhaps Gustaw's friends were afraid of being overheard—or that one or more of them was already under surveillance. He had expected the short notice to work in their favor, but anyone monitoring their telephone or email traffic could've easily found out about the meeting and blended into the café clientele.

The café's other customers were drinking, eating, chatting, and looking at their phone and laptop screens, not seeming to take notice of James and Natalya's gathering at all. No one looked particularly furtive or suspicious. Still, he was no expert at spotting eavesdroppers.

"Maybe this isn't the best place for this conversation," he suggested, sotto voce. "I'd be happy to join you somewhere else so we can speak more candidly."

The engineer/administrator actually rolled her eyes. "I don't think there's anything we would report to you elsewhere that we can't say here. Do you?" Around the table, heads shook slowly.

"If we're not telling you anything, it's because there's really nothing to tell. Our conversations with Gustaw were about political messaging and strategy. We didn't send him on a secret mission to Ukraine, I can assure you."

So much for that theory. James tried to keep them talking.

"OK. Tell us about his mood, then. Was he anxious or upset about anything?"

"You mean besides the fascist takeover of Poland's government?" a third participant piped in. "Sidelining the Constitutional Tribunal? Turning the state-owned media into the mouthpiece of the ruling party? We were all angry and worried about those things."

"Of course. Well, how were your meetings going? Are you optimistic you'll be able to make progress in the next election?"

"It's not as simple as that, really." The man speaking now had a neatly trimmed mustache and a pocket protector. Perhaps *he* was the engineer. "Many people in Poland are as outraged as we are by our current leaders. But many others think everything they do is correct. So, winning more seats in the legislature could help to overturn some decisions, perhaps." The man sighed before continuing.

"But Gustaw wasn't just unhappy about what the government was doing. He was disappointed in the people who voted to let them do it, in those who don't understand that Law and Justice is undermining the very democratic institutions that brought them to power in the first place. I believe he was disillusioned with the Polish citizenry as a group, and convincing some of them to support a different message next time might not change that."

"It's like he took the whole thing a little bit personally," someone else explained. "Like if we'd done something different in the past, Poles would've known better—seen through the empty promises and shallow justifications. Remember, Gustaw lost a lot fighting the Communist system—his scientific career, his family. A lot of us did."

"Do you think he was depressed, then?" James saw Natalya's face whiten at the question, as if that was one possibility she hadn't considered.

"Discouraged maybe." There were nods from the others. "I wouldn't have thought he had given up, though, if that's what you're suggesting."

Surely he hadn't come all this way only to learn that Gustaw's friends didn't think he was suicidal? That was the question in Natalya's eyes as James paid for a dozen pastries and cups of coffee and they left the café, having extended the commiserations and small talk to the point of awkwardness in the hope that someone in the group would linger to give them a more promising lead.

"What do you think?" James asked Natalya as they headed toward her car. "I didn't get the sense that anyone was hiding anything, but then, I've never met these people before."

"I barely know them myself, but I agree. They all seemed shocked and confused at the idea that their work could have anything to do with his disappearance." She choked slightly on the final word but quickly recovered her composure. "So, what's next?"

"I suppose I could go to Polish Academic Publishing and find out if they know anything new."

"Wouldn't Ludmyla have called if they heard something?"

"Presumably." He had seen her checking her phone for new messages at frequent intervals throughout the day. "Do you have another idea?"

Natalya shrugged, and they walked the rest of the way in silence.

He had come too far to give up in one afternoon. And while he wasn't ready to rule out an official Polish connection to his friend's disappearance, James couldn't immediately see how to proceed with that theory either. Were they to believe that Gustaw had been kidnapped off the streets of eastern Ukraine by Polish government agents while his co-conspirators were munching paczki here in Warsaw, unmolested and oblivious to his fate? Maybe one of them would think of something later and come forward with an idea they could pursue.

Meanwhile, the people at Polish Academic Publishing were his contacts on the ground. He had made his career leveraging local talent to get things done, so the publishing house was his logical next stop.

"Do you know how to get there?" James inquired awkwardly, realizing that Gustaw had left Polish Academic Publishing before the move to the current offices. That had been during Gustaw's second marriage, before he and Natalya were even together.

"Yes," she confirmed curtly as the car swung out into traffic, leaving James to wonder if she had accompanied Gustaw on recent visits or looked up the address only after his disappearance. Anna had been a part of James's life since adolescence, and he sometimes marveled at how his friends managed to integrate new mates into their lives already in progress. What did Natalya know of the hard times at Polish Academic Publishing or James's role in her husband's departure from the company? Did she blame him for sending Gustaw on this latest trip to Ukraine?

"How did you and Gustaw meet?" James asked. "I'm not sure he ever told me."

He saw her hands tighten on the wheel, then relax. She turned briefly to smile at him.

"A friend of a friend introduced us. It was a—what do you call it in English—'blind date.' I didn't expect anything to come of it, to be perfectly honest. He was older than me. We didn't have common interests. But he was so charming at dinner, I didn't care what he talked about as long as he was paying attention to me."

She laughed—a little ruefully, James thought—before her smile faded. "Anyway, that was years ago. People's lives grow together over time, I suppose."

Or apart, he added silently to himself.

Natalya's expression was all business by the time they arrived at the publishing house.

The suburban office block had a modern sleekness that was a long way—architecturally and geographically—from the nineteenth century palace downtown that had housed the business for most of its history. Gone was the imposing central staircase leading to the gilded Hall of Mirrors where the board used to meet. Here, an anonymous bank of shiny elevators in the front lobby led to the upper floors. The pounding, mechanical heartbeat of the press in the old palace basement had also been silenced. Most of the company's books and periodicals never even made it to headquarters anymore. They were instead shipped directly from the low-cost printer in Slovenia to the central warehouse in Lodz.

The relocation, more than a dozen years ago now, had traded a cramped, dilapidated structure full of nooks and warrens—charming but inefficient—for a larger space with an open floor plan that fostered teamwork. The proceeds of selling the palace had improved the balance sheet at a difficult time, too, but James still harbored some regret at the cold practicality of the move.

Natalya parked her compact car in the ample lot—another improvement on the old facility in the city center—and they headed inside.

A tense and respectful silence followed them through the building, turning to quiet murmuring in their wake. More than a decade after his reign ended, Gustaw's fate apparently had the entire business holding its breath. James shivered as he walked under his friend's official portrait hanging in the hallway along with those of other hallowed leaders of the past.

Ludmyla welcomed them into her office—which might have been Gustaw's if things had gone differently—as if they had an appointment. She looked nearly as sleepless as Natalya.

"I called UkraineLaw and spoke to Marko this morning," she said, waving them toward an upholstered settee in one corner before sitting in a leather wingback chair across from it. "He didn't have anything new to tell me."

"And you believe him?" James asked, recalling a conversation with Gustaw nine months earlier about accounting figures from Kyiv that didn't add up.

The question caused both women to turn sharply toward him, Natalya with a slight gasp.

"Is there some reason that I shouldn't?" Ludmyla said.

"Not that I know of. Just that Gustaw told me he thought Marko was taking money out of the joint venture." He had hoped to be discreet, but he had to consider every possibility.

"Stealing from it, you mean?" Ludmyla pressed, waiting for his nod. "And you didn't tell me about this? Polish Academic Publishing is the joint venture partner, James, not you personally. That's company money he's taking if Gustaw is correct." Fatigue had clearly sapped her patience, and he could see her anger venting in the easiest direction—toward him.

"He didn't have any proof, certainly nothing we could take to court," James rushed to explain. "And I didn't ask him to look for any.

"I didn't," he insisted in response to Natalya's glower. "But that doesn't mean he wouldn't try on his own. Which brings me back to my original question: How much do we trust Marko?"

"You're the one still clinging to the idea that that company can be salvaged," Ludmyla snapped, scraping the scab off of the old argument with a flick of her long, manicured fingernails. "Isn't that why you started sending Gustaw there? I barely know Marko and haven't had time to conduct a psychological profile on him. There's enough to keep me busy here in Poland."

James held his palms out in a placating gesture.

"I know you have your hands full here. That's why I brought Gustaw in. He was the one who closed this deal twenty years ago, and I believe he still has that entrepreneurial mindset to try to make it work. UkraineLaw needs some innovative thinking, not a memo from the head office. No offense intended, Ludmyla."

"And what sort of *innovative thinking* were you and Gustaw planning?" She couldn't quite keep the sarcasm out of her voice.

"The same kind I've been trying to talk Marko into for years: technological upgrades. I always thought his wife was the problem, but even after their divorce, he's no more interested in digitizing content than they were at the beginning."

James could recite the conversation practically verbatim, they had had it so often. He would explain the necessity of evolving with the times while Marko calmly assured him that what had worked in the company's past was still working just fine.

"And how was Gustaw supposed to change Marko's mind when you hadn't been able to, especially in today's economy?" The questioner was Natalya now. "From what I understood, UkraineLaw has become a ghost town since the Crimea invasion."

"He told you that?" James hadn't thought Gustaw and Natalya were communicating that closely these days.

"Certainly. It was right there in the email last week."

"Did he give you any more details about what he'd been doing in Ukraine?" James asked.

She shrugged her shoulders. "Nothing that seemed relevant to his disappearance, if that's what you're suggesting. Don't you think I've already been over that?"

"Of course you have. I apologize. We just don't have much to go on right now." James turned toward the publishing executive. "Ludmyla, did you and Marko make any progress on finding a private investigator who could help us?"

"Marko says there are retired police detectives available, but if you don't trust him, should we really trust his recommendations? I'm not sure how we would find someone on our own, though. You could end up hiring an organized crime syndicate or a kidnap and ransom operation."

"Maybe that's the kind of expertise we need. I don't suppose there's any insurance to cover kidnapping?"

"Not unless you bought it for him. He wasn't there in an official Polish Academic Publishing capacity, exactly, was he? And even if he had been, we don't provide that for our independent consultants." The publishing company chief snorted. "We don't provide that for me, either. Besides, there hasn't been a ransom demand for Gustaw. K&R people wouldn't know whom to negotiate with."

"I'm still trying to understand what Gustaw was supposed to be doing in Ukraine, other than maybe investigating embezzlement on his own," Natalya said tartly. "I thought this was a routine visit—a quarterly check-in sort of thing. Now you say Marko hasn't changed his way of doing things in decades. Where was this entrepreneurial approach supposed to come in?"

Two worn-out, increasingly suspicious, and angry-looking women stared unblinking at James, who looked down at his lap, then locked eyes with each of them in turn.

"What I'm about to tell you isn't for Marko's ears. Not yet, anyway," he said.

They both glared at him, and he looked down again before continuing.

"Okay, it's not really a secret. We figured since we couldn't convince Marko to change the way *he* does things at UkraineLaw, then we would start a new company that would buy his content and sell digital subscriptions to it like we've wanted him to do. Gustaw was talking about Ukrainians living in Poland—that is, hiring Ukrainians immigrants who already live here to do the work from here. But he may have been interviewing people in Kyiv, too. Or somewhere else in Ukraine. It's not as if he had to check in with me about every little detail."

"Unfortunately, those 'little details' could be the clues we're missing now," Ludmyla observed unnecessarily.

"You have to tell Marko about this," Natalya said, slapping her knee for emphasis. "I don't care whether he's angry that you didn't include him in your plans. It might give him some new ideas about what Gustaw was doing or who he was meeting with."

"And if Marko is involved?" James asked. "I'm willing to tell everyone I know from here to Siberia if it will help us find him, Natalya, but I'd rather not help a potentially guilty party cover up what happened."

"Tell them, then. I don't understand why you wouldn't have done that already. Call them all right now and ask for their help!" Natalya's words accelerated and amplified in a crescendo of insistence that petered out just short of hysteria.

A few shaky breaths later, she continued in a calmer tone. "And while you're at it, I think it's time we went to Kyiv and spoke to Marko in person. Maybe then we'll be able to figure out whether he's hiding something."

3

Gustaw

One week earlier
Mariupol, eastern Ukraine

They were to meet in the hotel bar at the younger man's suggestion. Gustaw knew that most public places would be closed by the time of their evening appointment, but he still thought it an odd choice for a business meeting. He imagined walking in to find Feliks tossing back a shot of vodka to pluck up his courage for their discussion. Later, he would regret not having done so himself.

In the end, they never entered the bar area, let alone ordered drinks. When Gustaw bounced down the wide, carpeted staircase from his room, he found Feliks lounging furtively near the entrance, his tall, lean form trying to meld into a conveniently located column. The Pole approached with his right hand extended, smiling broadly to put him at ease.

Even as he matched Gustaw's firm handshake, though, the young Ukrainian was shrinking into the shadows, his glance darting from the hotel's front door to the reception desk to the lightly populated bar.

"Let's take a walk," Gustaw suggested, hoping to defuse the other man's restless energy with physical activity and fresh air. In the underground days, he had used this approach on plenty of nervous recruits. The cover of darkness might help Feliks to open up, too, if, as Gustaw suspected, he had some secret to share.

But Feliks shook his head firmly, slipping around the column to the side furthest from the street door.

"Can we talk in your room?" he asked, voice soft as he frowned toward the few customers sipping cocktails and chatting with the bartender, indifferent to anything beyond their one-meter orbits. "There are too many people in there tonight."

Gustaw cocked an eyebrow toward the younger man. *Could this be some sort of setup?* But Feliks had been highly recommended for the sort of skills they needed, and Gustaw had traveled quite a distance to meet him. Anyway, the kid's jumpiness seemed genuine, and talking to him was probably the only way to find out what had him spooked. So, the Pole shrugged and agreed to move the conversation upstairs.

Half an hour later, when the young man's outpouring of revelations had subsided, Gustaw swallowed hard and began speaking.

"I've been where you are, Feliks. I guess you have no reason to believe that, but it's true," he said, grateful to hear that his voice was steady despite the knot that had formed in his stomach while Feliks spoke. "Oh, I never took a job working for organized criminals; that's not what I meant. But you've figured out something that a lot of people of my generation never wanted to understand—fought like hell not to know, even. Because once you realize that your personal success in life depends on supporting an immoral system, your choices are to support it anyway or to fight against it with no guarantee of winning. You can either follow what you thought were your principles *or* pay your bills, support your family—maybe even stay alive, given who *you've* been working for."

The sandy-haired youth in the corner remained motionless, his hands lying limp in his lap, staring into the imaginary distance, as if his confession had wrung all the energy from him.

"I'm right, aren't I?" Gustaw probed. "As I said, I've been there. The difference between you and me, though, is that when I made that discovery, I didn't have anyone like me offer to help."

The young man shifted in his chair and turned his eyes to meet Gustaw's, hope and doubt playing against each other on his face. He didn't say the words aloud, but Gustaw heard them anyway: *We've just met. Why would you want to help me?*

"Like you, I was once a smart, ambitious kid trying to earn his place in the world," the older man said, answering the unspoken query. "It was a different time, of course—Communist Party rule; a socialist economy where the government owned and ran everything; the Soviet Union breathing down Eastern Europe's neck. What do they teach you about the Soviet Union here, in this place that used to be a part of it?"

Gustaw waited for a response, but when the younger man didn't answer, he kept speaking.

"Well, it doesn't matter, I guess. Anyway, I've seen that look on your face before, when I tried to talk to my own children about the Communist days and the underground. It was a Disney movie to them, too, long ago and far away. The world has changed so much, how could any of it be relevant today?

"Maybe that's why my own parents kept their stories to themselves," he mused. "They lived through the Second World War, but anything I learned from them about those years was an accident. Their generation seemed to think all the horror was best forgotten: the Nazi invasion; death camps; Soviet 'liberation'; massacred Polish soldiers in the Katyn forest."

Gustaw's voice trailed off as a memory emerged: his mother standing at the sink, soapy droplets erupting from the dishrag she waved at his father during one of their arguments. "I could have had a good life there!" she shouted, lamenting her decision to return to Poland after the war instead of going to Western Europe as a refugee. "A young man in the camp was madly in love with me." The way she said it, it seemed like marrying Gustaw's father and suffering under the Soviet system were part of the same tragedy for her.

That was the only time he ever heard her mention the German work camp where she had been sent after the Warsaw Uprising against the Nazis failed. Years later he did the math and realized she was barely fifteen then.

"Your country has its own nightmares from those times, of course," Gustaw said, shaking off the memory. "I guess people my age had gentler experiences than our parents had, and that must have left us with more hope. We all knew the Communist system was bullshit, of course, the older generation included, but they were too afraid to do anything against it. My parents begged me not to join the Solidarity trade union in the 1970s. They said it was too dangerous, for me and maybe for them, too."

"How did you know trying to change things wouldn't make them worse?" Feliks asked, almost defiant.

"We didn't, obviously," Gustaw said. "The way I saw it, though, things were already going from bad to awful in Poland. The question was whether to sit back and let that process continue."

He ran his fingers through his hair, trying to contain the flood of images gushing through his mind—the empty desks in his classroom; the pre-dawn knocking at the door that preceded a raid; an Austrian child casually peeling a banana in the snow. Those early days were never far from his thoughts since the election last fall. Why had so many voters assumed they couldn't go back to all that? Why had he?

"We wanted our living conditions to improve, of course, but the lies were the real problem—the enemy at the heart of all our other issues," he said.

He was trying to circle back to Feliks's situation, but the look of incomprehension on the other man's face impelled him to a digression. How to explain that critical link between the way things are now and the way we want them to be? Without understanding the former, how could anyone work effectively to achieve the latter?

"When I was a teenager, my friends and I read books smuggled into Poland from the West," Gustaw began. "George Orwell was my favorite author. Do you know his work: *1984*, *Animal Farm*? He invented the term 'doublethink' to explain how everyone in an oppressed society pretends to believe things they know are lies because anyone who challenges the official story will be punished. I understood instantly that he was writing about my country and others like it. Yours, too, of course, though you are too young to remember those days.

"You see, Feliks, we'd been hearing about the greedy capitalists in the West our whole lives, but the two systems were kept separate. There was little trade back and forth, and travel in or out was virtually unheard of. When I was in high school, though, Poland started to open up a little thanks to Western pressure. My girlfriend and I managed to get visas to visit Austria and West Germany one summer. We were allowed to purchase one hundred American dollars from the government and figured we would find work as we traveled to earn more."

He shook his head as he recalled their giddiness while planning that trip. They had been so sure things would be wonderful there, in those unimaginable lands—like visiting Oz or Shangri-la, though he hadn't yet heard of those places.

"It was a great adventure, I suppose," he continued aloud, "but the way I remember it, we were hungry and cold most of the time. We couldn't afford hotels—barely food—and spent a lot of time hitchhiking and sleeping in parks. Some of the drivers who picked us up assumed that since we were Polish, we must be Communists, maybe even Communist spies. Why else would we have been allowed to leave Poland?"

He sighed and leaned back on the bed, propping his weight behind him on flattened palms.

"It wasn't much fun, to be honest, but I learned a lot about the world they'd been keeping from us. In the West, everyone owned cars, wore stylish clothes, ate delicious-looking food in beautiful restaurants. And there we were, two waif-like children of Communist Eastern Europe, literally peering through windows at a lifestyle our whole country could not possibly afford. In Warsaw, I didn't know anyone who lived like the people I saw, even my aunt, who had a Communist Party job and government connections. Why wouldn't I want that life for everyone in Poland? Who wouldn't be suspicious of the people whose lies kept us from having it?"

He couldn't keep the bitterness out of his voice as he almost spat out the word "lies." In his day, even with all the official dishonesty, it was a charge that had meant something, morally as well as factually. But he shouldn't blame this young man for being born at a different time.

"I guess it's not so obvious to your generation, the damage lies do," he continued. "On the internet today, people seem to say anything they like, and everyone can choose whether to believe it or not: no filters, no accountability. That's not how truth is supposed to work, though, online or anywhere else."

Gustaw saw Feliks's guilt in his walling-off expression and heard the lecturing note in his own voice. He stopped talking and took a deep breath before trying again.

"If I seem frustrated, it's because those of us in underground publishing spent years making sacrifices and taking risks to get accurate information to people even when it was illegal. We never knew when the secret police were going to harass or arrest us or confiscate our publications or equipment—even our family cars, for those few who were lucky enough to have one. After all that effort, I hate to see the truth being treated as if it's irrelevant—as if your made-up stories are just as valid as legitimate articles about events that actually happened. Reality is not determined by how many people you can convince to click on a link or even to believe the same lie."

He smiled gently.

"I must sound old-fashioned to you, talking about truth like there is only one version of it—*the* truth, Truth with a capital *T*, as the priests and philosophers would say. If not *truth*, then *facts*, at least, should be a matter of common agreement. People can argue all day about why the facts are what they are and what we should do about them, but I will never accept the idea that it's okay to invent them."

The younger man frowned, looking sheepish, but he made no move to defend himself or end the conversation.

"I do understand better than most how dangerous it is to get in the way when powerful people are lying to the masses," Gustaw said, softening his tone again. "But when I say it is possible to fix something that is wrong in the world, if you are brave enough, I'm telling you what I know from my own life."

"So, you got home to Poland after visiting the West and started trying to overthrow the government?" Feliks asked, incredulous.

"Not exactly," Gustaw laughed. "I attended university and studied biochemistry, which I loved and could happily have immersed myself in forever. For me, science was an oasis of facts in the desert of Communist misinformation. Even the threat of Soviet tanks can't change the laws of chemistry and physics, so Polish scientists were permitted to do their work in the real world, not that parallel 'doublethink' universe that Orwell wrote about. Some of my friends who had traveled to the West like me wanted to find a way to relocate there. I figured I could escape just as easily into the scientific community without having to leave my home."

He sighed at the remembered innocence of his younger self.

"A few years after my trip to Austria, though, there was a factory workers' strike in Poland. It was centered in a city called Radom about an hour outside Warsaw, where I was a student.

"A lot of the striking workers lived in rural villages and spent three or four hours a day traveling back and forth to work. These were very poor people who scraped by with a vegetable patch and a few chickens. They needed those factory paychecks to survive.

"Then the government, which you'll remember controlled every aspect of the economy under Communism, suddenly announced that food prices were going to double overnight. These guys lived in houses where the windows were covered with wood and newspaper instead of glass. They couldn't even afford windowpanes at the old food prices. Where were they supposed to find extra money to continue to feed their families?

"So, they took to the streets to protest the price increases. 'Hooligans,' the government called them and sent in the riot police.

"Some of my university friends and I got together to help the families of the men who'd been arrested. We collected money for them and gave them rides to meet with attorneys who could represent their husbands and fathers in court. As I got to know these families and understand the conditions they lived in, which were much worse than my own life in Warsaw, I couldn't help thinking about the West Germans I had seen, their dinner plates heaped with sausages.

"By the end of the protests, hundreds of people had lost their jobs, but the government had to rescind the price increases. The authorities had worse problems by then, anyway, because we, the intelligentsia, were in contact with the working people now, and that's just what our leaders should have avoided at all costs."

A question mark appeared on the face of the young man in the corner. Gustaw smiled and held up his index finger.

"Because we could explain things to them that the government didn't want them to understand. They knew the official version was full of lies, but before the strike, there was no alternative. I'm not talking about a sophisticated philosophy here, just a few basics."

Feliks crinkled his eyebrows, and Gustaw switched seamlessly to professor mode.

"Okay, in those days, the Polish Communist Party was described as the 'vanguard of the proletariat.' Do you know this term? It's the story my generation learned in school. Do what the Party says because they understand best how to help the workers prosper. So, if the people weren't prospering—and they knew that they weren't—it had to be the Party's fault, right?

"If people believed the Party was responsible for their hardships, though, it would undermine the Communists' whole excuse for being in charge. That's why the government was so quick to blame Poland's problems on the Jews during the 1968 purges or on foreign spies in later years. They would say anything to explain why the Party wasn't delivering on its promises. Those of us trying to convince the workers to form independent unions must be working for the American CIA, right?

"But I had seen with my own eyes the better life in the West, even for workers. The government couldn't convince me with their propaganda about how capitalism was on the verge of collapse. When I told the factory workers in Radom what I had seen, some of them, at least, believed me and not the Party. That was the real beginning of my underground career. Soon, I moved on to publishing books and information the government didn't want Poles to have access to, like those George Orwell books I'd read as a kid."

"But you got arrested for that, right? And put in prison?"

Gustaw wasn't sure whether to read worry or excitement in Feliks's breathless question.

"A lot of people got arrested after martial law was declared," he said as casually as he could. "It was the Communist regime's last gasp attempt to keep everyone in line. When they locked me up, I saw so many people from my old high school, it seemed we should be wearing nametags for the class reunion. That makes a difference in how you experience internment. I wasn't just locked away from my family; I was locked in with friends."

He remembered that first night so clearly—how their jailers had broadcast General Jaruselski's speech declaring martial law on the loudspeakers over and over until morning. Packed into holding cells, too wired to sleep, there was no escape from its maddening logic. The mass arrests of regime opponents would protect the detainees, the general had explained, since they couldn't violate the new laws and get into legal trouble while imprisoned. It was almost funny the first few dozen times they heard it, that crazy Orwellian language.

"I won't say I was never scared or depressed about being there," Gustaw admitted aloud to Feliks. "There was a lot of uncertainty. After we'd been held a couple of weeks in Warsaw, the guards told us to collect our belongings and started to separate us. When my name was called, I was loaded onto a bus with a group of other prisoners and driven to a military airport."

There had been whispered rumors that they would be sent to Russia or East Germany, two countries where the secret police had a much worse reputation than Poland's goon squad. After years of being harassed, arrested, and released unharmed by the Polish authorities, suddenly they hadn't known what the rules were going to be.

At the airstrip, soldiers divided them into smaller groups, and Gustaw watched more familiar faces disappear into army helicopters. He tried to hide his trembling as they lifted off and flew out of sight. Then it was his turn.

As their chopper climbed into the air, the prisoners tried to keep track of which direction they were heading. First, they went north, so they knew they were still in Poland. Then the craft turned toward the west, and they were certain they were in trouble. *Shit, it's going to be East Germany,* Gustaw thought.

Long after darkness had ended their ability to track the topography below, they landed in a forested area and were moved into barracks. As guards hurried them inside, Gustaw glimpsed a Polish license plate on one of the vehicles parked there. *So, we're either in Poland or they want us to think we are,* he had told himself, not ready to trust that anything was as it appeared anymore.

He nodded at Feliks now.

"They flew us to an isolated army training camp, but we were still in Poland," he said. "It was a surprisingly pretty place with trees and a lake—not that we were allowed to enjoy these amenities. The real purpose of moving us was to separate intellectuals like me from the masses of Polish workers in the cities. I guess the government thought the Solidarity trade union movement would fizzle without us around to spread our counterrevolutionary ideas.

"The worst thing about the location was how difficult it was for family members to visit us. The typical route from Warsaw involved two or three buses and a train, totaling fifteen hours or more of travel each way. Thirty hours of travel, with a one-hour visit in the middle.

"My family was luckier than most because we had a car. It was risky to come, though, because of the chronic shortages of gasoline. They had to make sure they had enough for the return trip before they left Warsaw. Otherwise, they could have been stranded halfway home.

"At the end of summer, the soldiers moved us to another isolated place, this time near the Baltic Sea. There, we could see but not approach the shimmering blue ocean instead of a lake, and we still had armed guards all around us."

He waited for the boy to make eye contact before continuing.

"We weren't beaten or starved in these hidden places, if that's what you're imagining, Feliks. No cigarette burns, electric shocks, or simulated drowning. We got to wear our own clothes, use a toothbrush and soap; our basic dignity was respected.

"I was even able to work on my PhD thesis using notes and research materials my wife brought me during her visits. She would take my handwritten pages to my professor, then return with his comments the next time she came. The writers and artists among us did their best to pursue their work as well. I was touched afterward to learn that, while he was incarcerated, one friend had written a poem which he dedicated to me."

He sighed and smiled to himself, letting the memory of that honor permeate the air a moment before leaning forward to confide in the young man.

"We *did* undergo interrogations where our captors tried to get us to name our colleagues in the underground or agree to spy on them in the future. And they tempted us with the prospect of leaving Poland for the West. But this was no Stalinist gulag.

"The real torment of it was the indefinite nature of our detention. If we'd been tried and sentenced to five years in prison or ten, we'd at least have known how long we would be there and been able to count down to our release date. Instead, every morning we woke up not knowing if they would let us go before bedtime or if we would be there for the rest of our lives. Each day spent with that uncertainty felt like wasted time, the past stretching out ever further behind us while the future of our imprisonment never got any shorter. Then one day it *was* over, and they sent us all home."

Gustaw looked up, gauging the effect of his narrative on the younger man, whose face had settled into a satisfied, almost smug expression.

"It took several more years before Communism ended in Poland. Then, everyone could finally say out loud that the lies had been lies. There were no more secret police for collaborating neighbors and co-workers to inform about the slightest whispered disloyalty to the official regime, no more danger of becoming a political prisoner or prevented from advancing in your career or getting approved for a better apartment because of such allegations.

"It's one thing to recognize the lies, though, and something else again to know the truth. I became the head of a publishing company in Warsaw around that time. We specialized in reference books—dictionaries and encyclopedias that everyone in Poland knew by name. Suddenly, with no more government censors, we could publish the first uncensored encyclopedia in decades. People couldn't get enough of it."

Gustaw doubted he would be able to keep his visitor's interest by talking to him about reference books, but he was too deep in the past to stop himself now.

"Poles were hungry for real facts," he insisted brightly. "It wasn't enough to expose the old lies. They wanted knowledge and understanding of what was objectively true, and they gladly paid to get it. We sold out the first print run, then ordered another and sold that out, too. Our six-volume encyclopedia was so popular we began planning for a full-length, twenty-volume Great Polish Encyclopedia that would be a necessity for every school and library in the country."

"You got what you worked for then, didn't you?" Feliks said, shaking himself to alertness. "No one in Poland is keeping people from publishing what they want to today. That's progress, right?"

Gustaw was silent while he pondered that question.

"Maybe there are two ways to lie to people," he suggested, trying the idea out loud. "You can suppress the truth, like the Communists did, with official censors and laws to punish people who say or write things you don't approve. But it's hard to keep it up over time because the government needs to have spies and informants everywhere.

"Besides, evolving technology has made it harder to control all the ways people spread and access information. When I was growing up, everything was either broadcast on television or radio or printed on actual paper. Even manual typewriters were considered contraband back then because they could be used to copy uncensored documents. There was a time in the Soviet Union when everyone who received an illegal pamphlet was expected to type up five or ten new copies and give them away to people, each of whom would make five or ten copies of their own to distribute, and so on."

He chuckled. "You wouldn't believe the effort it took to smuggle mimeograph machines into Poland in the 1980s, disassembled and hidden among shipments of innocent products like canned ham or gardening tools. Then we had to collect all the pieces and follow the instructions to put them together and get it working. Can you even imagine that today, when everyone has a printer sitting right on their desk at home?

"What's different these days is that people who want to mislead the public don't need to seize control of the government or even a major media outlet. They can just bury the truth in a pile of bullshit so it's harder to distinguish one category from the other. The internet is filling up with nonsense like your bosses' fake news mill, set up to look like real newspapers with articles written by professional journalists. In the name of honest competition and press freedom, reality has become a matter of personal taste, like picking your favorite ice cream flavor."

"Isn't it better to have it all out there for everyone to sort through and judge for themselves what's accurate?" Feliks suggested. "Besides, from what I've seen, people like to believe bad things about people they don't like. If we don't write it for them, someone else will."

"That last part may be true," Gustaw sighed. "If so many people weren't so eager to believe the garbage, your bosses wouldn't be trying to make money from it. On the other hand, your professional presentation gives readers another excuse not to be skeptical."

"I'm not proud of what we do, but it's a paycheck," Feliks said softly. "I didn't have a lot of options when I took this job. Now it feels like I don't have any."

"That's where I might be able to help," Gustaw said. "I'm not saying it's going to be easy, but if we do nothing, then nothing is going to change. Is that what you want, knowing what your bosses are up to?"

"I was just trying to be honest with you about my background," Feliks said. "Because I do want to get away from it—from them."

He hesitated, and Gustaw saw fear play across his face before he spoke again.

"If you really want to stop what they are doing, though," Feliks continued quietly, "you should know that there's more to that operation than fake news articles."

4

James

Kyiv, Ukraine

This wasn't what he'd intended when he left California. Still, James reminded himself as they passed through customs at the Kyiv airport, he hadn't broken his promise to Anna either.

Despite ongoing tensions with Russia and the war in the east, he reasoned that Ukraine's capital was no more dangerous than Warsaw. He would exercise the caution that he always did in his travels, keeping his office staff updated on his whereabouts and not taking any unnecessary risks. Natalya had insisted on accompanying him, begging the question of why she hadn't come earlier if she thought it was so necessary. They'd had no discussion about who would be paying her expenses for the trip. If they got some answers about Gustaw's whereabouts, though, he'd consider it money well-spent.

They would see Marko first, they'd decided during the flight, arriving at the UkraineLaw offices before he knew they were coming, just in case he tried to give them the slip.

The first step through the publishing house door was enough to validate Gustaw's recent descriptions of the operation. What had once been a thriving open office filled with cubicles had shrunk to a handful of desks arranged on an area rug just inside the front door. The rest of the cavernous space was unlit, the clicking footsteps of the receptionist echoing off the invisible far walls as she hurried to her station to greet them.

She didn't recognize him. No surprise there. James had been counting on Gustaw to keep an informal eye on the business lately. He asked for Marko, and her eyebrows lifted slightly at the familiarity, but when he introduced Natalya, the last name she shared with the missing man brought a stiffening of recognition.

"Please come into his office and sit down. I'll try to telephone him. Did he know you were coming?"

The other woman reached for the telephone. Natalya held her by the arm. "When do you expect him back?"

"I wasn't," she responded with a momentary frown. "At least, I didn't think he'd be back today. He had some meetings out of the office."

"Do you know anything about the search for my husband?"

"Yes." She paused, reconsidering. "That is, I knew he hadn't been in touch in several days. I don't know anything more than that, I'm afraid. I believe there was some discussion about hiring a detective to look for him. I have those names and telephone numbers, if you'd like."

James ignored Natalya's expectant look before nodding. "We haven't decided on that yet, but I'd like to have the information in case we do go forward."

"Of course. I'll go and get it for you. And my name is Nina, if you need anything." Not that there were many other people around to ask.

Left alone in Marko's private office, they quickly scanned the room: leather-topped executive desk, bookshelves filled wall to wall with the monochromatic bindings of UkraineLaw's legal tomes. Was there anything here that would help them find Gustaw? Probably not, even if the head of UkraineLaw had been involved in the disappearance. What were they looking for, a signed contract for a kidnapping?

With a contrived show of fatigue, Natalya sat down behind the desk, leaning over to rub the back of her leg with a rueful pucker of her lip. Then, glancing briefly toward the door, she set about shuffling through the papers on Marko's desk. When she finished, she leaned back in the chair, all innocence, before sliding open the top desk drawer.

James sat up straight and broadened his shoulders, trying to make himself as big a shield as possible for a room surrounded by glass on three sides. Which direction had their hostess gone again? He stood, making a point of stretching his back and neck before swiveling toward the open door. No sign of Nina.

The large room outside the glass had once held a bustling operation where young lawyers and copy editors wrote up-to-the-minute commentaries on the legal developments of the day, which were distributed to a robust mailing list of subscribers in the legal and judicial professions. Now, even the diminished furnishings managed to dwarf the two or three employees listlessly occupying those desks. Maybe some workers had taken advantage of the boss's absence to attend to their own interests outside the office, but there was little indication out there that the company was even functioning.

Marko had overseen this business for decades, from the government-owned Communist era to its private sector days before the joint venture with Polish Academic Publishing. From James's understanding, it had never been very profitable, but they had made a go of it. Today, it seemed clear at a glance that he would not be able to hold on much longer. James wondered how much of the joint venture's money he'd managed to siphon off for that day.

Perhaps UkraineLaw's problem wasn't about digital technology versus paper-based publishing, as James had always believed, or even about the stressed, shrunken, and war-torn Ukrainian economy overall, as Gustaw had implied when they discussed the company's recent struggles. Maybe it was simply that there was no more demand for legal expertise in a place where laws had such limited sway despite years of outside encouragement toward reform.

Law—the rule of law—was supposed to be the great equalizer in free societies, where the rules were meant to apply equally to rich and poor, influential and unknown citizens. In Poland today, this very concept had brought the new government into conflict with its Western European counterparts. How should he read the failure of a Ukrainian company meant to capitalize on the evolution of laws? Was the very idea going extinct here? International aid was contingent on Ukraine's leaders promising reform. In practice, though, there was growing concern that foreign money merely kept the till full for Ukrainian government officials on the take. And in places like Hungary and now Poland, legality was increasingly interpreted to mean whatever the ruling party wanted it to mean.

So, what hope did UkraineLaw have, really, embezzlement or not, high-tech content distribution or not? Maybe Gustaw had disappeared for a goal that had no chance of coming to fruition anyway. It was the most depressing thought James had had in ages, and the very person he wanted to share it with was unavailable.

How many times had he and Gustaw sat together over a brandy at a pub or a cup of tea in a café, parsing the news of the day not as quotidian gossip but as a clue to the direction of history, to the evolution of humanity itself? They came from such different backgrounds but had arrived at remarkably similar worldviews. Given their disparate starting points, James found it reassuring to see Gustaw drawing conclusions that mirrored his own. It gave him hope in objective truth.

He glanced over at Natalya, still shuffling through the contents of Marko's desk as if they would tell her where her husband had gone. He wondered if she and Gustaw ever discussed, for instance, Muslim sharia law or China's brand of Communism as governing systems that might compete seriously with liberal democracy. James and Anna certainly had not; the life they had built together revolved around other shared interests.

A flutter in the corner of his eye alerted him to Nina's return; he had just enough time to murmur "She's back" before she entered to find Natalya sitting quietly in Marko's desk chair, her hands folded neatly on the blotter.

"Here's that list." Nina wavered uncertainly between them for a moment before handing it across the desk to Natalya. From where James was standing, it looked like there were four or five names and phone numbers.

"What do you know about them?" Natalya asked, reaching for a pen from Marko's pencil cup.

"They all speak English," she ventured. "I think they're mostly retired policemen, but you'd have to ask Marko."

"Were you able to reach him?" James asked.

"Not yet, I'm afraid. If you tell me where you're staying, I'm sure he'll want to come over as soon as he hears you're in town."

Natalya looked a little miffed at the dismissal, but James thanked Nina for her help and ushered Gustaw's wife out the door. They had more important concerns than a high-handed receptionist sending him away from a company of which he was part owner. And there was no sense hanging around waiting for Marko if he wasn't expected back anyway.

"Now what?" Natalya demanded when they were back on the sidewalk, as if this whole enterprise hadn't been her idea in the first place. She was still clutching the list of detectives in her fist.

"The hotel, I suppose. It's where Marko will expect to find us."

"If he tries, you mean. If she gets in touch with him today. How could he be unreachable, though? Doesn't everyone carry a cellphone now?"

It was a reasonable question, though not one he felt required to answer. Perhaps the Ukrainian publisher had gone to see a movie.

"We could walk around the city, if you'd prefer," James suggested. "I wouldn't mind stretching my legs. I doubt we'll find Gustaw that way, though. I don't know anyone in Ukraine other than Marko. Do you?"

"No. I've never even traveled here before. What about these investigators? We could try to meet with some of them."

They'd begun walking as they spoke, somehow agreeing on a direction without discussing it. They seemed to be headed toward a brick-paved plaza at the end of the street filled with kiosks, food carts, and umbrella tables.

As they plopped down at one of the tables, James considered her suggestion. Why not talk to some of the people on Marko's list? If Marko's contacts were suspect because they came from him, then Marko himself was equally tainted, wasn't he? So, waiting for his return was no more prudent than proceeding on their own.

"Okay," he said. "Let's see if any of them are available to meet today. Do you want me to make the calls? Or we could go to the hotel and ask the concierge to do it."

Natalya already had her phone out and was dialing the first number on the list. He heard voicemail pick up on the other end of the connection. She left a message in English with her name, telephone number, and a request to follow up about a search for a missing person. Her voice was steady throughout. She fished a pen from her bag, made a quick note on the page, and moved on to the next name.

Before James could decide whether to buy a cold drink from one of the nearby carts, Natalya had exhausted the list, tallying up two voicemail messages, a busy signal, a wrong number that was still wrong on redialing, and an accommodating gentleman who would be delighted to meet with her upon his return to the city in three days' time. She folded the paper and tucked it into her purse.

"What's next?" she said.

"Now I suppose we go back to our hotel and wait for one of your calls to be returned."

"Or we could have an early lunch and explore Kyiv while we're here," she proposed briskly. "I can't just sit around waiting for someone to phone me back."

Did she really intend to go sightseeing while her husband was missing? The idea was both outrageous and practical; perhaps the activity would be a distraction when they could do little now to further the search. But shouldn't he have been the one to suggest it?

He studied her across the table as she spoke purposefully to the concierge desk. What had become of the weepy, trembling woman of a few days ago? He knew he should be relieved that she'd decided to take charge of the search for Gustaw. And the less emotional drama, the better. He would be lost himself if he dwelt too much on the years of friendship that hung suspended between himself and the missing man.

It might have been Gustaw's boyish grin that had reeled James in. He was sure it wasn't his new acquaintance's bona fides as an anti-Communist agitator or the seriousness with which the Pole was trying to make a business case for investment in his no-longer-underground publishing company. All that, explained at their first meeting in Washington, D.C. in the summer of 1989, was enough to spark James's interest, sure, and even get him on the plane to Warsaw several months later. Gustaw had tried to discourage that February visit. "May would be warmer," he had said. But the Californian was eager to get behind the Iron Curtain and see what Communism had wrought there.

What James found was a society in flux—and his first whiff of opportunity to participate in its change. He had asked to meet local entrepreneurs, hoping to launch a chapter of the international business group he represented at the time, but Polish entrepreneurs were still a rare commodity then and that idea quickly fizzled.

Instead, Gustaw showed him around and regaled him with stories of life in Communist Poland and his publishing work in the underground—how confederates at the official publishing companies printed their illegal books during the chaos of shift change, when supervisors weren't paying attention; how the printed works were smuggled out to a decentralized network of locked storage closets, where students and professionals with duplicate keys came to fill their backpacks with books, returning later to leave cash after selling them at their workplaces and universities; how equipment and supplies had to be moved frequently, smuggled from hideout to hideout to stay a step ahead of the secret police. James listened intently to these tales that offered just the right mix of moral clarity, danger, and, now that Communism was over, the desired and deserved happy ending.

"What now, though?" James asked over lunch at a simple cafeteria in Warsaw's Old Town. "You got what you've been working for all these years. What's next?"

"Now the real work starts," Gustaw had said.

A lot of people might have said that ruefully, sighing at the realization that after years of exhausting struggle, success had presented them with a brand-new set of challenges, like a mountain climber finally cresting a tall peak only to discover more summits stretching forward into the distance. Not Gustaw. His eyes sparkled when he spoke, and he seemed energized at having finally reached the fun part of the project to put Poland on the correct path.

Then Gustaw brought up his dream of opening a bookstore, and James chimed in with descriptions of his local Barnes & Noble in California—the coffee bar that sold drinks and pastries, the overstuffed chairs in quiet corners where customers could sit and read unpurchased books for hours as if it were a library. The magazine section alone encompassed hundreds of titles, with topics ranging from current events to scientific discoveries to all sorts of hobbies and interests. Imagine such a place in Warsaw, James had suggested, featuring newspapers and magazines from around the world.

Gustaw grinned—actually grinned!—at the idea. How could James not want to participate?

After lunch, he and Gustaw had walked the streets of Warsaw together, faces bundled against the frigid wind, stepping around puddles of icy slush and chattering about their plans without a moment's thought for the cold. Before he left, James wrote Gustaw a check to get the project started.

In the end, the bookstore hadn't come together, for reasons unrelated to James or Gustaw, but the seeds of their subsequent collaboration had been sown. Later, Polish Academic Publishing opened some retail storefronts to sell the company's own products. Perhaps those shops had somewhat fulfilled Gustaw's original aspirations, James told himself. Towering dreams often lose stature in the light of day.

Now that he thought about it, though, he wasn't sure when Gustaw had stopped smiling reflexively to welcome the challenges ahead.

With the weight of personal history already upon him, James joined Natalya in exploring Kyiv's past as superficially embodied in museums and statues in public squares. This wasn't how he liked to get to know foreign places—he preferred to interview the locals directly about their individual stories and worldviews—but he welcomed any distraction that might mitigate his feelings of anxiety and helplessness. In this goal, their efforts were only marginally successful. Ukraine's past encompassed the suffering of hundreds of thousands of Gustaws.

Perhaps the fate of one missing man was insignificant compared to the mass casualties of Stalin's starvation policies under Communism and competing invasions of Ukraine over the centuries. But isn't that what Western civilization really came down to: the idea that one individual *was* infinitely important?

If a single life is so cheap—after all, there would still be seven billion people on the planet no matter what happened to any one of us—then why fuss over human rights, civil liberties, or individual autonomy and choice? If human worth were purely a numbers game, then the individual would constantly be subservient to society as a whole—whatever that might mean—and never able to prioritize his own happiness. And if James believed in anything, he believed in the importance of personal freedom—so long as no one else got hurt in the process of exercising it.

For most of his adult life, James had managed to avoid the petty tyrannies that he saw stifling creativity and slowly smothering the souls of friends and colleagues, whether by a clingy, controlling spouse or through rigid workplace processes and agendas. He could never have been happy letting someone else dictate his daily activities, especially when consequential matters were being decided. Maybe even life-and-death.

The botanical gardens were a welcome relief from James's reflections, turning his mind in more uplifting directions about the persistence and resilience of life in all its forms. He and Natalya spoke little as they moved through the galleries and greenhouses, merely conferring occasionally about where to go next and whether it was time for a rest or a bathroom break. As far as he could tell, Natalya was genuinely absorbed in what they saw, pausing to read placards and examine exhibits like any other tourist. Glancing toward her when he thought she wouldn't be looking, he saw nothing to suggest the strain she'd been under beyond a propensity to reach up and fidget with the teardrop-shaped silver pendant she was wearing, sliding it back and forth along the chain a few times before letting it drop inside the collar of her blouse.

Eventually Natalya's cell phone rang. A private investigator she'd called earlier requested they come to his office. Marko had been looped in somehow and would meet them there. She jotted down the address and strode off to hail a cab, leaving James to follow as best he could, his long legs pumping to catch up. Sliding into the seat after her, he wondered whether she would've waited for him if he'd been caught in the press of the crowd.

5

Gustaw

One week earlier
A dim room, eastern Ukraine

"Gentlemen, I assure you, these measures are unnecessary. My purpose here is completely innocent. Please untie these ropes and let us talk like civilized men."

Gustaw noted the calm, suave timbre of his own voice, and it relaxed him a little despite his bindings. He had always had a way with people, from his teachers at school to nervous recruits in the underground to union leaders and foreign investors threatening to derail things at the publishing house. He didn't get everything he wanted—far from it in that last instance—but he always came out better for turning on the charm, regardless of the circumstances.

Until now, though, those circumstances had never included being physically restrained by criminals. Unless you counted internment during the martial law period.

Gustaw smiled slightly at this thought, then frowned when he caught one of his captors scowling at him. It was the tall, burly one with the bulbous nose, whose hopeful leer suggested that he would enjoy dismembering Gustaw at the slightest excuse. But he was restraining himself for now, which probably meant that the slight, cleanshaven man with the expressionless face was the one calling the shots. Gustaw addressed his next words to him.

"I came here with a simple business proposition, Mr. . . . ?"

As expected, his implied question was ignored. He paused only a moment before continuing.

"I have recently made the acquaintance of a young man whom I would like to hire for a new venture of my own. I understand he already has a position here, and I would like to compensate you for the inconvenience of losing him."

"Where is this young man, then?" his captor answered softly in a voice that matched Gustaw's for gentility. "Why isn't he here to explain for himself why he prefers to seek new employment?"

"He did want to come," Gustaw said. "I asked him to wait and allow me to speak to you first. You see, he was afraid you would be offended when you learned that he was considering another offer. I'm sure you can appreciate that. I thought we should talk things over, reassure him that everyone could be made happy if he were to come work for me."

The tall, meaty figure spoke then. His voice was gravelly, like an old smoker. "So, he would rather work for a Polish spy than for us?"

Gustaw chuckled. "Polish, yes. A spy? Of course not. Surely a man can travel to a neighboring country and start a business there without being accused of espionage."

"Who sent you to Ukraine?" It was the first questioner again.

"No one sent me. I work alone," Gustaw said. Immediately, he regretted telling these rough men that he had no backup. He forced a guileless smile.

"Now that I think about it, though, I suppose it must seem unusual that I came here so late in the evening. The young man I spoke of said his work shift began at this hour. I was hoping to speak to his supervisor directly."

He made a show of glancing around the grungy office with its dented metal furniture and a darkened rectangle where an observation window overlooked the vacant factory floor.

"I must have come to the wrong address entirely, though. I expected to find a building full of technical workers busy at their computer stations, but whoever works here must have gone home for the night."

"Tell us who your young friend is, and we'll decide if you're where you should be," promised the shorter man, whose quiet voice was somehow more ominous.

"His name? Well, if I'm in the wrong place, then you are not the gentlemen I expected to talk to about him. You cannot help me with my problem, and I have already taken up too much of your valuable time. I will gladly be on my way. It'll be as if I was never here."

The big guy took a sudden step closer and towered over him.

"Do you think we're stupid, then?" he shouted. "That we'd just let you leave?"

"No, I am not insulting your intelligence," Gustaw answered calmly, though his pulse was racing. He extended his open palms in a conciliatory gesture made farcical by the ropes tying his ankles to the cold metal chair legs. "I am happy to give you whatever information you require about myself and my purpose here, but I fear you will be disappointed, as my answers haven't changed."

"Then I am afraid we have a long night ahead of us," said the gravelly voice, cracking his knuckles in an almost-comedic show of menace.

"At my age, gentlemen, a good night's sleep would be more beneficial," Gustaw said, adding a half-chuckle that was not reciprocated. "Besides, I have a train to catch in the morning."

Now his captors laughed full-throatedly, their derision echoing off the bare walls of the unadorned room.

"Well, I am clearly at your mercy," Gustaw sighed. "Tickets can be exchanged, I suppose."

Dammit! He was supposed to have walked out the door hours ago leaving only goodwill and the promise of cash behind. The longer these guys were occupied with him, though, the more time Feliks would have to complete his task. The Pole shifted in his chair, giving the appearance of settling in before he spoke again in his resonant, storyteller voice.

"If we are going to spend some time getting to know each other better, then it might interest you to learn that you are not the first people to develop such a keen fascination with my humble, ordinary life.

"The Polish secret police wasted weeks—perhaps months—of manpower on me when I was barely out of high school, a mere university student with a young wife. I wasn't a spy then, either. I had signed a petition, you see, disagreeing with some proposed changes to the Polish constitution."

"Such as?" prompted the smooth interrogator.

"What they were isn't important. It was the usual nonsense of those times. *The Polish Communist Party is the driving force in society . . . The Soviet Union is a special friend to Poland.* I put my name down against it, so I was on a government list from then on.

"The agents assigned to monitor me didn't even bother to hide. I would come out of my apartment in the morning, and there they were, standing on the street corner smoking cigarettes with a lazy eye turned to my front door. They wanted me to see them, to be sure I knew that they were watching me.

"I learned to recognize all the people they had following me around town throughout the day—five or seven different faces at different times, all with the same telltale nonchalance."

Gustaw chuckled, warming to the memories.

"They didn't even bother to question me, then. That started a few years later. They used to search our apartment first thing in the morning when my children were very small. They would throw all our belongings on the floor, start the babies crying, then drag me off for forty-eight hours in jail. We all knew they couldn't charge me with anything, so after a couple of days, they had to let me go.

"It *was* a hassle, but I figured if the government was expending all those resources on one man because he signed a petition, the system could never survive. I was right about that, wasn't I?"

Blank faces stared back at him, not answering. Did his captors have no feelings of their own about the Communist days?

"The truth is, I started to feel a little sorry for those guys," Gustaw continued. "Sure, they had an easy job, but it couldn't have been very interesting for them, hoping to turn up evidence of some high-profile traitor and instead they have to watch me attending lectures and running experiments in the science laboratory.

"I always did wonder about the person who gave the order to have me followed, though. Lech Walesa and the other Solidarity bigwigs were off plotting to overthrow the whole system, and instead of keeping better track of *their* plans, the secret police were spending all that effort on me."

He clucked his tongue, then rested his chin on his fist in a tableau of puzzlement.

"Do you suppose there were consequences for that sort of screw-up in the Communist days? I bet your bosses would care if you made that type of mistake, wouldn't they? I've certainly worked for some people who didn't take kindly to having their money wasted."

"What's that supposed to mean?" snapped the raspy voice as the other man moved closer, eyebrows arranged in a threatening glower.

Gustaw shook his head.

"Nothing. I'm only pointing out that you're not the first people to get the wrong impression about me. It wasn't just those idiot Communists. Something similar happened again years later, when we were all happy capitalists in Eastern Europe.

"The company I was running had taken on a couple of investment banks as partners, and a few months afterward, sales of our encyclopedias and dictionaries dropped from couldn't-keep-them-on-the-shelves to almost nothing. The new investors thought they'd been duped into putting their money into a failing enterprise. They couldn't believe the timing was a coincidence, and they got very insistent trying to prove we had hidden the true state of the business from them.

"So I was summoned to a meeting in London with their lawyers, and I tell you gentlemen, even the Polish secret police, who imprisoned me during martial law, weren't that scary.

"They sent a car and driver for me, very posh, and we went straight from the airport to the office. I had no time to prepare for anything—not that I'd have known how to prepare for what was coming.

"I was escorted into a room, and there were the three of them, sitting at a long table with windows behind and the sun streaming in so that all I could make out were their silhouettes. It wasn't unlike this office, I suppose, with the lamp bulb shining directly in my eyes. It's much too harsh a light for this space, to be perfectly candid. Your ophthalmologist will have something to say about it if you continue to work in these conditions, to say nothing of your interior decorator."

Gustaw smiled and winked like they were all friends sharing his little joke, then continued.

"Anyway, there was one chair in the middle of the room on the other side of that table, and I was told to sit in it before they started firing questions toward me about how we had misled them.

"'How did you hide the losses? Who prepared the phony account statements? Where are the real books kept?'

"Logically, I could have stood up and walked out of that room at any moment. No one would have prevented me. Yet to do so would have been impossible. I was there representing my company, representing Poland and our other investors and every good faith understanding that there were people in the former Soviet bloc who wanted to play the capitalist game on its own terms. If I had walked out on them, then all the absurd questions they were asking me would have looked legitimate, and they would've assumed I had something to hide. Do you understand this, how people choose to sacrifice their own freedom and dignity in the name of reputation and honor?"

Gustaw paused, though he couldn't have said whether it was for the rhetorical effect on his captors or just to savor his own poignant thought. A part of him couldn't believe they had let him chatter on for so long, but he didn't want to waste the opportunity.

"So, I sat there for I don't know how many hours—no food, no restroom breaks—denying as calmly and politely as I could that there was any truth to the picture they were trying to paint. It's hard not to feel guilty in such circumstances, even when you know you are innocent. Perhaps you have observed that phenomenon in your own work."

The shadows shifted ominously, so Gustaw quickly resumed his narrative.

"At the end of the day, they thanked me for my time and sent me back to the airport with the same car and driver, who helped me with my bag and wished me a safe journey home, as if I were a valued colleague and not a suspected con man and thief."

"What's the point of all this chatter, Spy?" the smooth voice asked softly. "We are not Polish police or London lawyers."

So, they had been listening.

"Why did I tell you this story? Because I learned from that experience that the most terrifying people in the world are the ones who can look you in the eye and respectfully call you "sir" while calmly promising to tear your life apart if you don't give them exactly what they want."

He paused for a few beats, then gave a relaxed laugh.

"But I couldn't tell those lawyers what they wanted to hear, because we hadn't done anything wrong. It was just bad luck that their clients bought into the company at a high value and then business declined.

"So, ask your questions again, and I will give you the same answers," he concluded, a clipped firmness in his voice now as he sat up straight and tall despite his restraints. "Eventually, you will be satisfied that I have told you the truth, and then we can all go home. As I said, I've been through this sort of thing before."

6

James

Kyiv, Ukraine

Whatever James had expected from the office of a retired cop turned private investigator, this was not it. Instead of a dark-paneled hovel with battered desks and a grimy tile floor, this gentleman inhabited a bright, airy three-room suite with tasteful if forgettable décor and a middle-aged secretary to greet clients and offer them coffee. Perhaps the war had been good for the missing persons racket.

Marko was waiting for them in the reception area, looking relaxed and well-groomed in a casual blazer with an Oxford shirt and no tie. Even his chin stubble seemed to have been tidily trimmed to a uniform length, as if to portray a precisely calibrated level of nonchalance. He nodded in greeting, and they were all ushered into a small room with a round table and four upholstered armchairs. The investigator's assistant removed a large vase of flowers from the center of the table and took it out with her.

The detective was a fiftyish man of medium build and height wearing a dark suit. He introduced himself as Stepan, waved them to their seats, and listened to Marko's brief synopsis of Gustaw's disappearance, the police search of his hotel room in Mariupol, and the ensuing silence.

"While it is near the Donbas region, where there is fighting, Mariupol has been a safe city for travelers and businesspeople to visit," he explained, presumably for James and Natalya's benefit. "We have no reason to think Gustaw was involved in anything related to Ukraine's war with the separatists."

For the first time, James understood that Gustaw had disappeared not in rebel-held territory but on the government side of the battle lines. Not such a foolish place to be, then?

"I've spoken to the Mariupol police detective every few days since Ludmyla called me," the Ukrainian publisher assured them. "It's always the same answer: 'We have no new information. We'll let you know if we find anything.' Frankly, I doubt they're even looking."

"What was his business in the Donbas region?" the detective asked, addressing all three of them.

"I don't know why Gustaw went there, but I know he'd been trying to find candidates for a technical job here in Kyiv," Marko answered without so much as a glance in James's direction.

James blushed and looked down anyway.

"I gave him the name of one young man whose parents are friends of mine," Marko continued. "But I haven't been able to learn if he tried to contact him or not."

The investigator's pen hovered over the page in his notebook. Marko dug his phone out of his pocket and scrolled across the screen for a few seconds.

"Here it is." He read off a name—Yuri something or other—and telephone number. "I sent him an email over the weekend but haven't had a response."

"Well, where does he live?" Natalya was on her feet. "Why don't we just go see him?"

"I could do that for you," Stepan offered. "That is, if you intend to hire me."

"Maybe we should all go," James suggested. "I'd like to hear what he has to say for myself."

"That might be a little intimidating, four people appearing on his doorstep to ask about someone he may never have heard from who is now missing," the detective said. "I'd prefer to approach him alone. If he knows anything that will point us in a helpful direction,

I should follow up as soon as possible. We're already several days behind."

"Also, I'm not sure he speaks English," Marko said. "Mrs. Bogutsky, do you speak Ukrainian?"

"No."

"Well then, I will go with our friend here, and if we can find him at home, we will talk to him and bring you a full report."

"Then what?" James asked. "Do you search for missing people in the east?" Something about the man's scrubbed, buttoned-down appearance belied the image of him operating on a battlefield. To James, he had more the air of a tax attorney.

"Certainly. Many people find themselves misplaced on the wrong side of the front line. This can happen by accident. I can only look and investigate, however. I cannot guarantee that I will find him. Perhaps he is no longer in the east. Perhaps by now he has traveled or been taken to another place."

"How many people have you looked for in that area?" Natalya asked.

"Oh, half a dozen or so, maybe ten over the past couple of years."

"And how many of them were you able to find?"

"Four, I think, though I'm afraid one was no longer alive. It is a dangerous part of the country, as you know. But the man who died was a Ukrainian soldier who disappeared during a battle."

"You two find out what you can, then, and let's meet again in a few hours to decide how to proceed," James instructed, taking charge.

Natalya's taut face said she didn't like it, but the detective had a point; they couldn't all go barging in to knock on some unsuspecting kid's door demanding answers.

Besides, Marko had thrown him for a loop knowing about Gustaw's hiring mission. If Marko was angry about their plotting behind his back, however, he was showing no signs of it. He smiled easily as the group disbanded, patting Natalya on the shoulder and shaking hands with James to send them on their way.

Whatever Natalya might have in mind for the rest of the afternoon, James was going to his hotel room for a shower and some fresh clothes. There was nothing more they could do for Gustaw right now anyway.

They reconvened in the hotel restaurant for dinner. When James came downstairs, Marko and Natalya were already seated, their heads together in an animated exchange.

"Well, where are we?" James interrupted as he sat down. "Was your contact at home?"

"His father was, and we were able to reach the son on his cell phone. He said he did talk to Gustaw and gave him a couple names of other people who might be better suited for the job."

"Great. Did you try to call them? Was one of them in Mariupol?"

"We don't have the details yet," Natalya said. "His phone ran out of charge or something, but he's going to meet us here, along with the detective."

"That sounds like progress." James turned to Marko. "I'm curious, what did Gustaw say to you about the position he wanted to fill?"

The publisher gave a dry laugh. "He said I shouldn't tell you I knew anything about it because it was supposed to be a secret."

James shifted slightly in his seat, feeling caught out. "I wasn't sure how you'd react to the idea. We've talked about technology upgrades so often, and you've made your opposition to the idea pretty clear."

Marko nodded. "Maybe I have been slow to adapt, like you've said, but business was fine until this damned war started. Now, even your Bill Gates couldn't make technology profitable in Ukraine. But don't blame Gustaw for telling me about your new enterprise. He kept it to himself—all the way until I told him I was ready to close the company and retire from publishing."

"Oh, when did you decide that?"

"When civil war and economic meltdown drove away my customers. But Gustaw told me I should hang on a little bit longer, that maybe there was value in the intellectual property we'd been storing up over the years. I didn't believe him, of course, so he told me what the two of you had been discussing." Marko shook his head. "Now, I don't claim to be any more convinced than I was before, but if you think you can use our content on the internet, then your new company probably wants to buy it, am I right?"

"We'd been discussing more of a leasing situation, assuming that would help stabilize the *joint* venture." James couldn't resist putting a slight emphasis on the term to remind Marko that UkraineLaw wasn't his alone to shutter or sell.

"Not that that matters now, right? Until we find Gustaw anyway." Marko seemed genuinely pained as he said the name and shot a sympathetic glance at Natalya.

"Well, where do you think he is?" Her voice was sharp, dismissing his sympathy for a laser-like focus on the problem at hand.

"If I had an idea where he was, I would have someone looking for him there, of course," Marko insisted, stroking the back of her chair soothingly. "Gustaw has many friends and interests, yes? He is a publisher, a scientist, a political activist, even a runner of marathons. For all the years I've known him, his life has been like this. I think he could be doing something unrelated to UkraineLaw, Polish Academic Publishing, and all the rest of the activities I am familiar with. In that case, it is very difficult to know where to start looking."

Was Gustaw really so mysterious? There had been those times, back in the era of the investment banks, when James hadn't known which side his friend was on. Or rather, he had been fairly sure Gustaw was trying to cut James and his investors loose to save his own skin. Over the years, however, that certainty had faded to a not-very-urgent question mark. There were undoubtedly villains from that period, but neither he nor Gustaw were at the top of the list—not each other's anyway. Who knew what the bankers thought about it all by now? Or the hundreds of employees forced out by the turmoil of the free market transition.

They had done what they could to help the workers adjust, though, hadn't they? Short of keeping them on when the company couldn't afford it, of course. James recalled being in Warsaw during one round of layoffs when consultants were brought in to run a networking and resume-writing workshop for those affected. Dark-suited and somber-eyed, the laid-off employees mingled in hushed groups in the hallway between sessions, clutching their free notepads and pens to their chests as if they would provide some protection against the uncertain future.

Afterward, James had spoken to Gustaw about hosting a job fair at Polish Academic Publishing, perhaps in concert with other publishing companies.

"We could try that," the Pole had responded, shaking his head as he spoke. "But the whole book industry is struggling to make sales. No one else is hiring either."

"Maybe some related businesses, then," James had pressed. "Newspapers, magazines. There must be some field where their skills could be useful."

Gustaw had seemed open to the idea, but James had a plane to catch, so who knew what had come of it in the end. And, really, what did it matter now anyway? Polish Academic Publishing's dislocations were a drop in the bucket for Poland then, but the whole country had emerged strong and growing fast from the austerity measures of the time. And that had been good for everyone, hadn't it?

Stepan the private detective arrived, interrupting James's musings about the past. He was leading a young man wearing a jacket, a tie, and a nervous look. Maybe it was from knowing why Gustaw had contacted him in the first place, but to James he looked for all the world like someone arriving for a job interview.

Natalya watched their approach like a lioness ready to pounce. James stood up and crossed in front of her to introduce himself, temporarily blocking her view. He waved them to empty seats before retaking his own, jostling her chair slightly as he slid up to the table.

"I'm very sorry," he said, forcing her to turn and acknowledge him. "Please forgive my clumsiness."

"Of course," she agreed shortly, then turned to the new arrivals with a slightly less ravenous demeanor. "Now, what have you gentlemen figured out that could help us locate my husband?"

Marko spoke to the young man in Ukrainian, presumably translating her question. He answered softly with a brief glance in her direction.

"Yuri tells me Gustaw did contact him about the job he was trying to fill, but they decided he wasn't the best candidate for it," Stepan explained. "So, he gave Gustaw the names of some people he had worked with in the past."

"And have they heard from him?"

"Did either of them live in Mariupol?" Natalya's and James's questions burst forth together.

"Yuri has agreed to contact his friends to find out," the detective broke in. "He needed to plug in his phone to get their numbers, so we stopped at the concierge desk, where they are charging it for him."

"Thank you for your help," James addressed the young man and waited for Marko to translate. "Could you tell us whose names you gave to Gustaw and a little bit about them?"

The boy chattered for a couple of minutes before Marko turned back to answer in English. "He said the first one is his cousin, who lives here in Kyiv now but was originally from the east. He said his cousin is very clever and can do anything with computers. He has had a few different programming jobs, but Yuri isn't sure what the company names were. The other man is a former co-worker who mentioned a few months ago that he was looking for work. Yuri is not sure what either of them have been doing recently and didn't contact them to let them know Gustaw had their information."

"Why didn't you want the job yourself?" Natalya asked.

Yuri spoke, then Marko explained. "He likes what he's doing now, and Gustaw said there was a chance the operation would use Ukrainian workers living in Poland. He didn't want to leave Kyiv. His girlfriend and parents are here."

A harmless enough reason, James thought. "So now we are waiting for a phone to recharge."

"We don't have to, of course," Marko said, making him realize he'd spoken aloud. "Now that it's plugged in, we can get the numbers and Yuri can call on a different phone for privacy. I think that would be a good idea, before it gets too late." He turned to Yuri and spoke in Ukrainian, presumably repeating himself. Then the two of them stood and headed out of the restaurant toward the reception desk.

James gave the private detective a critical look. "How long have you known Marko?"

"A long time. Thirty years, maybe? He was a trainer for the police academy before he bought UkraineLaw. Did you know that?"

"I probably did, at one time. It had slipped my mind. Have you done any detective work for him before?"

"Not that I remember. We hadn't been in touch recently, but of course I want to help him find his friend."

"Gustaw is a good man," James agreed. "It's important to all of us to get him home safely."

"Of course. Which brings us to a few questions I have. I believe he was in Ukraine on assignment from you, Mr. Jensen. Is that correct?"

"He was in Kyiv for me, visiting our joint publishing venture with Marko and, as you've heard, trying to hire someone to help us launch a technical business. That's how my investments operate, you understand."

"Really? How does that work?" Stepan reached into his breast pocket for a small notebook and pen, which he opened expectantly.

"I partner with local champions to start companies," James began, pausing for the detective to keep up. "I provide capital and business expertise, and they supply the legwork and knowledge on the ground. It's a model I've used all over the world."

"I see. And Gustaw was looking for your next 'champion' in Ukraine?"

"Exactly."

"It must be difficult finding just the right person for such an important role. I'm surprised you would leave the choice up to Gustaw."

"Well, he was one of my champions, too, years ago. He negotiated the UkraineLaw joint venture when he was still managing Polish Academic Publishing in Warsaw. So, even though he's not Ukrainian himself, he has some background here. Of course, I would've had to meet and sign off on his choice eventually."

"And how closely did he communicate with you on his progress?"

"I see him when I come to Warsaw a handful of times a year. Also, he would've sent an email update after his trip. Or we might've Skyped if there was something specific to discuss. I'm not sure how these details will help you find him though."

Stepan stopped writing and looked up.

"Right now, I'm just trying to learn about his habits, routines, how unusual it is that he's been out of touch for so long. Did you realize he hadn't sent the expected update before you learned he hadn't returned home?"

Somehow the conversation had become an interrogation. Where had Marko and that kid disappeared to?

"No, but I didn't have a specific date to look for it," James answered with clipped patience. "He sets his own schedule and itinerary, obviously."

"Naturally." Stepan turned to Natalya. "What about you, Mrs. Bogutsky? How closely does your husband keep in touch with the family while he is traveling?"

"Every few days, I suppose. It depends on the trip and what everyone is doing."

"So, no nightly calls with you and the children?"

"No, our children are all adults now."

"And when did any of them last hear from their father?"

Stepfather, James thought to himself. Had anyone thought to contact his ex-wives and their kids?

"Before I did, from what they told me," Natalya said. "He doesn't spend his evenings checking in with everyone. When he's working, that's what he does, especially when he's traveling. He says he has to use every minute being wherever he is doing whatever he went there to do." Her voice took on the edge of someone reliving a dozen petty arguments—or the same petty argument a dozen times.

"Did you ever have any concerns that he wasn't?"

"Wasn't what?"

"Doing what he went somewhere to do."

A frigid silence blew across the table. James held his breath while Natalya absorbed the question, a version of which must be uttered to the spouse or partner of everyone whose disappearance is ever investigated.

"Gustaw never gave me any reason to worry."

"What about you, then?"

"What do you mean?"

"Well, he's out of touch for days at a time. Maybe you get lonely when he's away, find a friend to keep you company."

"No." From his spot beside her, James could see her winding the edge of the tablecloth tightly around one finger. He stopped himself from reaching over to pull it from her hands.

"Did he ever get suspicious about how you spend your time when he's gone?"

She was silent so long that James began to wonder if he should intervene, though whether to defend her honor or recount what he knew of their stormy marriage, he hadn't yet decided.

"Our marriage isn't perfect," Natalya said finally, releasing the purpling finger from its tourniquet with a wince. "We have disagreements, like other couples, but infidelity has nothing to do with it."

"I'm sorry to have to ask these questions, Mrs. Bogutsky. I don't know enough yet to know what information might be relevant, so I'm trying to learn as much about your husband as I can. What did you argue about?"

She looked down, swallowed hard, sighed, and met the detective's eyes again, unblinking. "The usual, I suppose. How to spend our money. How he spends his time. Ever since the election last fall, it's like he's on some damned crusade."

"He wasn't happy with the results?"

"Of course he wasn't, and I don't blame him for that. I just wish he'd let somebody else fight the system. Relax. Stay home. Think about retiring in a few years."

"But he doesn't want to stay home and relax?"

"He used to. At least, I thought so."

"Until the election?"

"Exactly."

"But he's not going to fix the Polish government from Ukraine, is he? So why would he delay his return from Kyiv to go to Mariupol?"

"That's the question we've been asking ourselves," James said.

"Yuri's cousin might be able to help us figure that out," Marko said, coming up to the table with Yuri beside him.

"You reached him, then?" Natalya asked, pouncing on the news with a ferocity that unraveled all the coolness she'd shown since they arrived in Ukraine. She stood, pressing her palms to the table. Maybe she was just eager to change the subject.

"Well, no," Marko admitted. "But Yuri spoke to his aunt, and she said he'd done some work for a company near Mariupol. She wasn't sure of the name of it. We explained how important it was that we speak to him, so she's going to call his apartment manager to check and see if he's home. She promised to have him call Stepan as soon as she reaches him."

"And the other guy?"

"Never heard from Gustaw, or so he says. Also, no connection to Mariupol that he would share. He says he is looking for work, though, if the job's still open."

"Not at the moment." James dismissed the idea as in poor taste. "I guess we're back to waiting."

This time, no one was prepared to dispute that. Fortunately, the detective seemed to have run out of questions for them, so Natalya signaled for a waiter, and they were able to have an uninterrupted, if subdued, dinner together.

As they ate, James looked around the table at this ad hoc search committee. There was the estranged wife—okay, maybe not estranged, exactly, but recently strained in her relationship with the missing man; the Ukrainian business partner whose honesty Gustaw had questioned; the Ukrainian private investigator whose degree of loyalty to that partner was unknown; and James himself, the former colleague turned employer, a long-ago friend, then former friend and now a friend and employer again.

Should they trust the two Ukrainians? Marko and Stepan had done nothing to suggest otherwise, but between the language barrier and their homefield advantage, how were he and Natalya to know? James had dismissed the idea that she was somehow involved. So, she and Gustaw were having a rough patch, maybe even heading for divorce. To all appearances, she just wanted to find her missing husband. If not, why drag James to Kyiv to look for him?

Over coffee and crème brulée, he allowed the helplessness and absurdity of the situation to sink in. What were they doing dining in a fine—okay, decent—restaurant while Gustaw was who-knows-where suffering who-knows-what? And after an entire day in Kyiv, all they had accomplished was to make some phone calls that only led to more questions and more phone calls. How would this seemingly logical but incremental process help them find Gustaw?

This frenetic feeling—desperately treading water without going anywhere—was one he did his best to avoid. And at this point in life, he was fortunate to have the means to do so. Over the years he'd established a reliable network of personal assistants, interns, and contractors who were paid to help him resolve any problems that arose in his life, whether in business or private matters. Of course, it hadn't always been that way . . .

The long-ago day when the floor dropped out of his Poland dreams had started routinely enough. It must have been fifteen years earlier or more. James was in Warsaw for a quarterly board meeting. The mood was grim at the company since encyclopedia sales had plummeted, taking revenues down with them, but until that point, everyone seemed to be working together to find solutions.

As they often did, the Supervisory Board members—some Poles, some not, but all representing different groups of company shareholders—had met for breakfast together before going to the publishing palace to meet with the management team. There, the bankers' representatives had demonstrated that the bloom was definitely off the rose on their new investment.

"We're going to get you for dragging us into this mess," one of them had spat across the table at James. And by "you," it was obvious the banker didn't mean the publishing house or even James's investment group as a whole, but James Jensen himself.

By the time James arrived at the publishing palace for the meeting, he thought he'd adjusted mentally to the rancor in his fellow shareholder's tone. Certainly, the man had reason to be frustrated with the company's sudden drop in sales less than a year after the investment banks bought in at a high valuation. Maybe the bankers even had a good excuse for being suspicious. But the venom and the personal threat came as a shock to James, who'd hoped that the bankers would be his allies in guiding the company toward standard Western business practices. Instead, they turned against James and tried to paint him as the one who had cut ethical corners. He shrugged off his disappointment, prepared to focus on the decision making ahead.

Then he heard the clapping.

It wasn't applause. As meeting-goers climbed the wide staircase to the Hall of Mirrors, slow clapping punctuated their ascent. The noise sounded like a mockery of that congratulatory gesture—or perhaps the drumbeat of a hunting party closing in on its prey.

Black-clad workers lined the stairway, stone-faced, refusing to make eye contact as they continued that eerily rhythmic clapping, as if the trade union's members had merged into one giant human metronome. James had tried to speak to a couple of the workers, but they ignored him. He looked for the leaders of the demonstration so he could talk to them directly, but he couldn't tell who was in charge.

James entered the Hall of Mirrors and looked around. Mirror-lined walls, ornate crown moldings, and a huge crystal chandelier still telegraphed the room's original purpose as a ballroom, though a long board table now sat at its center. When the Communists came to power, in Poland as elsewhere, they had been better at appropriating what already existed for their own purposes—in this case, a publishing house—than at building something new of their own.

At the head of the table, Gustaw shuffled through papers, seemingly engrossed in reviewing his presentation. James made a mental note to speak with him afterward about how they should respond to the demonstration.

The workers protesting on that day at that time surprised James, but he didn't have to guess what they were upset about. Falling revenues meant budget cuts and layoffs throughout the company, and the board was scheduled to vote on a painful package of them at that meeting. The workers, who were also shareholders since privatization, had already forgone the annual dividend checks they'd come to expect. James had talked himself hoarse trying to explain that shareholder dividends depended on the company's profitability and were not an automatic perk of private ownership, but it was a tough adjustment for people who thought of them as guaranteed bonuses.

Obviously, the workers were now picketing for their jobs, hoping the board would postpone some of the bloodletting. But there was something else going on as well, James learned soon after the meeting started.

They had just settled into their agenda, moving through the day's business with something like normalcy, when the heavy oak doors of the hall shook with a thunderous banging. Three knocks and a pause. Three knocks and a pause. Death himself, when he came knocking, would not startle James more than that deep explosion of noise behind his shoulder. In the palatial setting of the Hall of Mirrors, he felt like a courtier caught at Versailles on the eve of the French Revolution.

Outside the door, the workers started chanting in unison. Gustaw stood up and volunteered to go talk with them. When he opened the door to slip out of the room, James got a brief glimpse of the giant log the protesters had used as a battering ram. Then the head of the publishing house, who wasn't even a member of the Supervisory Board, brought the union president back into the meeting with him and invited her to present the workers' grievances to the assembled group.

That's when James learned that their primary complaint was directed at him and his investors, who were accused of stripping money out of the business just when Polish Academic Publishing needed it most. The employees demanded that James put the money back, solving the company's liquidity problem and saving everyone's jobs.

But the truth about that money was more nuanced, as James spent half the meeting trying to remind the board. The investment banks themselves, when they bought their shares in Polish Academic Publishing, had insisted that James and his partners sign a non-compete clause forbidding them from making any further investments in Eastern Europe. At the time, the banks wanted to be sure the publishing company they were investing in would not end up competing with the obvious business geniuses who had already succeeded so spectacularly in Poland. They were happy to pay James and his associates $4 million to formalize the arrangement.

Should James have turned down an offer that put that kind of cash back into his investors' holding company? It was never Polish Academic Publishing's money to begin with, just a side payment between shareholders, but that's not how it looked now to the Poles who were seeing their country's publishing legacy diminished by changing fortunes.

Neither Gustaw nor the bankers had spoken up to defend the arrangement, at that meeting or amid subsequent tensions with the trade unions, lenders, and others blindsided by Polish Academic Publishing's reduced circumstances. Everyone wanted to recast that transaction as provisional, a borrowed pot of gold subject to a reverse osmosis that could suck the money back into the business's coffers, where, of course, it had never been. Nor was it still sitting in an account somewhere waiting to be reclaimed, having already been invested in a publishing startup in China.

Gustaw's silence on the matter continued even after the Warsaw press learned of the side payment and trumpeted the least-flattering interpretation of it to the entire country. James and his fellow investors were caricatured as just another group of greedy foreigners who were indifferent to the fate of the companies where they parked their cash in search of a quick buck. At the time, James couldn't help wondering if Gustaw had secretly informed the press about that aspect of the sale, deflecting public ire from his own management mistakes to the foreign investors' supposed opportunism.

Truthfully, he still didn't know, having never wanted to jeopardize their latter-day détente to press his friend on the subject. The most Gustaw had volunteered about it after the fact was that, since the bankers considered that $4 million to be part of their investment in Polish Academic Publishing, Gustaw was unfairly expected to provide a high return on the full amount without having the full amount available to deploy within the company.

It was a fair point, James was willing to concede today, but it wouldn't have made a difference. As he told his fellow board members at the time, his shareholder group should not have been asked to single-handedly bail out the business now that performance had taken a bad turn. It was up to all of them, from workers and management to shareholders large and small, to right the ship.

Unfortunately, righting the ship had taken much more than a rousing speech to a semi-hostile crowd around a board table. By the end of that meeting, Gareth Gordon, a veteran British publisher James had recruited to sit on the board and one of very few men he would call mentors in his life, had seen the writing on the wall.

"I've done what I can to help this company transition to a modern free-market enterprise," Gareth had told James as they waited for their flights at the airport. "That's the challenge you set when you asked me to join the board, and I'd like to think I've risen to meet it. All this drama is a younger man's task. Do come visit us in Marlow when you're passing through."

With those words and a reassuring pat on his shoulder, that eminence grise of international publishing had flown out of Poland and away from Polish Academic Publishing's problems to resume the well-earned retirement James had interrupted when he brought him onboard. His protégé was left standing at an emptying airport gate, abandoned on all sides.

From the heaviness in his chest at the memories of that day, it occurred to James that fifteen years wasn't such a long time ago after all. His current feeling that life had taken a sideways turn had faint echoes in that earlier upheaval. He hoped fervently that it would take less time and energy to sort out the present mess.

At the end of dinner, James escorted Natalya to the door of her room, waving off her expectant comments about getting the detective hired and on his way to Mariupol. More than a week after Gustaw disappeared, the trail had probably grown cold by now. Did it make sense to send someone else into what could be harm's way? Could inquiring actually create more problems for Gustaw, wherever he was? And if they were lucky enough to find out anything about their missing man, then what?

Alone in his own junior suite, his mind shied away from the possibilities, most of them bad. Stretching his arm along the back of the sofa, he turned his torso and looked out the window. The glare from the table lamp bothered him, so he reached over to shut it off and stare into the darkness. There wasn't much of a view from his lower-floor, back-of-the-house, booked-at-the-last-minute hotel room, but he wasn't really focusing on the scenery anyway.

World events had first intruded on James's own life in October 1962, when he was a young boy at boarding school in Switzerland. His father had called during the Cuban Missile Crisis to tell him about the precautions his family was taking in case of nuclear war. Suddenly, the years of dinner table lectures about the threat of Communism were real, menacing his own family while James was halfway across the world in a neutral country. The phone call alone, in an era when such communications were enormously expensive and cumbersome to arrange, was enough to terrify him. Night after night, he lay awake in his dormitory bed, shining a flashlight on his wristwatch under the covers so he would know what time it was in California, thinking about his parents and his brother going about their days, potentially minutes from annihilation.

And while that particular crisis lasted less than two weeks, the effect on his consciousness had been permanent. Faraway happenings, like the international news he digested with interest on his shortwave radio, could alter his world forever.

So it was only natural he would be drawn to people like Gustaw who had fought that cancerous Communist system from within, sacrificing personal comfort and ambition to help bring down a totalitarian regime, seemingly against all odds. That his friend was able to go on to a second act as a successful publisher in a free Poland validated James's own early involvement in Eastern Europe.

Losing Gustaw, if that's what was happening now, was going to hurt. More than parting ways with his young peers cut down in that long-ago Vietnam War few of them had chosen. More than the mentors and friends who, as the years advanced, had started to give in to disease or despair. The fiercely independent Pole, with whom he'd spent years barely communicating after Gustaw's ouster from the publishing house, was still a touchstone for James's understanding of how the world was evolving.

Recently, as geopolitical events had spiraled in a direction neither of them approved, he appreciated being able to let off steam and compare notes with Gustaw. Together, they would try to predict how history might unravel forward into a future that seemed both dimmer and more complex than James had believed just a handful of years ago, before Islamic extremism, an ascendant China, and rising nationalism around the globe threw all his settled assumptions into turmoil.

James wanted his friend back. No, he *needed* him back. Badly. Or the world might never make sense again.

Ever since he learned of Gustaw's disappearance, James had been waiting for him to make contact and render this whole exploration unnecessary. Instead, they kept getting drawn deeper into the mystery of what could've happened to him. Could an innocent employee search lead to a disappearance? Or was Gustaw involved in something none of them had thought of, as Marko supposed?

The moment James feared the most, perhaps even more than the possibility of finding Gustaw dead, was the point when they ran out of clues about where to search for him. Because he was going to hire that private investigator. He couldn't fool even himself into imagining otherwise. He should've signed the papers at dinner so the man could leave early in the morning. Having that administrative detail out of the way might have been good for a few more hours of sleep than he was likely to get now.

He turned away from the window, a rectangle of blackness surrounding the lights of Kyiv. What was this whole eastern conflict about anyway? The rights of ethnic Russians? The European Union knocking at Putin's door? Nothing to do with Gustaw in the slightest. Not worth whatever risk he had taken to be there. Forty million people in Ukraine, unemployment off the charts and economic growth stagnant, and he had to head straight toward the war zone to find someone to hire? Rash. Foolish. Unacceptable.

James had never been a risk-averse person. He knew empirically that he would die one day, but that wasn't going to stop him from living every day until then. He didn't go out of his way to be reckless, though. He was a man with responsibilities, a family and employees and businesses to take care of. What threats or enticements could've lured James himself to the edge of a war zone? Days of pondering hadn't given him any obvious answers.

It was almost midnight, probably too late to contact the detective at the number he'd so graciously shared. But what was the point of being a boorish American abroad if you couldn't feign ignorance when circumstances called for it?

"Stepan, I hope I didn't wake you," he was apologizing a few minutes later. "I understand you Europeans stay up pretty late, and I couldn't sleep with worrying about Gustaw. How soon can you leave for Mariupol?"

He told Natalya the next morning. It wasn't even 7 a.m. when she knocked on his door, chattering about breakfast and an early start while he stood there in his bathrobe trying to shake the fog out of his head. He'd barely slept.

"You mean he already left?" she demanded, pacing a little in the width of his narrow doorway. "Maybe we can catch up with him at the airport. How quickly can you be ready?"

"Let's take a few minutes and think about this," he said, resting his left temple against the wood of the doorframe. "I believe he's driving there. He said there is only one flight a day, and it doesn't go all the way to Mariupol."

"Well, we could get our own rental car, then. Or do you think Marko will come with us? Does he have a car?"

"Slow down, Natalya, please. I just woke up."

She took a breath, exasperated. Then another, continuing in a calmer tone. "I'm sorry, James. I have had a lot of coffee this morning. I don't think I slept at all."

"Did you eat anything yet? Why don't we meet in the dining room in twenty minutes and figure out what to do then."

"I can't just stay here and do nothing."

"For now, we can. The detective is already on his way. It's his job to look for Gustaw now. He'll probably make better time without us slowing him down and asking a lot of questions."

That argument seemed to make an impact. She sighed, nodded, and floated off down the hallway like a deflating balloon. He told himself he'd made the right call—Gustaw would not want his wife following him onto a battlefield—and headed for the shower. By the time he got to the dining room, he hoped to have manufactured some way they could help with the search from Kyiv, or even Warsaw.

Marko joined them at breakfast. It wasn't anything they'd planned, unless Natalya had called him while James was dressing. Perhaps he'd been lurking in the dining room waiting for them to appear.

The legal publisher wore a bit of a hangdog look that James couldn't make sense of. Was he feeling somehow responsible for Gustaw's disappearance? If he'd been more receptive to James's interest in digital technology, perhaps there would've been no need for a separate Ukrainian business or a search for someone to lead it? That logic would be a stretch, though, even for a more conscientious soul than James imagined Marko to be.

Perhaps it was something simpler: his detective friend Stepan was overcharging a little for his investigative services, and Marko wasn't telling him about it. Well, given Gustaw's suspicions about embezzlement from the joint venture, padding the PI's contract probably wasn't the half of what Ukraine might be costing James. The important thing for now was that Marko was distracting Natalya from wanting to hop on the next bus to the east.

"We don't even speak the language," James had reasoned. "We would be no use at all there." And if there were any danger, bringing Gustaw's wife within arm's reach would only give "them"—whoever "they" might be, if there were a "they"—more leverage over him.

Because whatever the difficulties in their marriage, James was sure that Gustaw wouldn't willingly put her in danger. He'd always tried to protect those in his care, whether the lowly couriers of the publishing underground or the rank-and-file workers of Polish Academic Publishing, even to the point of going toe-to-toe with James and his investors, to the detriment (demolition?) of Gustaw's own career.

So, the greatest favor James could do for his friend now was to coax his wife away from the danger zone. In this goal he seemed to have an ally in Marko, but even their combined efforts were not enough to convince her that a return to Warsaw made sense.

"So, we've come all the way here only to hire a detective we could've engaged over the phone?" she huffed, as if traveling to Kyiv hadn't been her idea to begin with. "We don't know what that man could be walking into, and he's just as alone as Gustaw was. No, I'm going to Mariupol to help him look. You do what you want."

"We *are* helping, Natalya," James insisted, trying to convince them both. "We spoke to his friends. We've hired Stepan, and we should let him do his job. And if Gustaw does try to contact you or Marko or someone at Polish Academic Publishing, how would we even know it if we're out of touch ourselves in eastern Ukraine?"

"There are two possibilities, Mrs. Bogutsky," Marko explained soberly. "Either your husband does not wish to contact us, or he has been prevented from doing so. If it's the first option, then our appearance could compromise whatever he is doing, possibly putting him in danger. If the second, then whatever danger he is in, you would be exposed to that as well."

"I don't care about that."

"Well, I imagine he would. And you showing up asking questions could alarm the people he is involved with. Perhaps they believe him to be someone other than a Polish publisher with a wife back in Warsaw."

"Well, who else would they imagine him to be? He's no secret agent."

"Of course he isn't," James agreed. "But he has been involved in his share of under-the-radar activities over the years. If there's any chance that's what he's doing now, we have to be discrete about how we look for him."

"We are looking for him, though? You did send the detective to Mariupol?" Sudden doubt made her voice plaintive.

"Of course he did," Marko chimed in. "I got a text message from Stepan first thing this morning saying he was on his way. He should be there by tonight. He'll be in touch again tomorrow."

"You see," James added, opting to reassure rather than be annoyed by her suspicions. "If we were to head back to Warsaw now, we'd be traveling at the same time he is, so we wouldn't miss any updates."

"No. I'm staying here," she said, stamping her foot under the table. "We've already come this far."

7

Gustaw

One week earlier
A dim interrogation room

"My journey? A little bumpy, perhaps. And the bag over my head was new, of course. Let us say that I am glad to have reached the end of it. Of whose hospitality am I now the beneficiary?"

The question was met with terse silence from the balding man in the green uniform sitting behind the metal table to which Gustaw's hands were shackled. The man looked irritated, possibly because he had not, in fact, inquired about Gustaw's journey. More likely he resented being saddled with this unwanted prisoner, who now had to be dealt with somehow. En route to this cell, Gustaw had seen him glance regretfully at a card game raucously underway at the end of the hall.

His minder had allowed him to stop for a few minutes in the washroom. There, Gustaw had glanced into a hazy mirror over the sink and been appalled at the battered wretch who cringed back at him—bloodshot eyes; hair sticking out in all directions; a raw, seeping scrape over his left eyebrow; and a visible lump on the right side of his head. Jagged lines of dirt accentuated the wrinkles in his normally tidy, white shirt. He felt as bad as he looked, tender bruises all over, stiff muscles aching, cold and hungry and filthy.

He couldn't believe it had only been a day or so since he and Feliks were confidently plotting their move. He had had plenty of time after he woke up in the van—feigning unconsciousness to avoid further violence from his captor—to consider how thoroughly they had miscalculated. At least they had discussed worst-case contingencies. He'd given Feliks all the information he needed to carry on alone. If the kid had been successful himself. If he followed through without Gustaw there to encourage him.

Gustaw had always been an optimist in the face of long odds. His parents had called him a fool for joining the underground in the 1970s. His underground colleagues had called him a fool for that column he wrote admitting to his involvement in the illegal publishing company. After martial law was declared a few months later and he was arrested and thrown in prison, he was inclined to agree with them. They said it again in 1989 during the Round Table talks with the Communist government. Gustaw had joined the activists trying to negotiate a way forward when some of his allies preferred to keep pressure on the government until it collapsed. Still, he had fought his corner, advocating more communication, openness, and searching for common ground.

Gustaw *had* gone through a dark period in the mid-Eighties, after martial law but before Communism ended. He wondered if anyone was even reading the books they risked so much to publish. Maybe the only people seeing their work were the ones who already agreed with it. Meanwhile, as government repressions had eased, so had public outrage about them. Having your car confiscated might be better than a three-year prison sentence, but it was still a hardship for the activist and his family. Morale was sinking in the movement, and Gustaw's along with it.

After Communism was over, though, Gustaw met many people who told him how much reading their publications had meant to them in those years. He had been wrong to doubt, back then. Maybe someday he would realize that his pessimism about today's Poland was also misplaced.

But then along came Feliks's gangsters with their online fake news operation—and worse—threatening to send not just Poland but the whole world hurtling back into the past.

He had known an old woman, back in the underground, who was in Yalta at the end of World War II when the Allied leaders met to plan the post-war order. She wasn't involved in the diplomatic negotiations but had worked at one of the hotels where the American delegates were staying. They were wonderful guests, courteous and appreciative of her efforts, she told Gustaw decades later. Good tippers, too. Well, who wouldn't be charmed by the good, strong Americans helping to save Europe from itself for the second time in as many generations?

So, when the war ended and the details of the agreement between the Great Powers became known, she was devastated, not just because of Eastern Europe's subordination to the Soviets but for her own naivete.

"Whatever lofty principles they claim to support, whatever rules and institutions they create to enshrine them, in the end the powerful look after themselves," she told Gustaw, fury glinting in her eyes despite the intervening years. "When the price of upholding those ideals gets too high, the little people get sacrificed."

He hadn't wanted to believe she was right. What standards could leaders be challenged to live up to if the whole pretense came crashing down? And now Gustaw was a prisoner, locked up where he could do nothing about any of it. He addressed his silent captor again.

"If you will not tell me who you are, sir, could you enlighten me as to where I am? Which organization you work for? No? Well, then I will start.

"My name is Gustaw Bogutsky, and I am a businessman from Warsaw, where I am overdue to return, thanks to this unplanned excursion. I hope I will not be delayed much longer.

"I spoke to the gentlemen who just departed for several hours and answered all of their questions many times over," he explained reasonably. "I can't imagine what I could have said to them to warrant this detour. I'm afraid you will find my visit with you to be an unfortunate distraction from your other important work. Please tell me how you think I can be of assistance so I can be on my way . . ."

The man met his eyes civilly enough but did not smile or speak. How much did his captor know of what Gustaw himself was pretending not to know? Very little, he supposed, which would make any normal interrogation pointless. Then he had been brought here not to be questioned but to be kept out of the way.

Gustaw kept his tone conversational.

"If it is going to be a while, then, could I borrow a book to pass the time?"

There was a curt head shake from the man, who looked down and pretended to ignore him while flipping through a file open on the table. Surely the gangsters hadn't had time to write a report about Gustaw? They hadn't seemed like the paperwork type.

"A magazine then?" Gustaw pressed. "Not even a newspaper? That's a shame. I suppose reading isn't what it used to be. Certainly not in my own country. Did you know, sixty percent of Poles fifteen and older don't read even one book in a year? Not a single one! Hungarians read five times as much. I was involved in a study that looked at these statistics. It was very depressing to me. I worked all those years as a publisher, and the audience has gotten so small. Of course, even a few hundred copies of an important book are worth getting into the hands of the country's top leaders and thinkers. But what happened to the old notion of changing ordinary citizens' minds by introducing them to good ideas?"

"You publish books?" Eyes elevated from his file again, the man appeared almost interested despite himself. He removed the dark-framed glasses that had slid down his nose and tossed them on the table, waiting for his prisoner to continue.

"Yes, I am in the publishing business. Did our mutual friends not tell you? I used to run the largest publisher of dictionaries and encyclopedias in Poland. It's all on the internet now, of course, but at that time, every school and library had to have a set on their bookshelves.

"Before that, I started an illegal publishing company that printed books the Communist censors would never have allowed. Do you recall those times? I'm afraid I can't tell anymore who is old enough to have lived through all of that. I have to look in the mirror every so often to remind myself how much time has passed."

Gustaw shivered at his own mention of mirrors, recalling his garish reflected image from earlier and wondering what it might look like a day or two from now. He was better off focusing on the past; at least he knew how the long-ago events had turned out.

"In 1980, I attended the Nobel Prize ceremony in Sweden," he bragged fondly. "That was probably the high point in my underground career, coming at a time—we called it the Solidarity Carnival period—when we thought we were winning the battle for more freedom. The Polish poet Czeslaw Milosz was that year's winner for literature, and since our operation was the only one publishing his work in his homeland, he invited me and a few other Poles to see him receive it."

"You were allowed to travel there?" If his captor didn't remember those days himself, he at least knew something about the times.

"The Communists had to let us go," Gustaw explained. "The Polish economy was dependent enough on Western assistance by then that the government couldn't risk upsetting those countries. Our flight was delayed for a few hours, though, so the people in Stockholm thought maybe we weren't going to be allowed out after all.

"Our hosts greeted us at the airport with the latest issues of *Time, Newsweek,* and *Der Spiegel*—weekly news magazines that were popular in the West then. Every cover had a variant of the same graphic—a tank emblazoned with the Soviet hammer and sickle rolling over the Polish eagle. The entire Western world assumed we were on the point of being invaded."

He paused, but his captor didn't respond, his eyes once again on the documents in front of him. Gustaw kept speaking.

"*I* thought it was anti-Soviet hysteria. We had only left Warsaw a few hours earlier and everything was fine. But it turned out that the Soviets *had* been massing troops just across the Polish border. The CIA knew it, but we fools inside the country didn't have the first idea that there was a real threat. I figured the Soviets were too busy with their year-old invasion of Afghanistan to open another front.

"Luckily for Poland, Ronald Reagan would soon be elected president of the United States. Before he was even in office, he warned the Soviets that his administration would not stand by while they invaded a satellite nation. And they must have believed him; I'm sure that's when they started planning for martial law."

Still no sign of interest from the man, who Gustaw could see perfectly well was too young to have lived through the Communist period. It wasn't so much his smooth skin or trim figure as the absence of a subtle darkness behind his eyes. One old soul would recognize another, and Communism had aged everyone it touched. Gustaw switched gears.

"The prize ceremony itself was beautiful, with all the pomp and circumstance you would expect—the red carpet, a speech from the King of Sweden, everything lavish and sparkling."

Nostalgia crept into his voice as he was transported decades into the past, trying to bring his captor with him.

Gustaw had borrowed a tuxedo from a friend who played violin for the Warsaw Philharmonic, because of course he didn't have any formalwear of his own. The suit had fit him well enough, but there was a shiny patch of fabric underneath his right arm where the violinist's sleeve had rubbed back and forth against the jacket as he moved his bow back and forth. It was the fanciest occasion he could ever hope to attend, with cultural icons, diplomats, and actual royalty, and he was wearing a jacket of two different colors. The whole night, he held his right arm stiffly against his side to hide the shininess. Other guests probably thought he was paralyzed.

"On one hand it was a dream to be there," he told the man in the green uniform now. "I was so proud of the work we had done to get us invited to such an important international event. But I was uncomfortable with the pageantry—afraid of doing something inappropriate, you know, because we didn't have such events in my life back home, and I didn't want to disgrace myself."

Gustaw's palms began to sweat, and there was a fluttering in his stomach as he recalled the anxiety of those glamorous hours. It was strange to be having such a physical response to this distant memory, he thought, rather than to his present peril. Perhaps he hadn't enjoyed that ceremony as much as he had always told himself. He wasn't going to admit that now, though.

"The following year, in June 1981, Milosz was allowed to visit Poland," Gustaw continued. "He spent a day with me in Warsaw, and I drove him around to see how the city had changed. He had been living outside of Poland for a long time by then, and he had never seen the Palace of Culture and Science, built in 1955. Have you been to Warsaw? Do you know the monstrosity I'm talking about—Stalin's 'gift' to the Polish people? He saw it and immediately started cursing. 'Oh, hell, this is impossible! I've never seen such a piece of architecture.'

"In the afternoon, he came to a reception with fifty or sixty workers from the publishing operation. It meant the world to them to be able to meet with him, ask him questions, get his autograph. And he was clearly touched as well by the risks they had taken to get his poems and essays published when they were officially banned.

"That was six months before martial law was declared, and the underground was barely underground at that point. My family's apartment was a de facto office; people came and went all day long, collecting books, reviewing manuscripts, delivering supplies and equipment. I never imagined we could go back to how it was in the 1970s, let alone that most of my colleagues and I would be in jail by Christmas. At least we had a common sense of purpose, and that helped us to get through those years."

Gustaw wasn't sure why he was telling all this to his minder, who probably didn't care about the ancient history of the Soviet days—or recognize the similarities in current events. People just didn't understand how much things had improved in a short generation. How easily it could all disappear again in a fraction of that time.

"When I was in the underground—even before, when I was in high school and got my first taste of banned literature—I thought it was ridiculous that an entire country could be denied access to certain books. Even as a teenager, I could tell that these were thoughtful, important works. If everyone were exposed to those ideas, I knew people would see that they were better than the Communist Party's ideas, and things would change in Poland.

"And somehow, after more than a decade of persistent work to print and distribute uncensored writings, everything did change. I allowed myself to believe that the better ideas had won because people recognized that they were objectively better. Later, when Polish Academic Publishing was selling uncensored encyclopedias to every family in Poland, I knew I was right."

He sighed and proceeded in a subdued voice.

"Today, I'm not so sure. How are we supposed to convince all those Poles who like the current government's message that they've bought into an illusion? They'll figure it out eventually, of course, just like they did with the Communists, but how much economic growth and political freedom will we have lost by then? How many young people's aspirations thwarted? Attitudes perverted by suspicion and scapegoating? Real people's lives irreversibly hurt. It all seems to be going backward. And it isn't because the better ideas weren't out there; it's because the majority of people apparently didn't like them anymore."

Gustaw tried to make eye contact with the younger—but not so young—man who had yet to ask him a single question unrelated to his own narrative. At last, he looked up, but his expression was flat, his thoughts unreadable.

"You probably think I'm being a bad loser," Gustaw suggested. "The other guys won the election, so the sky must be falling, right? But there are certain rules to being in power in a democracy. Winning an election doesn't make you dictator for the duration of your term. There are supposed to be checks on political power—courts, media, civil society. That's not how this latest crop of leaders sees things, though.

"They don't like the judges on the Constitutional Tribunal—that's the highest court in Poland—so they invalidate their appointments. They don't want to risk having their legislation overturned, so they change the rules on what order laws must be reviewed in. It's boring and bureaucratic stuff to have to explain to people, but it effectively means they can pass whatever laws they like and then claim the court has no authority to challenge them.

"They replace the leaders in state-owned companies and tighten government control of public television stations. Sure, they won the election, so they can appoint new people to those jobs, but the results are very dangerous for Polish freedom. Now they are trying to consolidate their power by controlling the message. And the sad part for me is how well that strategy is working.

"Of course, I understand the problem. Poles have been sacrificing financial security and material comforts for years for the sake of economic growth, and it feels like we should all have more to show for it by now. I just didn't realize so many Poles would buy into their proposed solution.

"It was the cultural piece we missed somehow," he mused. "We invited the world in, young people went off to England and Germany to work, and apparently some of us ended up feeling that our Polish-ness had been overlooked in the transition. I think there's some laziness to this attitude. People don't like having their ideas challenged, and most of the discontented people in Poland these days are ethnic Poles and Catholic. They're comfortable when society caters to them.

"Remember, though, that in the nineteenth century my country was carved up three times by its neighbors and completely ceased to exist for over a hundred years. Now we're in the European Union and NATO, and most Poles want us to be there, but those organizations haven't solved as many problems as some of my countrymen expected. So when some bureaucrat in Brussels tells us to take in Syrian refugees or stop burning so much coal, some Poles see that as threatening our national sovereignty, as if other European countries don't have to follow the same rules.

"It's like all the ideas that come from other countries can't be trusted—except for Hungary, of course. We seem to be just a few steps behind them now in defying the very idea of international norms or standards.

"You should hear the things they say about non-governmental organizations in Poland these days—but perhaps it's not so different than what they've been saying in Moscow for a decade now. I know many of the people from these groups—they work hard for low pay—but the ruling party wants them out because they don't like the competition. The former president's daughter works for one of them—that alone is enough to raise suspicion in some minds. Now donations are drying up. Morale is down. And most of these groups are just doing good, charitable work trying to help people, animals, the environment.

"It was groups like these that helped us work our way out of Communism. What was the Solidarity trade union if not the first non-governmental organization of that era? I even founded my own NGO in 1989."

"Did you really?" the man asked, latching onto a potential offense, albeit one decades old and committed under an obsolete regime. His pen hovered above the dossier as he prepared to take notes.

"It was called the Free Speech Society, and the idea was to publish uncensored books and take their authors around the country on speaking tours to its members. Sounds crazy, right? Why would the government ever allow such a thing?"

As the interrogator's pen scratched across the page, Gustaw answered his own question.

"Because I had very cleverly tricked them into it, or so I thought. It was during the Round Table talks between the government and Solidarity. I convinced the government negotiators to agree to end censorship on the internal publications of NGOs. It was a loophole big enough to drive a tank through. Who was to say that a novel was not a publication or that every citizen of Poland couldn't join an organization that published them?

"They didn't have time to figure out their mistake, though, because the Communist Party lost all the contested seats in the legislature that June. After that, it was obvious things would never be the same in Poland again."

Gustaw sighed, oblivious to his audience, before continuing.

"At least, that's how it seemed at the time. Now, it feels like we're headed right back to that same place, where only one version of events can be told. They haven't brought back the censors yet, but the government has begun subtly pressuring Polish companies not to advertise in newspapers and magazines they don't like.

"I have publisher friends in other countries. Do you know what they tell me? Our government goes to international conferences trying to sell books that are so laced with propaganda, foreign companies won't touch them. They simply aren't credible, but the Law and Justice crowd thinks their job is to sell a positive image of Poland. I thought our image was positive when we were leading Europe in economic growth rates."

He snorted in disgust. These days, he couldn't even convince his own family that things were going wrong. No wonder he was venting his frustration at this stranger, whose own country had already gone back down the authoritarian path.

"My adult children *love* the new child credits," Gustaw said, sarcasm accenting the verb. "Finally, someone is helping their families a little bit. They aren't bothered by the religious agenda either, but their mother always was a devout Catholic. I used to be, too, back when we were married. Did you know I helped build an illegal church when I was at the university?"

"I thought you were a book publisher," challenged the jailer. "Now you are also a construction worker putting up buildings?"

"Yes, with bricks and mortar, hammer and nails, my own two hands," Gustaw insisted. "The Church was a pillar of the anti-Communist movement, but the government didn't dare go too far in repressing it. They might refuse to grant a building permit now and then, but they wouldn't raid the churches. The religious presses printed a lot of our underground publications. The challenge was to get the materials out of the building and distributed without getting caught.

"Maybe I've lost my faith since then; maybe I never really had it. It was a liberal priest I worked with on the church, though, not like these conservatives who want to run people's lives their own way, just like the Communists used to. Communism and Catholicism; they're just different ideologies for people to force on each other, control people with."

"So is your Western capitalism, isn't it?" The interrogator was finally interested again.

"No, I don't think free market democracy is the same," Gustaw answered. "We have choices now that we didn't before—not just what consumer products to buy or political party to join but which job to seek or city to live in. Of course, there are no guarantees that we will be hired for the job or be able to buy a house in the place we prefer, but I think we all deserve the chance to try to build the lives we want."

"Not much point being allowed to try if there's no hope of actually getting it," the other man said with some bitterness.

"It's a start, though," Gustaw conciliated. "Anyway, I've been a fan of freedom for most of my life, at least since my rock-climbing days. I was barely out of high school then, and I spent a few years of weekends climbing the hills that passed for mountains in Poland. The fresh air of that pastime was figurative as well as literal. I found a life outside political oppression and away from the secret police when I packed my knapsack and joined my friends on a climb.

"It was a good way to recruit for the underground, too. Not only were other climbers drawn to that same sense of personal freedom, but I knew which ones could be relied on in difficult circumstances. Your climbing partner literally holds your life in his hands; if I could trust them on the mountain, I figured I could trust them to keep our secrets.

"I didn't do it for long, though. Once I was married with young children at home, I knew I needed to keep myself safe for my family's sake. And I did lose friends to climbing accidents—falls, rockslides, exposure.

"Years after martial law, when I finally met General Jaruselski, I thanked him for saving my life. He had no idea what I was talking about, of course, until I pointed out that if his government hadn't confiscated my passport, I might have climbed higher, more dangerous mountains than the Tatras."

"General who?" The questioner's pen stopped moving across the paper.

If he weren't a prisoner chained to a table, Gustaw might have told him to get out his phone and Google it. Instead, he ignored the question, unwilling to interrupt his train of thought just because no one knew their history these days.

"As a young adult, I could escape to the mountains for a few days or the chemistry lab for a few hours. Even earlier, playing smuggled-in rock albums from the West in my aunt's apartment, my teenaged friends and I could imagine that we lived in the free world, if only for an afternoon.

"You couldn't overstate how much I loved that music—Pink Floyd, Led Zeppelin, The Rolling Stones, The Who. That's how I improved my English. A few times, my friends and I competed to see who could come up with the best Polish translation of the lyrics. For a while, I even wrote reviews and submitted them to a jazz magazine—not a student publication, you understand, but a magazine for adult readers. Sometimes they printed my columns, sometimes not, but I was so proud of being a real journalist."

Gustaw's exhilaration at recounting those long-ago pleasures fizzled as his focus returned to the present, with its danger and uncertainty.

"I just hope my grandkids will find that kind of escape somewhere, too, if they need it," he almost whispered. "I don't want them to think that the world as it's taking shape for them is truly free just because today's leaders tell them so. Those of us who remember when things were different will need to keep saying so until they believe it."

The man before him suppressed a yawn, looking like he didn't understand much of anything Gustaw was saying. The prisoner shrugged his shoulders again, resigned.

"I do realize that every generation grows old and has to accept that things aren't the way they used to be or didn't turn out as well as they had hoped. At least we had the chance to be young and rebel against important things and see our dreams come to fruition for a time.

"When you're twenty-five years old, it's easy to throw yourself into the hope for change and expect to live long enough to enjoy the transformed world you are building. At my age, it's depressing to see everything we thought we had accomplished start to crumble and know that I might not have the time or energy left to help turn it back around."

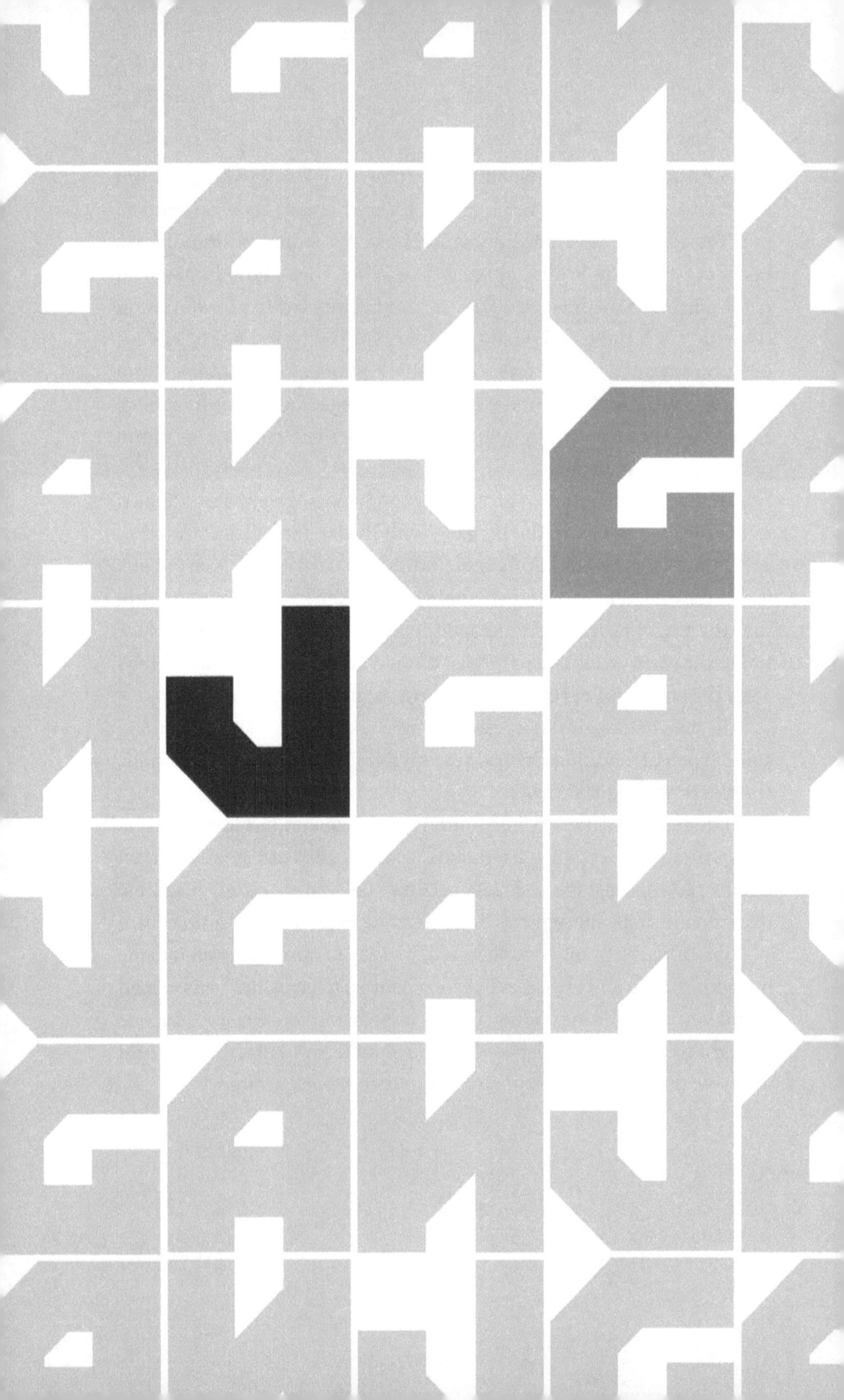

8

James

Kyiv, Ukraine

Natalya was not about to retreat to Warsaw, so James stopped at the concierge desk on his way back to his room and arranged for them to stay a few more nights.

Stepan checked in from Mariupol the following morning, as promised, and then a wall of silence descended.

"He said we might not hear from him every day," James explained, trying to reassure an increasingly anxious Natalya. "He could be traveling through dead zones—uh, areas where he can't get a cell phone signal."

As time passed, they distracted themselves as best they could, checking in with home and office so frequently that the lack of new updates grew maddening.

James made daily visits to UkraineLaw, which Marko accepted with more graciousness than he might've expected. Perhaps the Ukrainian realized that there was little danger of James discovering his secrets, even if they were right under his nose, as long as they were transacted in Ukrainian. Or maybe whatever subterfuge he'd engaged in previously was no longer possible given the company's dwindling circumstances.

There was still a breath of life in the business, though, James decided after a couple days in the cavernous office space. A few customers came and went with what Marko told him were new orders, and the last handful of employees stayed at their desks looking industrious all day.

He sat with Marko to go over the books, brainstorm new product ideas, and try to pump some optimism into the demoralized management of the company. It was an uphill battle all the way around. Scant weeks before, James had intended to invest capital in a brand-new Ukrainian company. Now he couldn't see that happening unless Gustaw were to reappear with a perfectly innocent (though undoubtedly infuriating) explanation of where he had been. The idea of putting money directly into UkraineLaw under these circumstances was equally unthinkable.

And what of Polish Academic Publishing, the joint venture partner? The Polish publishing company's leaders had been dismissive of, if not downright hostile to, the Ukrainian affiliate since Gustaw's departure from the company fourteen years earlier. If they'd been more interested in bolstering the business, James and Gustaw might never have started planning the second company intended to save it. They certainly weren't going to have a change of heart now that one of their own had disappeared in the process.

The broader news from Poland was not good, or at least more of the same. Was it worse to see the country's political polarization hardening in the spring than it had been watching the nationalists triumph unexpectedly the previous fall? Where did his stake in Polish Academic Publishing even fit into the changes going on in Warsaw?

James had always assumed his company was above the fray, promoting universally relevant values like knowledge and intellectual rigor, too apolitical to be caught up in Poland's shifting policies and governments. Sure, they had had those growing pains fifteen years ago, when he and his investors were blamed for the investment banks' decisions, but Polish society had matured since then. Hadn't it?

A notorious American criminal had once been quoted as saying that he robbed banks because that's where the money was. The Law and Justice Party of Poland wanted to write tax policy the same way. And, for all their anti-Communist allusions, in some ways they were no different from those antecedent leaders, looking to large, foreign-owned businesses for the funds to underwrite their ambitious economic program, just as the Communists had scapegoated, robbed, and purged the successful classes when they came to power. Anyone in Poland today who suggested that this approach was unwise or unfair was branded as part of an international conspiracy of the moneyed elite, an ill-defined group whose main characteristic seemed to be economic success in a world where too many Poles were still struggling.

"It won't touch us," Ludmyla had tried to reassure him. "This company is a Polish institution, like Webster's dictionary or Encyclopedia Britannica."

"Majority-owned by Americans."

"Run by Poles."

"Let's hope that means as much to them as it should. They don't hesitate to vilify the old guard in the Polish government to undermine *its* preferred policies."

"Old guard" wasn't the Communists in this context either, but the previous administration, somehow lumped into the same pot as the pro-Soviet rulers of decades ago. This was the new government narrative: the Communists had never really left power because post-Soviet administrations had failed to purge their influence. So, the old exploiters kept right on exploiting under the new, open system, aided by an eleventh-hour asset grab during the privatization of state-owned resources at the end of Communism. That's why ordinary Poles had failed to prosper after all these years—and what the new regime would save people from.

Was Law and Justice trying to carry out a long-delayed housecleaning, sweeping the former powers out for good, or was this rhetoric just a weapon used to discredit the people who spoke out against their agenda? Mere months into the new administration, it was too early to know for sure, but James suspected the latter.

Which brought back the question of Polish Academic Publishing. His own group's stake in the business went back twenty-five years, growing in that time from half to more than ninety percent of shares. They were still the premier publisher of dictionaries and encyclopedias in Poland, a name synonymous with Polish learning and culture. It would be easy for the government to launch a campaign against foreign ownership of this national treasure, as the trade unions had fifteen years earlier. It could happen anytime they needed a distraction, provocation or no.

James hadn't considered selling in a long time—not since those darkest days butting heads with the investment banks—but maybe it would be better to get out ahead of that possibility rather than lose his investment in a fire sale sometime down the road. Were there oligarchs in Poland? Not yet, perhaps, but he could imagine the day when the keys to Polish Academic Publishing would be turned over to some Law and Justice-linked businessman happy to rewrite history for Jaroslaw Kaczynski, the party's—and country's de facto—leader.

For now, though, as they waited in Kyiv for word from the private detective, James tried to make UkraineLaw his focus. He was talking through the company's limited prospects with Marko one morning when three flat-faced, flannel-clad men appeared in the office doorway, the alarmed receptionist Nina barely visible behind them.

"I'm so sorry, sir. I tried to stop them," Nina stuttered breathlessly, trying to nudge her way inside in some misguided attempt to place herself in their path.

"No trouble at all," Marko said smoothly, rising to cross the brief distance between them before the visitors could fully occupy his office.

James, who'd turned slightly in his chair at their approach, was already standing, though whether to greet the new arrivals or for some more defensive purpose he wasn't sure. He stood half a head above the average Ukrainian man, and these guys were no exception. But then, their intimidation quotient came more from the girth of their beefy forearms. Marko was no slouch, but three were still more than two.

"How can I help you gentlemen?" Marko's voice took on that soothing, almost sedative quality that had disabled James's own well-reasoned arguments at times. For now, he hoped their visitors were similarly susceptible.

"We're looking for an, uh, associate of ours who we understand is coming here," said a mustachioed man, craning his neck to one side with an audible crack. "Perhaps you can tell us where to find him."

"We're always happy to meet with new clients, of course," Marko smiled benignly. "I'm afraid we don't have any such meetings scheduled for today, but if you gentlemen would like to take a seat in the conference room, we can order in some refreshments and talk about whatever project you have in mind. Perhaps your friend is late?"

It occurred to James to wonder why this conversation was taking place in thickly accented English, accustomed as he was by this point to adopting a mildly interested expression while incoherent discussions went on around him. He'd thought about hiring a professional translator for the rest of his stay.

"I don't think you understand," the group spokesman answered, placing special emphasis on each word. "We're not here for your business. We just need to speak to the boy. Feliks."

"There is no Feliks here. You must be misinformed. What address were you given?"

"I'm certain we are in the right place," the visitor answered with a smoothness to rival Marko's own. "It does not matter. If he is not here now, we will wait for him." And he moved as if to sit in the chair James had just vacated.

"I'm afraid not," Marko said, erupting into motion. He grabbed the invader by the arm and pushed him back out the door with enough force that his compatriots tumbled backward through it ahead of him like bowling pins. James barely got out of the way in time.

He heard the gun cock before he saw it. Marko's hands were still wrapped around their unwanted guest, who was now frozen in surprise as he stared down the barrel of a pistol pointed at his forehead. Nina blew a wisp of hair out of her eyes, her grip on the firearm steady as she looked to her boss for direction.

Marko chuckled darkly, choosing to address James rather than the routed ruffians or his frosty-gazed receptionist.

"I seem to remember you asking me once many years ago if we had enough security around here, James. What do you think of our current system?" With a wide-arced kick, he swept his captive's legs out from under him and let him drop to the ground on top of his friends. Then he pulled his own handgun (!?) from the back waistband of his suit pants, deliberately disengaged the safety, and pointed it at the more agitated-looking of the remaining men.

Figuring he should help out, James moved toward the third man and assumed what he hoped was a vaguely threatening stance above him.

"Have you contacted the police?" Marko asked calmly.

"They're on their way," Nina assured him, her gun still trained on the apparent spokesman for the group. "I told them to hurry because we might have difficulty containing this bunch. The chief said he understands that anything could happen before they arrive."

"James, do you have your phone with you?" Marko asked. "Please take these gentlemen's photograph so we can file an accurate report."

Relieved to be wielding a camera instead of a gun, James did as requested, trying to make sure each man's face was clearly visible in the frame.

"Thank you. Now, you fellows have until the count of five to get out of here," Marko explained softly to the men on the ground, who had all raised their hands in surrender. "And if I see any of you again, I won't be summoning the police to deal with you. I think we *are* finally beginning to understand each other, yes? One!"

The three men scrambled to their feet and were out the door before he got to "four."

The whole incident happened so fast that James didn't start shaking until it was over.

"Who were they?" he asked in bewilderment. "And who is this Feliks they were asking for?"

"No one here," Marko explained, calmly resetting the safety and placing the gun back in his waistband. "Any ideas, Nina? Then perhaps we should get those pictures to the station as soon as possible to see if someone there can identify those men. James, please forward them to me and we'll take care of it.

"I think we had better triple our security detail for a few days as well," Marko continued, addressing the receptionist again. "Once the reinforcements arrive and set up a perimeter, send the workers home and close the office for the rest of the day. I don't want to risk having anyone followed when they leave."

Nina nodded calmly, as if he were giving instructions for a catered lunch. She clicked back to her desk in her high heels, still holding the cocked pistol at the ready.

"Formidable, isn't she?" Marko observed with a smile as James watched her walk away. "I suppose you thought your country was the only place where ordinary people were equipped to defend themselves."

As if his own executive assistant back in California were packing heat—or needed to.

"But who were they looking for?" James sputtered. "And why did they come here? Do you think they knew something about Gustaw? Maybe we should have asked them some more questions. Or does this kind of thing happen all the time around here?"

"No, it doesn't. Most people know better. But that doesn't mean there's a connection to Gustaw's disappearance either."

"But what if there is? We need to reach your detective friend. Maybe he knows something by now that would help explain this."

Marko looked like he wanted to argue, but then he nodded. "I think you are right. I'll make a few calls, and if we can track him down, I'll ask if he's come across any 'Feliks.'"

James was turning to go, relieved to retreat to the relative security of the hotel, when Marko called after him.

"And James, be careful yourself. If these goons have been in contact with Stepan, they might know where you and Natalya are staying."

The suggestion was enough. James and Natalya checked out of their hotel within twenty minutes of his return, catching a taxi to the airport and going inside to cool their heels for half an hour before quietly exiting to find another cab to a different accommodation across town. The subterfuge was probably pointless, James told himself, as there were only so many decent hotels in the city, but it distracted Natalya for a few hours until Marko called with an update on the morning's visitors.

"Guns for hire," he explained. "They could be working for anyone. The police will be on the lookout for them, though, and if they show up back at UkraineLaw our security guys will get some answers for us."

James felt a frisson of excitement at Marko's assurances. The Ukrainian might not know how to make a legal publishing house thrive, but he did act to protect his turf and people without losing stride.

With the abrupt move across town, Natalya seemed finally to be taking the potential danger seriously. She'd agreed to James's plan soberly and with minimal questioning, packed calmly and efficiently, and waited out the detour in patient silence. Once they'd checked in to their new rooms and met up again in the hotel lounge, however, a steady stream of words erupted out of her.

"Who are they working for? Who was this boy they were trying to find? Were they talking about a child? What do they know about my husband? I can't believe Marko didn't find out what they knew before letting them go."

At her insistence, James showed her the photo he'd taken that morning—the uncropped version where receptionist Nina's pistol was visible in the foreground.

"Oh my God, someone could've been shot. Or killed. What if those men had had guns?"

"They may have, Natalya. Our friend Marko moves quickly. But honestly, with men like that, I think most of the time their appearance is enough to scare people into doing what they want. They didn't seem prepared for resistance."

"Well, if they come back, they might be. Does this have anything to do with Gustaw?" Her words came faster, and her voice took on a shrill tone as she spoke. "How could it not? How many conspiracies can one company be involved in?"

James sighed and folded his hands in his lap.

"I have as many questions as you do, Natalya," he said. "At least the police know to watch out for these guys now, and so do the guards at

UkraineLaw. If they're still in the city, I'm sure they'll find them soon. But if they are mercenaries, as Marko said, then they probably won't know much anyway. Regardless, I think it's time for you to return to Warsaw."

"Go home? Now?" She was indignant. "Who's to say some other group of hired thugs isn't already knocking on my front door there?"

What had started as a rhetorical point at the beginning of the sentence provoked genuine alarm by the end of it. "Oh, God, I have to call the kids and make sure everyone's okay," she babbled. "And my friend Hanna has been checking on the house. What if someone goes there looking for me and finds her instead?"

"I think that's a very good idea," James said to calm her. "I'm sure they're all fine, but they'll be glad to hear from you. Perhaps you could stay with one of the children until this situation gets sorted out?"

Natalya gave him a stubborn look but didn't bother arguing. She headed for the elevator.

James stayed where he was for a minute, trying to process the morning's events, then went into the bar to order a drink. He felt like he'd earned one.

Where was Gustaw? Who was Feliks, and what did those goons' employer want him for? Why did Marko, suspected embezzler and longtime impediment to technological progress, suddenly seem so helpful? And when would it all be cleared up so James could go home?

When he left California, he hadn't imagined being gone more than a few days. Neither had Anna, who took every phone call as an opportunity to ask what he'd achieved in Kyiv that he couldn't have done just as well in a Skype call from the comfort of his own ocean-view office.

It was a fair question. Did proximity give him the illusion of involvement? Was he more of an insider just because he'd looked Stepan the private investigator in the eye before signing his contract and arranging the wire transfer for his retainer? Mediocre food and an uncomfortable mattress aside, he was no more in the loop for coming to Kyiv than he would have been back in Warsaw.

Or was he? He *had* seen Marko, that old police academy trainer, in action. That was one revelation. And he might never have known about UkraineLaw's unfriendly visitors if he hadn't been there that day sticking his nose into company business. Who knew what other activities he'd missed by not being around to witness them? Or what he might be missing out on right now.

A sudden hunch propelled him outside the building, leaving his drink untouched on the table. He flagged down a taxi back to the UkraineLaw offices, both hoping and fearing that his suspicions weren't true.

He never saw them coming. The black-clad security guards intercepted him half a block from the building.

"Mr. Jensen, you weren't expected back today," said a man James had never seen before. "The office is closed now. We can't be sure it's safe for anyone to be here."

"Of course." James smiled broadly as his heart hiccupped slightly. "I just wanted to check back in with Marko. Is he still here?"

"We can pass along a message for you, of course. Perhaps he could contact you at your hotel?"

Giving their new location to this unknown enforcer didn't seem like the most prudent step, so James shook his head. "I only need to speak to him for a moment. Perhaps *you* could escort me inside. I'm sure I'd be in good hands." He smiled warmly to let the flattery sink in.

The guards exchanged glances. Then one of them stepped away and pulled his cell phone from his pocket. The ensuing conversation was incomprehensible to James, so he focused on body language. In the guard's deepening glower and ramrod straight spine, James imagined he saw the man's need to uphold his own authority warring with an ingrained habit of obeying orders. His head sank as the conversation continued. Then he gave a firm nod and ended the call.

"Please come with me, sir," he said and strode off toward the building, his partner bringing up the rear with a little more pretense of looking around for danger.

When Marko greeted them at the door, he was wiping his hands on a towel with dark smudges on it. "James, are you alright? How is Natalya? Has anything happened?"

"No, I'm fine. We're both fine. We've moved to a different hotel as a precaution."

"Good, good. I was just taking the opportunity to tune up some equipment that's been acting up lately." He smiled but didn't move out of the doorway.

"Shouldn't you take your own advice and go home in case those men return?"

"Oh, you don't need to worry." Marko sounded breezy, almost dismissive. "They aren't going to cause me any trouble."

He stood there another moment before ushering James in with an elaborate flourish of his arm.

He led his guest through the furnished portion of the vast room to the dark echo chamber behind and into an alcove in the far corner. The flip of a wall switch revealed a scene out of an action movie—or perhaps the aftermath of one.

The fiftyish man sitting in the straight-backed chair at the far end of the boardroom table looked like he was asleep, his head slumped over onto his chest, his shoulders pushed forward at an odd angle. It took James a moment to realize that the man's arms were stretched behind his back. Tied?

Damp splotches sullied the man's dark Oxford shirt. Alarmed, James looked again at Marko's towel. Were those spots really machine oil? He took a few more steps toward the apparent prisoner and craned his eyes until he could see the man's chest rising and falling.

James exhaled audibly. Only when Marko chuckled did he realize he'd been holding his breath. He took another look at the bound man, trying to recall if he was one of the morning's visitors. He pulled his phone out to consult the photos he'd taken.

As quickly as it emerged from his pocket, the latest iPhone skittered across the tile floor into the shadows. "What are you doing with that?" Marko demanded from his elbow, no longer smiling. James took a step back, suddenly aware that he was now a participant in this surreal drama.

"Is that one of the men from this morning?" he asked crisply, willing himself not to panic.

"No. He's the one who sent them."

"Did he tell you anything?"

"Perhaps we should sit down." Marko retrieved James's phone from the floor, brushed it off, and handed it back to him. He received it at arm's length and eyed the table warily.

"Not here, of course." His host was all smiles again. "I think my office would be more comfortable, don't you?" He turned on his heel and led the way without looking back, flipping the light off as he went.

James took a deep breath and followed, leaving the unconscious man at the table alone again in the dark.

They sat down at Marko's desk, much as they had been that morning when the intruders first arrived. James half-expected Nina to appear and offer them coffee.

Instead, Marko opened his desk drawer and pulled out a bottle of vodka and two cut-crystal lowball glasses. Without asking, he poured a generous shot into each and pushed one across the table. James waited until his host had emptied his own glass. He then took a tentative sip from the one in front of him.

"Clearly, we have some trust issues," Marko noted sardonically, the American term sounding surprisingly natural despite his accent. "Would you feel safer holding this?" He pulled his handgun from his pants and slid it across the desk, one eyebrow raised in mockery. James hesitated a moment before picking it up and placing it on the chair beside him, confirming that the safety was on before carefully pointing its barrel toward the wall.

"Who is that man in the next room?"

"Just a middleman, I'm afraid. One of our local unsavory types. He sent the muscle from earlier to retrieve someone they thought might show up here—a kid from the east, apparently. But he's not sure who hired him or what they want with their target. He was supposed to send them proof when they had him, then get instructions for where to deliver him."

"From the east? So, this is connected to Gustaw's disappearance?"

"Maybe. But this guy doesn't know anything about that either. Believe me, we discussed it at length."

James swallowed that information without comment. "Why did they think this kid would come here?"

"I don't know, and neither does he." He indicated the back room with a jerk of his head. "Maybe they were just covering their bases."

James's heart was pounding. He took a few deep breaths, willing it to stay in rhythm. He didn't want to have to find out how good Ukrainian hospitals were. "Did you learn anything useful from this guy?"

"Well, I did get a photograph of the young man they're looking for." He slid a grainy computer printout, creased from folding, across the desk. "Recognize him?"

The subject looked to be in his early twenties, with dark hair and sunken eye cavities. So, not a child then, but young and lost-looking all the same. James shook his head. "I don't think so. You?"

"No, but if he does come here, we'll know who we've got."

"And what about the guy you already have? Do I want to know what's going to happen to him now?"

Marko sighed. "Nothing's going to happen to him, James. We're not barbarians. We've had our little chat, and I'll drop him off with my friends at the police station when he wakes up."

"The police station?"

"I don't think he's going to file a complaint against me, if that's what you're thinking. Don't worry so much. He'll be released by lunchtime tomorrow. But I don't expect he'll be sending any of his colleagues back here very soon."

"You're pretty sure of yourself, aren't you?"

"For a near-bankrupt and soon-to-be forcibly retired publisher, you mean? I guess the old training never left me."

"Then I'm supposed to believe this is your first stint as a tough guy since then?"

"Tough guy, James? That means criminal, like Al Capone, yes? Remember that these men came into my place of business—our place of business—and threatened violence. I thought you Americans were all about protecting your territory."

Will Europeans always see the United States as the Wild West? James wondered. *The frontier has been settled for well over a century now.*

"Your determination to defend yourself isn't what's throwing me here, Marko," he retorted aloud. "It's that you're so damned good at it. An armed receptionist? Security guards who look like private mercenaries? I thought this was a legal publishing house. Why the hell do you need that kind of firepower?"

"I don't know, James. Why don't we ask Gustaw? Oh, wait, he's not here. I guess we'll have to wait until he gets back."

"You're blaming him? You've got guns all over the place—and people who obviously know how to use them. And you want me to believe it's all because Gustaw disappeared hundreds of miles from here last week?"

"Believe what you want, James," Marko said, throwing up his hands. "I didn't ask you to come here, let alone bring his wife. I didn't tell him to go to eastern Ukraine either. I'm just trying to adjust to the situation we find ourselves in. Isn't that your philosophy—resilience and adaptation to a changing world? You've spent years lecturing me about evolving with the times. And if you think that doesn't mean being prepared for dangerous visitors in Ukraine today, then just imagine how our uninvited guests might've behaved if Nina hadn't been alert to potential threats."

James took a moment to do just that. "Alright, I'm grateful you were ready for trouble, but I still don't understand why. Or at least how. Are there trained paramilitaries on the street corners of Kyiv waiting to be hired as day laborers?"

Back in California, groups of Mexican migrants could be found congregating near home improvement stores and truck rental places hoping to be hired for a few hours of gardening or heavy lifting.

"Fairly close to that, actually," Marko said, seeming to understand the reference. "Did you think two Russian invasions and an ongoing war, never mind our endless government corruption, has had no economic effect here?" Marko paused, looking James straight in the eyes. "Or do you still believe technology is the reason UkraineLaw is going under?"

Frankly, he didn't know what to think about any of it now. For a few moments, he'd even forgotten about the man tied up in the back room—a man being held and interrogated, probably roughed up, by his business partner of two decades.

James crooked his head toward the darkness at the back of the building. "How did you find him, anyway?"

"Oh, his pals never made it out of the neighborhood."

James's eyes widened, and Marko shook his head.

"No, that's not what I meant," he continued. "Our guys were able to follow them right to our friend in the other room. Stupid amateurs went straight back to the one who sent them."

"Whom your security people then kidnapped and brought here?"

Marko cocked his head thoughtfully before answering.

"Yes, I suppose that's a fair description."

"Why would it even occur to you to do that? Why not just tell the police? They're your friends, aren't they?"

"So is Gustaw."

"And this is how you think you'll find him?"

"Maybe."

Well, how would James know any better? He'd never searched for a missing person in Ukraine—or anywhere else—before. Was this the kind of local knowledge and expertise he had to rely on now? Whatever his preconceived understanding of his own relationship to vigilantism or violence, after the morning's events he could feel his standards evolving.

Which was why James didn't hesitate when his old Russian friend Anatoly sent him an email that evening. He had a lead on how to find Gustaw, but they would need a large amount of cash to proceed, Anatoly wrote, providing few details beyond the amount of cash to procure: $50,000. James contacted his banker and made the arrangements.

9

Gustaw

One day earlier
A dim cell

"I'll always be grateful for what James did for me, Poland, and our publishing company when we needed foreign investment, but he gets the story a little bit wrong, too. We Polish managers weren't the only ones who misjudged circumstances, and James's mistakes cost me a lot more than mine cost him, however stressful events were for him at the time."

Gustaw sat on the narrow cot facing the gray-haired man who claimed to know his American friend James and, by way of proof, seemed to have heard all about their tumultuous time together at Polish Academic Publishing. His visitor had entered carrying the folding chair in which he now sat, closed the door, and then unfolded it in the tight space between the cot and the wall. Both men's knees were turned partly sideways to avoid knocking into each other.

They were speaking in English—the Russian's idea, though Gustaw wasn't sure that was enough to prevent his captors from eavesdropping. Despite the incongruity of the time and place, Gustaw could not help trying to set the record straight about those long-ago years in Warsaw.

"When the dust finally settled, James bought back the investment banks' shares for pennies on the dollar, moving his investors firmly into majority shareholder status. From then on, their agenda could move forward unimpeded. I, on the other hand, was unemployed in a struggling economy, with the very public problems at Polish Academic Publishing hanging like a millstone around my future work prospects. Who wanted to hire the guy who sold out the crown jewel of Poland's publishing industry?

"We're past that now, of course. I've moved on, and he was very gracious in helping me survive financially after he pushed me out. For many years, we've been able to be friends again. But there's a reason I didn't tell him what I was doing in Mariupol. It's not that he would've objected; I don't give a shit about his approval. It's that he wouldn't have understood anyway.

"You see, James came from the free side of the Iron Curtain, and no matter how much time passes, those of us who lived behind it still view the world through a bit of a film, don't you agree? Our mutual friend has that wonderful American optimism. It's what brought him and his money to Poland to begin with. I envy him having lived in a place where the borders haven't budged in over a century, but we Poles can't afford to have blind faith in the status quo, not with the way things have been going lately. Maybe he can't either, given the state of American politics today.

"James also has that infuriating American attitude that history started five minutes ago. He would tell the story of privatizing a publishing company as if it began when the ink dried on the purchase documents. For us Poles on the management team, it started years, if not decades—even centuries—earlier, with Poland itself in a perpetual tugging match between the Cossacks, the Swedes, the Austro-Hungarian Empire, and the damnable Russians—no offense intended, of course."

"None taken," his visitor said graciously. "But I'm not sure what all those long-ago events have to do with James and your publishing company."

"How does Polish history relate to the technical and scientific publishing at Polish Academic Publishing? Only that what could be printed—truth itself—was a matter of constant interpretation of reality, permission of the occupier, forbearance of the censor. Even the language of the published work was a function of shifting borders and despotic whims; could Poles be trusted to write in their own tongue this year or were there rebellious rumblings to be squelched? So, let's not pretend that a decision not to publish, not to distribute, not to finance a particular project was always a simple matter of market demand and profitability.

"Twenty-five years ago, we thought that new encyclopedia was going to change Poland, inoculate us against authoritarianism, and make the revolution permanent. I remember the first time I told James about it; he was so excited he almost hyperventilated."

Gustaw chuckled briefly and was relieved when his visitor reciprocated.

It had been during one of those "due diligence" visits the American made to Warsaw to look over the accounting books. James had reached another impasse with the chief accountant, so Gustaw decided to take him over to meet some of the book editors while that situation cooled down. James did his best to show interest in some of the more technical works in progress, but when they sat down to talk to one of the encyclopedia editors, he was entranced. "The first one without Communist propaganda? That's wonderful!" he had gushed, looking like he wanted to march down and get the printing presses rolling immediately.

"He couldn't have been prouder if he'd written the thing himself, and that was before they even won the privatization bid," Gustaw explained. "By the way, it was also before we realized what a cash cow that encyclopedia was going to be."

His visitor's eyes seemed to glitter for a moment, as if sharing James's early enthusiasm—or perhaps it was the mention of the project's enormous profitability that excited the Russian, who had once built a fortune of his own, if he was the man Gustaw thought he was.

"The grandkids don't understand when I try to explain it to them, that there was no Wikipedia yet," the Pole continued. "If you wanted to know something, you went to the bookshelf, pulled out an encyclopedia, and looked it up. And in Communist Poland, if it didn't conflict too much with the worldview promulgated by Karl Marx and Josef Stalin, you might get an accurate answer. Otherwise not. Then our new encyclopedia came along, and you can imagine that everyone wanted a set."

The timing had been perfect for privatization. A new edition of the encyclopedia was almost complete when the Communists lost power, and all Gustaw's team had to do was edit out the bullshit. All the major development expenses were paid before James's investors bought into the company.

"James probably has you believing we just sat in our offices counting the profits and congratulating ourselves on our cleverness," Gustaw suggested, wearily defensive. "Of course, we were proud of the work, but not for even one minute did I believe it would last forever. That's why we made acquisitions, started joint ventures, initiated new projects—all so we would have money coming in from other sources when people stopped buying the encyclopedia. He hated our new distribution operation so much—the cost overruns on it were his excuse for demanding I resign—but it's the most successful part of the company today. Ironic, isn't it? You'd think in the digital age there wouldn't be so much demand for driving paper publications around Poland. If there's anything we should understand from the present, though, it's how hard it is to predict the future."

Gustaw held up his palm, as if the other man had raised some protest at his words.

"But I'm not trying to dredge up old arguments. As I said, today's problems were seeded long before James and I worked together to privatize a publishing house."

"What do you mean?" Gustaw's visitor leaned forward in their cramped space, patiently inviting more explanation. The Pole couldn't help obliging.

"There's the bullshit we understood instinctively from childhood. You know what I'm talking about. The untruths the adults were too afraid to call lies—the official story that everyone knew landed a few degrees aslant from reality. I was a teenager reading a smuggled-in copy of George Orwell's *1984* when I finally found the vocabulary for this phenomenon: 'doublethink.'

"The following year, my friends started to disappear. Not literally—Poland wasn't Argentina—but that's how it felt to me. One week someone was sitting at the desk next to mine, and the next he was gone. A few months later, a classmate would bring in a letter bearing greetings from Paris or Stockholm. It was no secret what the government was doing in 1968. They'd cooked up those anti-Semitic purges precisely for their propaganda value.

"'These foreign Jews have been spying on all of us. We, the Polish Communist Party, will protect you,' our leaders promised.

"Stalin *had* cynically installed Russian Jews into the secret police forces of East European countries. That had been decades earlier, though. Their children and grandchildren had grown up Polish, and those were the friends who would mail me Western rock albums from exile while I reciprocated with the latest Polish music, unavailable in a West that had no economic ties to the Soviet bloc.

"Then it was summer, and I watched Polish troops marching off to help the Soviets roll back reforms in Czechoslovakia. It felt like a science fiction movie. Military planes flew overhead as columns of tanks and army cars moved out to crush the Prague Spring. *What a disgrace!* I thought even then.

"I was living with my aunt at the time—my father's sister, a dutiful Communist Party worker. I got to meet a lot of her loyal Communist friends. I told them just how little I thought of the Communist Party of Poland, and they told me that I was a poor excuse for a Polish patriot who didn't understand that the Soviets had thousands of tanks ready to rumble across the border anytime we did something they didn't approve of. And, unlike the Hungarians in 1956, Poles would be too stubborn to back down from the fight. So, a Polish rebellion against Soviet influence would inevitably lead to a bloodbath, and we would have only ourselves to blame. Of course, they didn't mention that they also enjoyed having their own privileged place within the system."

His tone softened as the remembered cynicism of his youth gave way to nostalgia.

"All things considered, I guess they were pretty indulgent with me. As far as they were concerned, I was a foolish kid who didn't know how the world worked. I'm sure they thought I would figure it out soon enough, see the error of my ways, and follow in my patriotic aunt's footsteps.

"I got a lot out of those conversations, though. I learned how to argue against the official, government version of events without losing my temper. That skill came in handy in the underground. Unfortunately, it's gotten a little rusty in the years since then.

"Maybe age has something to do with it, but I really wasn't prepared for what happened to Poland in this last election. The nationalists have taken over, turning their backs on our international commitments and alliances. The way things are going, our American friends might be in for a similar surprise."

"Do you think so?" the other man asked with audible skepticism.

"You don't believe it? Neither do a lot of them. I'll be thrilled if I'm wrong, but I have a feeling that loudmouth real estate developer isn't going anywhere.

"I'm sorry," Gustaw continued when he got no response. "Here I am running on about events you remember perfectly well, even if you did see them from the other side. What should we talk about instead?"

"Our mutual friend is eager to learn what happened to you, where you have been the past couple of weeks," the Russian explained, leaning forward again with his hands on his knees.

"Weeks? Is that how long it's been? I'm sure James does have questions, but there are things I can't talk about here. Even if you are his friend, as you claim to be, we never know who else is listening. That's not a concern we thought we would have after 1989, is it? We thought Orwell's Big Brother was dead and gone, along with Big Neighbor, Big Boss, even Big Friend and Big Spouse. Everything is automated now, though. We don't need people to spy on each other when the technology can do it for us.

"At Polish Academic Publishing, we saw the very beginning of these changes, James and I. Jozef, my head editor, thought we were crazy to imagine an encyclopedia set could be anything but ink and paper. But we put each volume on a compact disc, releasing one every few weeks, and sold it at newsstands. People loved it; they always sold out on the first day. With all the financial stress the company was experiencing at the time, the digital encyclopedia was the one bright spot I remember.

"Jozef was furious when budget issues delayed our publishing the paper version of that encyclopedia, but James just smiled about how futuristic we were being, as if it were a deliberate strategy, not an unfortunate necessity. Technological progress might be the only history his kind really understands, other than watching societies advance headlong toward his own worldview.

"Of course, we couldn't know then that the internet was a Trojan horse, welcomed into every intimate corner of our lives before we knew the invaders were aboard. And even if we had known, how many of us would trade away the joy and convenience of smartphones, social media, and the online search engine? Where else can you immortalize your every fleeting opinion and share photos of your fancy lunch with envious primary school classmates? Imagine a world where people still read road maps to get their bearings."

"You think we'd be better off without so much technology." It was more a statement than a question.

"No, I'm not a Luddite at all. I use Skype and Uber, even Wikipedia, I'm embarrassed to admit. And I'm not talking about how all these conveniences have changed us—texting through dinner; the workday that never ends because the emails just keep coming; that reflexive lunge for a pinging device. No, there's a less philosophical concern here about how online banking has the potential to put a cybercriminal's hand in anyone's wallet. And so much worse.

"Power plants, medical records, and even the doors of hotel rooms can all be hijacked from half a world away. You've heard James talk about the possibilities, I'm sure? A nuclear reactor melting down with the engineers in the control room powerless to intervene or the refrigerators in giant warehouses suddenly switching off, spoiling a city's food supply. Today, you wouldn't even blink at the idea that a skilled-enough hacker could shut off your father's pacemaker or intercept the video feed from your grandchild's baby monitor.

"Big Brother is back, and his name is Legion. Now we never see them watching, but we know they're there, whoever *'they'* are. CIA, FSB, Google. Or some other 'non-state actor' you've never heard of.

"James thought his side had the high moral ground, until young Edward Snowden let slip just how *'by the people'* his government wasn't. Now we're all in the same soup, not sure who is monitoring us or why, hoping we can stay under the radar or rely on the odds to keep from becoming the next victim.

"Maybe the last twenty-five years were the aberration, and oppression is the real status quo. Do you suppose? Your people went from tsars to central committees to Putin with very little successful self-government in between. We thought we had done better, but our people let us know last year that they disagreed—and what nation can claim self-government when the governed themselves reject the definition?

"I suppose you must wrestle with these questions, too, from time to time. Weren't you a politician once? Did you ever find yourself at odds with the people you thought you represented?"

"I could ask you the same question," the Russian said.

"Oh, I was never in the government. I thought about it at first, though not as an elected official. I wanted to be an adviser, and I could have done it, too. I knew everyone in that first post-Communist administration. But some wise friends warned me against it, and they were right. There was so much political upheaval at the time that I would have been unemployed within a year, along with the rest of that government.

"You must know somebody, though, or they wouldn't have let you in to see me. I don't suppose you can get me out of here?"

"Not today, I'm afraid." His visitor's head shake seemed genuinely regretful.

"Well, I wouldn't believe you if you'd said 'yes.' *Just another interrogators' trick,* I'd have thought.

"The Communists offered to let me go during martial law back in '82. And they meant it, too. 'We can release you tomorrow,' they said, waving my confiscated passport in front of me. 'But you and your family must go straight to the airport and get on a plane to your friends in America.' They even had my wife pressuring me to take the deal. That was how they were going to get rid of us troublemakers, you see."

He chuckled for his visitor's sake, grinning broadly to squelch the memory of her final visit to his prison, where she delivered the ultimatum that ended their marriage. She was hardly the first woman to resent a man's loyalty to comrades and cause over his own family.

"'Absolutely, I'll go,' I told them all those years ago. 'I'll take that one-way flight to Washington so long as you take a one-way flight to Moscow on the same day.'"

The Russian smiled weakly and Gustaw sighed in response.

"I'll admit it was tempting to just leave. I had Western supporters who would've helped me get settled abroad. I just wasn't willing to be driven out of my own country for wanting to make it a decent place to live.

"Even after we won, though, I was never someone to argue for revenge. Ask James. I didn't fire the Communists at Polish Academic Publishing, and believe me, there was pressure to do just that. But they weren't all villains and oppressors. Some of them were probably true believers, like my aunt and her friends, or people who had only joined the Party to get ahead in the society it controlled, like those scientists who were too afraid to hire me years earlier. We all had to choose our own responses to the system we were born into. Once it was gone, I just wanted the new system to work. All this time, I've managed to convince myself that it did."

"You expect me to believe you weren't upset with anyone, after all you had been through?" The visitor snorted, drumming his fingers on his knee. "That you're not feeling the same way now?"

Gustaw cocked his head, then nodded slowly.

"Yes, I am angry about a lot of things happening today in Poland and other places. I don't like it when officials lie to us, any more than I did forty years ago. I think the public has been manipulated with bad information, and people like refugees and immigrants are being used as scapegoats, just like the Jews were in 1968.

"As I said, I was flabbergasted when the so-called Law and Justice Party won the election last year. I couldn't believe that people would fall for their xenophobia and pipe dreams of easy money. All that effort to keep the economy humming along—decades of lower wages and social spending to sustain growth and investment. We were Eastern Europe's miracle, outperforming all our neighbors on any metric you could name, and now it's all at risk because people want the government to pay them to have more children."

"And you think you can make people see reason? Turn back the clock maybe?"

"Well, of course I've been trying to do *something* about it. I'm not retired yet, my wife would be the first to tell you. But don't get my doctor started on the ways I should be slowing down. Sore joints, creaky spine. No marathon this year, he said. Which is a good thing, because I don't think our friends behind the glass are likely to let me train for it. What do you think?"

A polite chuckle from the Russian. "So what *have* you been trying to do about it, then?"

"What difference does it make what I've been doing? Those guys aren't Polish secret police, *are* they. I can tell you, Vladimir Putin doesn't like our new leaders any more than I do, which might be the only opinion we share.

"It's no secret, though, that I've been trying to get opposition thinkers together. Funny how, in a democracy, that sort of thing is legal and open. No need for infiltrators with hidden cameras and secret recording devices to find out who came and what we talked about. We met in a café for anyone to see—and hear, if they wanted to. How's that for progress?

"Of course, Law and Justice could always send some thugs in to break up our next meeting. Theoretically, that would be a risk with any government, but the longer a society goes without allowing that behavior, the less acceptable it will be to the majority of citizens. Or so I had hoped.

"I never called myself a hero, but I know James likes to say that. I'm sure it's what intrigued him about working with my associate Rudolf and me in the first place. And I suppose there's no harm now in admitting I played up to that image to keep him interested. I never lied about it, though.

"Rudolf had emigrated to New Jersey the moment martial law was declared, but he was only too happy to pretend he had spent years rubbing shoulders with Adam Michnik and Lech Walesa. They were the intellectual and the muscular industrialist leaders of that era. Look them up if you don't remember how important they were to my country then. But Rudolf was nothing more than an errand boy—a brave one, I will admit. We didn't have many people willing to take the risks he did moving equipment between hideouts, but that didn't make him a top-level operative. Anyway, his blustering caused me a lot of problems at Polish Academic Publishing."

"James told me you worked with Adam Michnik in the underground."

"Sure, *I* knew most of the Solidarity leaders of the 1980s and many of the government people in the early 1990s. Even today. A lot of the Law and Justice officials are old underground activists."

"They're betraying the freedom they fought for back then?"

"I think so. But it makes perfect sense to them. What they're doing now is what they thought they were fighting for all along, apparently. Catholicism, Polish families, and national pride. In their minds, the last quarter century probably looks like an absurd detour. Their history books will skip straight from World War II Polish heroism to the Smolensk plane crash they call a 'massacre' to the cultural renaissance heralded by their own election.

"It's not unlike what your friend Vladimir is doing here, by the way, assuming here is where I think it is. In the 1940s, we were all noble anti-Nazis in this part of the world, right? No collaborators to be found. Then gloss over the next seventy years, and now we're all proud nationalists. He is trying to make Russia great again, isn't he, never mind that that greatness came with a Soviet stench? A lot of people seem to believe he already has."

"I'm not one of them, I assure you," his guest said with solemnity.

"That's encouraging, although it's a dangerous opinion to declare openly. Of course, a skilled interrogator knows how to say what his victim needs to hear."

The visitor stood with an abruptness that suggested Gustaw's words had hit home. "I suppose it's time for me to leave," he said, folding his chair with a snap.

"Are you going now?" With a contented half-smile, Gustaw reclined back on his cot with his hands threaded behind his head. "Well, thank you for helping me pass the time. Give James my regards if you speak to him."

10

James

Mariupol, Ukraine

"I'm going with you," Natalya insisted for the tenth time.

"I'll have enough to keep track of with Gustaw, Anatoly, and all this cash he asked for," James repeated. "I can't be responsible for you as well."

"Nobody asked you to be," Natalya growled in a low voice.

Marko half-turned to speak confidentially to her, but not so quietly that James couldn't overhear. "I'm sure you don't need anyone's protection, but as Gustaw's friend, James thinks it's his duty to keep you safe, and he's not going to stop believing that just because you want him to. Shouldn't we let him and his friend concentrate on finding Gustaw?"

The messenger bag filled with cash sat on the table in front of them. James saw her glance toward it in unconscious acknowledgment that she had little leverage to press her case.

"I'll have a copy editor from UkraineLaw accompany you back to Warsaw," Marko offered.

So, James felt justified, if guilty, in finally breaking his promise to Anna. He had done all he could from Kyiv; she would have to understand that. And without word from the private detective, Anatoly's lead, whatever it was, was all they had to go on. He couldn't walk away from the search with an unexplored clue still on the table.

Besides, he didn't want to entrust $50,000 in cash to a courier. Not in Ukraine. It was risky enough hauling it around himself. "Surely this sort of thing is done by wire transfer these days," he had said in a follow-up email, but his old friend had ignored the hint, providing no further details about what he knew or how the money was to be spent—on bribes? Bodyguards?

Marko would accompany him to drive, translate, and look for his incommunicado detective friend. Anatoly, not knowing the Ukrainian publisher, had discouraged Marko's inclusion, and James had enough recollection of the bound man at the board table to be wary. Still, Marko's sidearm and low profile seemed the best way to get James—and the valuable luggage on which the whole errand apparently rested—to their destination.

They compromised. Once arrived in Mariupol, James would rendezvous with Anatoly to retrieve Gustaw, and Marko would search for Stepan separately. Perhaps, James suggested with awkward levity, the five of them could get together for a celebratory drink after it was all sorted out.

In accordance with Anatoly's instructions, Marko dropped James at an agreed-upon street corner and drove off in the direction of the hotel that was Gustaw's last known location. There wasn't much of a hospitality industry left in Mariupol, and it seemed safe to assume Stepan had at least contacted this one when he got to the city. It was as good a place as any to start making inquiries.

James stood at the intersection, cash-heavy satchel on one shoulder, his right fist gripping the handles too tightly, while his customary leather duffle dangled from his left. He felt encumbered, vulnerable, as if everyone in eastern Ukraine had X-ray vision to see that life-changing stash of U.S. dollars hovering above the pavement, with only this sixty-something language-limited American around to guard it.

The jowly man who approached him wore sunglasses, though it was late in the afternoon and overcast, and stepped in close before speaking.

"James, so good to see you again after all these years!" The man took a step back, grinned, then threw his arms around James's chest in a bearhug. James clenched his bags even harder before returning the gesture.

So, this diminished, graying figure was what had become of Anatoly, the first aspiring capitalist James had encountered as the world turned away from Soviet Communism. No, not aspiring. The man was a millionaire before James knew him, thanks to preferential contracts and lines of credit from the Soviet government. What he had become since then—failed business collaborator abroad, public enemy and frustrated politician at home—didn't matter much to the present circumstances. If he could come through for Gustaw, that was all that was important.

"Did you bring the money?" Anatoly whispered quietly, then smiled at James's brief nod. "Okay, let's get to somewhere we can talk."

He turned abruptly and led James down the street, then through an alley, across another intersection, and into a narrow street where he used a key to unlock the wrought-iron door to a courtyard. They entered, and he ushered James and his baggage across it and through another door into a dim, musty-smelling room. In the shadows created by closed blinds and the dwindling daylight outside, James couldn't tell whether they had entered an apartment, an office, or some little-used storage area.

"Anatoly, please tell me what you know. It's been two weeks since there's been any news of my friend, and you insist I bring a bag of cash to a war zone before you'll share what you've learned. What is the money for?"

"Ransom."

"Ransom? So he's been kidnapped? By whom? Where is he now? Is he okay?"

"Slow down, James. I'm going to answer your questions, but you've been on the road all day. Do you want to have something to eat? Take a shower? Rest from your trip?"

James sat down on a small loveseat in what was starting to look like a living room as his eyes adjusted to the dim lighting. "Are there any lamps in this place?"

"Of course." Anatoly switched on a torchiere in the corner and settled himself into a battered leather armchair.

James waited silently.

"You want to hear about Gustaw." Anatoly spoke from the shadows like an anonymous source in a crime documentary. "He's fine. He had been moved out of Ukraine, but the people who have him will return him here, in exchange for the money you brought."

"But who has him? Why did they take him in the first place? How did you find him?"

"I'm not without contacts and resources, James, even after all this time. I assumed that's why you called on me in the first place."

"Of course. And I'm incredibly grateful for everything you've done. Do you know why this happened? Was it just a straightforward kidnapping for ransom?"

"No, it was . . ." Anatoly stopped speaking in mid-sentence, but after a pause he still had nothing to add. "Frankly, James, you're better off not knowing. The men who took him made a mistake. They thought he had information he didn't have or was more important than he turned out to be. Now they know better, and they'd rather have the cash than hold onto this worthless old guy."

James winced at the description. But if the kidnappers' faulty judgment was his opportunity to bring Gustaw home, he would take it. "Okay. What do we need to do?"

"I've got the exchange set up for tomorrow. It's a two-person job, though. One of us will drop off the cash at one location while the other meets Gustaw at a second."

"Fine. Good. But how will the one with the money know Gustaw has been released and it's alright to pay?"

Anatoly scowled like a disappointed parent. "That's not how it works, James. You have to pay them first. Once they have the money, then they let him go."

Of course. He had seen enough movies to understand that. Why had he imagined it could happen the other way? And what choice did he have?

"But they will let him go?"

"Yes. I've convinced them he's not a threat. We just have to follow their instructions." Anatoly handed James a folded piece of paper.

The carefully typed message had details (in English) of how the money was to be divided and bundled before sealing the stacks in Ziploc bags, which would all be loaded into a black backpack of a style ubiquitous in the country. As the courier approached the drop site at a public playground, he was to wear the pack on his left shoulder, then sit on a bench, place the bag on the ground underneath, and, after five minutes, get up and walk to a nearby snack stand to buy a bar of chocolate before leaving the area. If anyone followed him to return the abandoned bag, he was to drop it in a trash bin around the corner. Meanwhile, the second team member was to wait at a café across town for Gustaw to join him.

"You should be the one to wait for Gustaw," Anatoly suggested as they were reviewing the plan. "I know how anxious you are to see him."

He was, of course. But the thought of sitting passively and nibbling a sandwich while waiting for something to happen was more than he could stand. It's how he had spent most of his time since leaving California. He had to *do* something, now that there was something concrete to do. Besides, it was *his* money, and he wanted to be sure it was handed off correctly.

"I'll do the money drop," James said. "You pick up Gustaw."

Anatoly agreed with a shrug. Reaching down beside his chair, he tossed a backpack with the tags still on it onto the coffee table, along with a box of plastic bags. He motioned for James to set his satchel beside it, inhaling deeply as he unzipped it to reveal the crisp piles of bills. They set to work.

Once the cash was prepared and packaged for the next day's delivery, Anatoly heated a dish of stew in a microwave for their supper. Then he brought out a bottle of vodka and poured a generous dose into a couple of glasses.

"How have you been, really?" James asked, forcing his questions about Gustaw out of his mind.

"It's been tough at home for a while now. I think I've told you that."

By home, of course, he meant Russia in general, not the marriage (marriages?) that had folded years ago, leaving Anatoly estranged and at arm's length from his now-grown children. Come to think of it, that seemed to be the story for too many of James's friends.

Maybe Anatoly didn't see things that way, though, imagining, as James did, the energetic visionary he had been decades ago side by side with today's humble, hollowed-out version. Because in between there had been activity and dreams and plans—so many of those. He was going to help make chess an Olympic sport, become an influential politician, build from his early fortune a pile of wealth to rival the oligarchs. But he had crossed swords with the wrong powerful people long ago, and over time, it had all fizzled.

Had Anatoly, like Gustaw, simply been endowed with more creative ideas than management skill to bring them to fruition? Was that another legacy of their shared roots under Communism, a system cursed with too many grand visions and not enough effective solutions? Or were they both merely examples of a type that would have revealed itself in that way regardless of geography? So much early potential seemed to be shipwrecked over time on the imbalance between people's abilities to envision and execute their dreams.

But Anatoly was here now, and he had succeeded where the professional detective apparently failed. Thank goodness this ordeal was almost over. James took a satisfied gulp of Anatoly's vodka, secretly regretting that it wasn't bourbon.

"Of course. I understand that Putin is making a mess of Russia's future prospects. And now we have Hungary and Poland going the same way. Even the Philippines."

He tried not to allude to the email blast Anatoly had sent out two years earlier, asking his Western contacts for funding—$2 million worth—to mount a final, "Hail Mary" political campaign for reelection to the Russian Duma. James himself hadn't replied to the request, which had shocked and embarrassed him on his old friend's behalf. Had Anatoly grown so brazen in his years out of favor at home, or had desperation driven him past the point of caring about propriety?

"The conditions are intolerable already," Anatoly said, draining his own glass. "But somehow, we must tolerate them, just as we used to do under the Soviets. Anyway, how is the life of the blessed in California?"

Well, James wouldn't deny it. "Going wonderfully, until all of this happened. Anna and the kids are doing well. My businesses are prospering. Did you know Polish Academic Publishing is the largest publishing group in Poland now?"

"Congratulations, James. I'm glad things have worked out so well for you."

Was there a sarcastic note in the Russian's statement? James reached for the bottle and poured another round.

Decades ago, Anatoly had been the one featured in news magazines and fêted at elite business gatherings. James had never had that kind of exposure personally, but he'd cultivated connections to many who did—people like Anatoly and Gustaw. And he'd done his best to introduce them around so they could prosper in the world of free minds and free markets that, with the discrediting of Soviet Communism, was finally open to everyone. For many summers, he had hosted networking weekends at his vacation home in southern Spain. The elegant house and beautiful coastal setting provided an inspiring venue for a salon-like exchange of ideas on topics from business to good governance to philosophy.

Nevertheless, while James calmly built up a prosperous life by increments, many of these luminaries had flamed and, as far as the wider world was concerned, flickered out. And though he couldn't remember ever having been jealous of their more-alluring origin stories, he felt a guilty satisfaction now at the realization that his quieter path had led to a happier conclusion.

Was it luck or a well-earned reward that accounted for this difference? Aware of his early advantages—and the number of his similarly well-off peers who had squandered theirs—he had always figured good fortune and good decisions were about equal as progenitors of his success.

But the outcome of the present moment was bound to affect this calculus—for himself, for Gustaw, and maybe even for Anatoly in his supporting role. Because if the end result of a quarter century of Eastern European involvement was to be calamity, then James could hardly retain the same pride of ownership in his accomplishments there. Poland had always been about more than money to him.

He watched Anatoly refill their glasses again and gamely took a sip. They had the whole night to catch up. Why not take the bull by the horns?

"So, what's the latest on your political aspirations? I never heard how your plans to run for election again turned out."

Anatoly frowned. "Not so well, as you might guess. Without Putin's support, I would have needed a lot more funds than I was able to raise to mount a serious challenge. It really wasn't worth trying."

James nodded. "We've seen a lot of upheaval in your country since we first met, haven't we? Any predictions about what happens next?"

"Who could have predicted half of what's happened in that time?"

The ruminating silence between them encompassed the sudden crumbling of the once-mighty Soviet Union; Russian President Boris Yeltsin's turn from democratic hero to disappointing cronyism and the rise of the oligarchs; the Chechen War; the Russian Flu economic crisis of the late 1990s; and, of course, the era of Vladimir Putin, a strongman whose cult of personality had mesmerized the majority of his countrymen for more than a decade, never mind the suppression of dissent, assassination of political opponents, and general authoritarian air of today's Russia.

Had the West botched the aftermath of Soviet Communism? For all the efforts of people like James, who brought investment dollars and intellectual capital in to help those societies adjust, had the transition been too painful for too many for too long, the opportunities for abuse too numerous for those able to convert power in the old system into wealth and influence in the new?

Was there anything Western governments could have done differently—*he* could have done differently? He had always prided himself on his fairness to the people who worked for him. He and his fellow investors had gone into Polish Academic Publishing with profit-sharing plans and generous terms for managers like Gustaw to buy stock in the company. Yes, the coming of the investment banks, with their impossibly high expectations, had nearly led to disaster. But he had stuck with Polish Academic Publishing afterward and done what he could to repair the damage. And the business was thriving again, still providing jobs to hundreds of Poles. Today's discontents weren't his fault.

"Your friend Gustaw has predictions," Anatoly ventured. "He seems to believe Hungary and Poland are just the beginning of a wave of authoritarian isolationism that will sweep across the West—even your country."

"I know. I've heard him say the same thing . . . Wait. You've spoken to him?"

"Yes, certainly. I've been to see him a few times. He's fine, as I told you. I made sure of it myself."

"So, whoever has him let you in to see him, then let you leave again? What kind of kidnappers would do that?"

"The kind with whom I have mutual friends. We're very lucky he was being held where he was. Otherwise, I would never have been able to find him, let alone visit."

"But why couldn't you get him released, then, if you know these guys?"

Anatoly rubbed his eyes, which James noticed for the first time were red-rimmed with irritation or exhaustion. But when he spoke, he exuded infinite patience.

"I *am* getting him released, James. That's why you're here. Look around you and think about where you are. People are desperate. They know someone with resources is looking for Gustaw. Do you really imagine they'd let him go for nothing?"

"So, who are they?"

"Like I said before, I think it's safer if you don't know."

Why? He wanted to ask, but stifling his curiosity seemed like a fair trade for bringing his friend home.

They slept that night in an adjoining room that smelled of damp and sweat. James's twin bed had a sagging mattress and unsightly rust-brown stains on the coverlet, but the rough sheets seemed clean. It had been a long time since he'd stayed anywhere this unkempt—perhaps his 1989 visit to Moscow to attend the conference where he and Anatoly first met—but the Russian insisted they were safer keeping away from hotels, particularly the ones that catered to Western visitors.

He could tolerate it for one night. James brought the bag with the ransom money to bed with him, looping his arms through the straps and hugging it to his chest like a lover, and slept uninterrupted until morning.

He awoke to sunlight slipping under the curtains, still clutching the backpack that would buy Gustaw's freedom. The unmade bed beside him was empty, and James felt a momentary fear that he'd been abandoned until he detected the smell of coffee brewing in the kitchen.

The surrounding squalor was more pronounced in daylight—dingy window glass, peeling paint, amorphous dirt pellets in the corners of the tile floor. Forgoing his daily shower until he could find more suitable accommodations, James quickly dressed, repacked his bag, and went to find Anatoly.

They laid low—was that the right term?—in the shady apartment for the early part of the day. They went over the plan a dozen times. A taxi arranged by Anatoly would drop James at the playground, circle around, and park on the other side of the square, then bring him back to the apartment afterward by way of a few more stops intended to discourage tails. Anatoly would make his own way to the café and return with Gustaw by a similarly cautious route. It all sounded absurdly dramatic to James, and yet here he was, guarding a pack full of cash, ready to abandon it in a public park on the promise that his missing friend would reappear afterward.

As the time established for the money drop neared, James began pacing in the diminutive salon, frantic to get on with it and finish the job. By the time Anatoly put him in the cab after a final review of instructions, he was both overeager and bitterly dreading the next hour or so.

He glanced suspiciously at the man in the driver's seat, with his grave expression and chin stubble. Maybe this was a setup, and instead of releasing Gustaw, James and his money would be taken instead. There would be nothing Anatoly could do to stop it; he would be across town waiting. And Anna? Well, if they took him, they'd better keep him, because he didn't want to hear her say, "I told you so." He hadn't told her about the planned ransom, hoping to delay his confession until they were all safely back in Warsaw.

Traffic was minimal, but the driver seemed to be taking his time. They threaded their way past interchangeable beige and yellow apartment blocks, the smokestacks of idle industrial plants visible in the distance. Somewhere, he knew, languished the cranes of a port struggling to survive since Russia's annexation of Crimea two years previously gave that hostile neighbor control of the entrance to the Sea of Azov.

James didn't know how close they were to their destination, but he suddenly found himself wanting to postpone their arrival, as if his lizard brain sensed the approach of danger.

Then they were at the cracked, debris-strewn curb, and he was out and on his way up the sidewalk toward the swing sets, with just enough recollection of the plan to switch the backpack to his left shoulder as he went. There was a bench, and he sat on it, breathing heavily, glancing around before stopping himself with a silent curse.

He heard the squeals of children playing behind him as he deliberately slid the bag off his shoulder and tucked it behind his knees, the strap sliding through sweaty fingers as he unwrapped them from the cargo he'd been guarding so carefully for two days. His legs shook as he sat there, willing them to straighten and carry him toward the coffee stand across the square.

On his third attempt, he was stumbling forward in the right direction. Halfway to his destination, he froze. Had he waited long enough at the bench? It had felt like a lifetime, but he knew adrenaline could make people misjudge. What if it wasn't five minutes? What if it was only three? Would that be a deal breaker for the men who had Gustaw? He should've checked his watch. How could he have forgotten such a simple thing?

He should go back—but no, that seemed worse than misjudging the timing. The people watching—as he knew they must be—might think he was trying to retrieve the money. So he slogged forward to buy his chocolate bar—thank goodness Anatoly had given him some local money for that purpose—and continued on to the other side of the square, where the taxi driver was waiting for him. It took all his willpower to keep from turning around and looking toward that bench to see if anyone had come to claim the money.

The cab dropped him at the same corner where he'd been picked up, a block and a half from the apartment where they'd spent the night. As Anatoly had suggested, James walked around the block to make sure the driver was gone before heading for the gated courtyard. When he got there, it dawned on him that he'd never been given a key.

He waited a few minutes for Anatoly and Gustaw, then started to worry that his presence would attract attention. What would be the point of all this secrecy if he stood outside like a lost tourist until the whole neighborhood knew where the tall American was staying?

So he walked around the block a couple more times, figuring he'd catch them on the way inside. The circuit only took a few minutes. Surely he hadn't missed them, assuming they would be approaching on foot as well? But maybe they needed more time to arrive. They were coming from farther away, or the kidnappers were counting the money before bringing Gustaw to the café.

He appraised the wrought-iron fence, calculating his ability to scale it without being seen or breaking his neck. James was a strong swimmer and an avid runner. He did not shy away from physical exertion, but he was not a gymnast either. Even if he did make it over, then what? He'd be locked in a courtyard for who knew how long, with nowhere to sit and no key in or out, visible to anyone who glanced through the gate. It wasn't a good option.

At Anatoly's insistence, he'd left his phone behind. "You don't want the distraction of calls or email," the Russian had said. "And you really don't want these guys to think you're taking pictures or trying to monitor them in any way." Remembering how Marko had separated him from his phone over similar concerns back in Kyiv, James had readily agreed. He didn't need any such misunderstandings with armed kidnappers.

A shop on the next corner sold groceries and incidentals, and he had enough money left in his pocket to buy a pen and small notepad.

"I'll be at the Neptune Hotel," he wrote on the top sheet. "Please contact me there when you get back."

Then he folded the note into the tiniest of paper airplanes, returned to that wrought-iron gate, and sent it sailing toward the door his friends would have to enter. It skittered to a stop where he was sure they couldn't miss it. Satisfied as only a middle school paper airplane design champion could be after all these years, he started down the street looking for another taxi. If he didn't have enough cash to pay, well, the hotel concierge could take care of it and add it to his bill. He was done with the cloak-and-dagger side of things. Anatoly hadn't outlined a Plan B for him to fall back on, so he might as well make himself comfortable while he waited.

Imagine James's surprise, then, when the receptionist at the hotel's front desk handed him a letter that had been delivered for him two days earlier, before he'd even considered coming here. Hands trembling in anticipation, he retreated to his new hotel room to open it.

11

James

Mariupol, Ukraine

Dear James,

Your Russian friend just left, and I'm not sure he'll be able to visit again, as my captors have been threatening to move me. I don't know why that would matter, though, since I don't know where I am anyway. But he left me some paper and pens, and the guards have not taken them, so I am writing even though I have no idea if these words will ever reach you.

It might all be a jailer's trick: he is not your friend at all, just another clever interrogator, and instead of being delivered to you, this letter will be read and laughed at by the people who are holding me here. But, in the absence of other diversion, I choose to hope, for old times' sake, that this communication will get to you somehow. And, if I am wrong, as I have been too many times to count lately, then at least it will help me set my thoughts in order before facing whatever fate they have in mind for me.

As you presumably know by now, I left Kyiv a few weeks ago (I've lost track of the days) and traveled to Mariupol to meet a candidate for the new company we have been planning.

The young man I was interviewing—his name is Feliks—already had a job and was reluctant to even speak about leaving it. A smarter man than I would have congratulated him on his good fortune and moved on, but I got a whiff of something amiss in his behavior. After we talked for a while, he shared his concerns.

Contrary to my initial impression, Feliks was very eager to separate from his current employers. He didn't like the work he was doing.

No, that's not strong enough. He didn't approve of the work he was doing.

He asked to use my laptop and pulled up a website filled with news articles out of a parallel universe. You would be amazed by the headlines I saw there. Only the most credulous fools would imagine they could be true, but this man's employers had hired an army of technically savvy workers to spread them online as widely as they could.

And here's the part that will really surprise you: these articles were written in English, and many of them were about your American presidential election. It was mostly anti-Hillary Clinton stuff, everything from the Catholic Pope endorsing Donald Trump to a child sex ring the Democrats were supposedly running out of a pizzeria. The Clintons have been vilified in America for years, and I figured this was more of the same. But why were these Ukrainian guys going to such trouble to spread these obviously absurd stories?

"No, people really believe them. The guys who hate Mrs. Clinton can't get enough of this stuff," Feliks assured me. "The bosses even pay bonuses when the stories we write get shared enough times."

So, it was an advertising scam, then. The more page views these fictional articles got, the more money the criminals—they had to be criminals, I figured—made. And since there was only so much of this stuff on the internet created by the usual conspiracy theorists, they had to generate new stories of their own to cash in.

You can understand why Feliks wouldn't be happy with his job writing nonsense and spreading it around through the rank and file of online idiots. But Ukraine is at war, and there are only so many jobs to be had.

I can see now that I should have left well enough alone, but what I saw then was a bright, ambitious kid whose aspirations were being thwarted by narrow-minded thugs. Sound familiar? It did to me. Thanks to Ukraine's infamous corruption, I figured I could grease a few palms and buy his freedom.

So I went to the address where Feliks said he worked, hoping to find his supervisor and discuss terms.

James shook his head in bewilderment. Reminiscing about his own youthful setbacks, Gustaw had marched himself into a gangsters' den to try to pay off people he didn't know on behalf of some kid he'd just met? With such a beginning, the rest of the story practically told itself, James thought as his eyes returned to the letter.

The visit did not go as planned. I approached two men in the quiet parking lot of what I expected to be a bustling technology center and woke up tied to a chair in a dim office. Nearby, a man sat at a computer with his back to me.

You might be surprised to learn, given my history of intrigue, arrest, and incarceration, that this was the first time I had been rendered unconscious in the service of my cause. (Though I'm not sure that our new Ukrainian company quite qualifies as one of those.)

If I were James Bond, of course, I would have jumped to my feet, untying the rope as I did so, bashed the man over the head with the chair, downloaded the contents of his computer to the thumb drive hidden in my shoe, and snuck away before anyone knew I was awake.

Instead, I did what any normal 60-year-old would do when waking up tied to a chair. I squirmed, groaned, and struggled unsuccessfully to free my hands. The man at the desk swiveled toward me with a polite smile.

That first questioner took his time, kept his cool, never lost his courteous demeanor. Soon, one of his colleagues joined us. He had a bulbous nose, a few missing teeth, and a leering curl to his lower lip when he spoke. We were in that room together for hours.

James shivered from a chill that had nothing to do with the hotel's air conditioning as he imagined the calm, relentless questioning of his friend. What brutal details was Gustaw omitting from his missive?

I can feel you wondering what they did to me during that questioning, and what has been done to me since. I think that does not matter very much. My treatment has been worse than I would prefer but certainly less horrible than you are imagining, so do not think of it. As much as I want to go home and see Natalya and my children again, I feel at peace with the idea that it might not happen.

What I'm trying to say is, if you do by some miracle receive this letter, don't spend your energy worrying about me and my situation. What I'm about to explain to you is the important thing.

I never mentioned the phony news articles Feliks had shown me. I figured if I could convince them I didn't know about that, then they would let me go. Of course, it's a little tricky to demonstrate that you don't know something that you're not supposed to know about. You can't exactly bring up the subject, right?

It took me a long time—too long—to realize that this whole episode wasn't about made-up news articles on Facebook, as troubling as that revelation was. That crew had far more important secrets.

I can sense your impatience now, James, as you wonder what terrible conspiracy I have discovered. I will explain everything.

First, though, let me remind you of an earlier time when the world was even more chaotic than it is today. This was before both of our births, though not by very many years. It won't be a new story to you, student of history that you are, but I don't think we've ever spoken of it before.

You know all about the Yalta Conference in 1945, I'm sure. The fighting was still underway when Josef Stalin, Franklin Roosevelt, and Winston Churchill met in that Crimean resort town to discuss the future of post-war Europe: borders, systems of government, occupation zones after the German surrender that hadn't even happened yet.

James vaguely recalled learning of this summit between the Allies at the end of World War II, but he wouldn't have remembered that it took place in what was now Russia-annexed Ukraine. Unsure of this historical event's current significance, in any case, he kept reading.

Depending on who is telling the story, your American president was either duped into giving too much away or made the best of a situation in which he had limited bargaining power. Either way, my own country paid the highest price for the Yalta agreement. The occupying Russians arranged sham elections and installed a puppet regime in Poland after the war that so many Poles had died to help the Allies win, and the world did nothing to stop them. Sure, there was handwringing and public expressions of regret, but the war was finally over, and nobody was prepared to start another one.

As you know, it was forty-some years before we extricated ourselves from that situation. Decades of political repression and poverty. Jews fleeing to the West. Old people waiting in line to buy bread. Schoolchildren forced to learn Russian. Hundreds of millions of people pretending to believe the Communist lies until the Soviet system finally collapsed under the weight of its own stupidity.

So, if I were to learn of another such gathering—this time in secret—where today's "great" leaders intended to divide up the world again, plunging a new generation into that same, old nightmare, what do you imagine my reaction would be?

Now, I don't mean to imply that Vladimir Putin and Xi Jinping were lurking there in that dark warehouse where I was told our prospective employee worked. Such men's movements are too closely monitored. But what if I were to tell you that some of their underlings were getting together to talk about things their bosses could never be heard saying publicly? You might reasonably wonder why such a gathering would take place on the non-Russian side of a war in eastern Ukraine.

Then suppose I were to tell you that China and Russia were not the only interests represented at this meeting, and that the third group of participants were stand-ins not for a current world leader but for a longshot candidate to become one? And now you will not have to guess who I mean, nor why such a rendezvous must take place in absolute secrecy.

I'm sure you would tell me there is no world war today, no deposed governments to replace or occupiers' role to allocate during an upcoming transition. Then I must tell you to think bigger, beyond literal occupation of bombed-out cities and the installation of puppet regimes. Today's powers project their will in other ways—through trade relations and sea patrols as well as the deployment of "little green men": those Russian soldiers who invaded Ukraine in 2014 wearing uniforms without insignia.

And now, I think you are imagining how the negotiations I am describing to you might proceed. How like-minded, power-drunk men might use their clout in the old, fraying order to establish a new one in their own self-serving image—a future where no one is immoral because everyone is.

But perhaps this is only a crazy story. How could I have uncovered such a fantastical plot? And even if I could escape this prison, what hope would I have of convincing people that it is true, as if anyone believes anything they don't want to believe—or questions anything they do want to believe—these days?

So what is this letter but a Hail Mary, my imagination conjuring up a final flare of hope that what I write will someday make it out of this cell, if not to you, James, then perhaps into an official file that will resurface decades from now, when all the implications and consequences of the present moment are fully known, to shed light on how and why things came to pass as they did?

We had our differences over the years, James, but I think we have shared one crucial belief: that the world is getting better. Nations and empires rise and fall; countless individuals suffer, toil, and die, their miseries and injustices unavenged and forgotten. But somewhere, in all of that, human history has a direction, and it points toward progress and prosperity for more people.

Do you still believe that, James, despite today's setbacks? Isn't there something wonderful about pretending it's true even if we're not sure anymore? A small Pascal's Wager on behalf of the human race. Only in this case, unlike with the existence of God, maybe believing in it will help to make it real.

For the first time since you and I started our endeavors together, I understand that I'm not going to be here to see how this all ends. Ultimately, I suppose, none of us are. The best we can hope for is to log some sort of accomplishment in the course of our lives. I thought I had done that, until the recent spate of unraveling began. I only wish I had been able to do my bit to stop it.

The last time we were together in Warsaw, you seemed so at-peace with the idea that Western Civilization is declining. You said that throughout history, dominant powers, like successive generations, have been pushed aside so the rising ones could flourish. You even seemed to think we deserved it a little bit, having grown too soft, not hungry enough to lead mankind forward.

Because I can see no other options at present, I will try to find that same peace now. And maybe someday in the future we will be able to meet and compare notes about how it all turned out.

Your friend for the ages,
Gustaw

He stared at the signature for a long time, trying to convince himself it might be a forgery. But he had seen too many faxes, memos, notecards over the years to have any illusions. Gustaw had written that letter, and he had done so with the expectation that he was not coming home. Had Anatoly not told him about the ransom arrangements?

Anatoly must have been the one to smuggle the letter out, so why not give it to James directly rather than leaving it here at a hotel he'd been specifically discouraged from visiting? Was this the backup plan he hadn't been told about? Could his friend guess what he would do if Anatoly and Gustaw failed to return to the dingy apartment? Or was there a copy of this letter waiting for him in every decent hotel in the city?

Because it was a copy, he eventually realized. An old-fashioned duplicate made with carbon paper. As he scrutinized the handwriting, he identified several characters that bore those telltale gaps where the writer hadn't pressed down hard enough to transfer the writing through to the second page.

Carbon paper. Did they even make that stuff anymore? And how in the world did Gustaw get ahold of it?

For a few hours, the mystery of the letter and of his friends' non-appearance obscured the weight of what Gustaw had tried to tell him. Eventually, though, it started to sink in.

His friend claimed to have stumbled onto a plot to take over the world—or at least control parts of it that the powers in question wouldn't be able to hold onto through more public means. James tried to envision the horse trading that that sort of a conspiracy would entail: China wanted Taiwan and the South China Sea, Russia to restore its influence over the Baltics and Eastern Europe. There would indeed be dark days for Gustaw's Poland if that happened.

But Poland was part of NATO now, as were the Baltics, Hungary, the former Czechoslovakia, and others. A Russian threat to any of those countries would pull most of Western Europe and America itself into the conflict. At least, that's what the founding alliance members had promised each other more than half a century ago. Would any future American leader really dare to renege on that commitment?

What could that billionaire real estate developer from New York want—or be convinced he wanted—badly enough to start negotiating away chunks of the globe before he'd even officially secured his political party's nomination, let alone an election few imagined he could win? Debt forgiveness, perhaps? Or preferential trade deals? Something to show for all the bluster of the campaign trail, if it were the candidate's own initiative, because self-aggrandizement seemed his one consistent goal.

Meanwhile, if they pulled it off, the entire post-war international system would evaporate or become an empty husk, nothing to smooth the clashes between individual nations' (and their leaders') interests.

But perhaps Donald Trump had cronies who were savvier and more strategic than he himself appeared to be. Gustaw's letter had implied low-level surrogates, probably the kind who could be repudiated if the whole thing ever went public. So why would Gustaw risk writing about the plot, and under the very noses of his jailers?

More importantly, what could James do about it? As horrifying as the prospect that Gustaw described was, there was hardly enough information here to prove anything. Did James even believe it was possible? A secret Yalta-like summit in a Ukrainian industrial building controlled by gangsters seemed like a stretch, even for Hollywood. Didn't such meetings usually take place in neutral island resort nations?

But then, here James was in eastern Ukraine, holding a document that was certainly written by Gustaw, whose judgment he trusted implicitly when it came to ferreting out political misdeeds. The man had helped bring down Soviet Communism, only to see authoritarianism making a comeback a quarter century later. If he said there was a secret plan to divide up the globe like pirates' booty irrespective of international law, established borders, and the principles of human rights and self-determination, then James would take him at his word. But what would strangers who didn't know Gustaw think? And how was his own belief in the truth of the report supposed to help James convince them?

Nevertheless, this letter, representing as it did the only known communication from his friend in weeks, was precious and needed to be preserved. There was a safe in his hotel room where the letter would be secure for now. On the way upstairs, he paused outside the hotel's business center. He could fax or email it immediately, ensuring the survival of its contents, but suppose Gustaw had been released after all? He wouldn't want to have caused unnecessary worry.

After stowing the letter, James finally took that long-delayed shower and, exhausted by the day's cocktail of anticipation, disappointment, and lingering uncertainty, fell asleep on the bed wearing a scratchy bathrobe embossed with the hotel's logo.

Eventually, of course, he had to get up, put his one set of clothes back on, and check in with Polish Academic Publishing and his office in California. They had heard nothing and were, in fact, expecting to hear him confirm that Gustaw had been successfully retrieved. His own lack of information was met with grim silence on two continents. His assistant promised to call Anatoly and Marko periodically and, if she made contact, tell them where James had ended up.

As the hours at the hotel crawled by with no word, James grew increasingly resigned to the idea that his friends weren't coming to find him. He ordered a tasteless dinner delivered to his room and picked at it absently while trying to determine his next move.

He could attempt to find the apartment where he'd left his bag and phone, but honestly, he didn't recall anything about where it was. Could they locate the cabbie who had brought him to the hotel and find out where he had been picked up? Track the location of his phone? That seemed like something that should be possible, but he didn't know for sure. He would ask next time he called California. From the letter, he knew that Gustaw had not been taken from his hotel. So it seemed safer to remain here, where there were (a few) other people around, until he could arrange his return to Kyiv.

There was no more point in delaying, so he also jotted down his office fax number, got Gustaw's letter out of the safe, and took it downstairs to be transmitted.

At least he'd succeeded in leaving Natalya behind. She would be safely in Warsaw now, where she could absorb the uncertain finality of her husband's absence surrounded by family and friends.

Because the moment he had dreaded for ten days had finally arrived. He was out of leads, out of options, out of steam. He slumped in one of the worn club chairs in the poorly lit lobby, staring straight ahead at nothing. The blood whistled through his ears with a soft swishing sound, echoing the hum of the fluorescent lights. The room was desolate, another casualty of the ongoing war to the east. No one was traveling to Mariupol these days—no one in his right mind, at least. What had made him think he was so much smarter and luckier than the rest?

12

Natalya

Warsaw, Poland

Marko's designated escort didn't leave my side for the entire trip, even watching the lavatory door from a discrete distance while I was inside. When we reached Warsaw, I figured I would buy him lunch and he would catch the next train back to Kyiv. He apparently had other instructions, though, and he intended to follow them to the letter.

So, I took him home, where he immediately did a walk-through of the entire house, locking all the doors and windows and opening the closets to look for lurking bogeymen, before settling down in the kitchen for a cup of tea. As tired as I was from the travel and the stress of waiting for word about Gustaw, I appreciated the company. I didn't want to be alone, at least until I knew my husband was okay, preferably not until he was safe at home again.

But I didn't want to call the kids until I had some good news to share with them, imagining the tension of everyone standing around the parlor waiting for the phone to ring. Let them come when we had something to celebrate.

We hadn't spoken much on the trip. The young man was solicitous enough, offering to carry my bag and bring me food from the dining car. But I was in no mood for small talk. Frankly, I was pissed off at being sent home like a helpless damsel just when we were getting somewhere, but that's how James insisted on doing things. I didn't have $50,000 in cash to pay his friend on my own, so I went along with their plan.

But once we were seated at my table drinking from my mother's porcelain cups, I figured I should get to know my protector. Marko had introduced us at the train station, of course, but honestly, I didn't even remember his name. He looked uncomfortable when I asked him to refresh my memory.

"Actually, ma'am, what we told you back in Kyiv is not my true name. It was Marko's idea; he said it would be safer that way. My name is Feliks."

Whatever he saw on my face at this news made him recoil a little bit. I tried to adjust my expression to reassure him. I needed to learn what he knew.

"You're the one those men were looking for in Kyiv?"

"Yes." He looked a little bit frightened, though whether of them or me, I couldn't say.

"Then Marko sent you here for your safety, not mine?"

"Yes. No. That is, both, I think. Anyway, it was Mr. Bogutsky's idea for me to come to Poland."

"Gustaw? What do you know about my husband? Where is he?" I was too close to him, breathing heavily in his face, trying hard not to grab his arm and wring the news out of him.

"I don't know. I'm sorry. I haven't seen him since he went to talk to my bosses." He lifted his eyes to meet mine, seemingly ashamed of his ignorance.

"Where? Why? Did you tell Marko and James about this?"

"I told Marko everything I know, Mrs. Bogutsky. I'm sorry it isn't more."

"And he told me absolutely nothing."

"He made me promise not to tell you until you were safe at home."

"Why not tell me himself? James is going to bring Gustaw back, so why couldn't I wait for them? What danger does he think I'm in?"

"Not you, ma'am. That is, not that we know of. I'm the one he wanted to get to Poland."

"Then why didn't he just tell me that?"

"I'm not talking about Marko, ma'am. Mr. Bogutsky told me to come here if he didn't return to his hotel that night. He didn't know you'd come to Kyiv, I suppose. He said you could help me."

I had no proof that what this young stranger was telling me was true, of course, but it sounded right, my husband sending home strays even in the act of vanishing himself.

"I don't know what Gustaw or Marko think I can do for you here that they couldn't do in Ukraine, but I'm willing to try. First, though, I want to know everything—who you are, how you met my husband, what happened the last time you saw him, and how you ended up in Kyiv masquerading as a worker at the publishing house."

He was not succinct, rambling at times, fumbling for words at others. I read his nervousness as guilt for causing all this trouble. He was wrong, of course. I know my husband well enough to know that no amount of cautioning on this young man's part would have dissuaded Gustaw from anything once he had decided to do it. But I didn't have time to reassure him.

His story, once he told it, became obvious. He was the young man Gustaw went to Mariupol to interview for James's new company. I'd have realized it immediately if I hadn't been so exhausted and distracted with worry. The ruffians looking for Feliks were hired by his employers, who for some reason did not wish to accept his resignation. Apparently, my husband got in the middle of this dispute and somehow it got him disappeared, because anything can happen to anyone in a lawless place like eastern Ukraine.

But what Feliks was doing here, well, that was a surprise. Because what this kid wanted from me was not money or a place to stay or even help finding a job in Warsaw. It was something he could have had in a hundred cafés between Kyiv and here. After he finished his tea and a sandwich, he asked if he could use my computer for a while.

Feliks emerged from Gustaw's home office after a few hours in which I paced the kitchen and salon, willing good news into the silence. He looked expectantly at me, but I shook my head and his eyes dimmed and dropped to the ground. I waited for him to explain himself, but not for long. I was days past the limits of my patience.

"What were you doing in there? What was so important that you had to come all the way to Poland to do it? Why not just use a computer in Kyiv? I'm sure Marko had one you could borrow."

You can do anything from anywhere these days. Isn't that the whole point of the internet? I saw I had made him feel guilty again, but he was not apologetic as he tried to answer my question.

"There was a secret meeting that the world has to know about right away," he said, sounding like the voiceover in a movie trailer. "I had to get the proof out of Ukraine before they found me."

"Who was at this secret meeting? What kind of proof?"

Then he showed me a thumb drive, the kind we've been using for fifteen years for digital data storage. No high-tech spycraft there.

"I'm supposed to give this to someone," he told me. "A friend of Mr. Bogutsky."

He had been unfailingly respectful in his references to my missing husband.

"I have sent him a message to meet me. A taxi will pick me up soon."

"But who are you meeting? What is on that drive? You can't just leave," I protested. "We don't even know where Gustaw is yet."

"Please, Mrs. Bogutsky. This was the reason your husband put himself in danger, so I could get these files to safety. I can't let him down now."

"Well, your taxi isn't here yet, young man." I allowed myself to slip into a motherly tone. "Why don't you sit down and tell me as much as you can while we wait for it."

So, he began to outline the circumstances of his first encounter with Gustaw—the possible job, the fear of trying to get away from his disreputable employers—all that he had already told me, followed by his absolute confidence in the unexpected information he had stumbled across at work. People from China, Russia, and America were getting together in that seedy factory for a secret conference, and no one was supposed to know.

I'm not sure how Feliks recognized that this surreptitious summit was a problem—legally, morally, geopolitically. Somehow, he knew that the attendees were not merely international crime bosses. Unknown or shadowy figures themselves, perhaps, they nevertheless represented powerful people with a bigger agenda than profit. Or maybe he just figured that if his crooked bosses were involved, it couldn't be aboveboard.

But Gustaw would have realized immediately the kind of catastrophic decisions that could be taken by such a conspiracy, especially where smaller, weaker countries and people are concerned. After all, he grew up in a country suffering the consequences of one such agreement and spent half his adult life fighting to overturn it. I can well understand how recklessly he would have tried to stop, undermine, or expose this new bout of international horse trading.

Apparently, Feliks wanted to tell the world about the conspiracy through his employers' own fake news mill, but when Gustaw got involved, he talked him out of it. Too dangerous, he insisted, and too easy to dismiss the information as yet more wild propaganda. Why not let the gathering proceed as planned and try to get more damning evidence of who would attend and what they were plotting to do? Why stop at easy-to-fabricate meeting agendas and guest lists when it might be possible to get photos or video or audio recordings of the meeting itself?

And so my husband took the risky plan of an insider—a complete stranger the day before—and made it even riskier, inserting himself into the heart of those events in the name of protecting his new protégé. Small wonder that he didn't make it out.

"What exactly is the plan now?" I pressed him for more information. "And what is on that thumb drive if Gustaw never returned with the desired recordings?"

He intended to answer me, I'm sure of it. But at that moment, there was a knock at the door, and he disappeared into the night. He was gone before it occurred to me that it does not take three hours to send an email and order a cab.

13

James

Mariupol, Ukraine

He decided to spend another day at the hotel hoping to hear from Anatoly or Marko or even Ludmyla or Natalya—anyone, really, with information of any kind about Gustaw or the missing detective. His assistant in California became the clearinghouse, making regular calls to Polish Academic Publishing, UkraineLaw, the Bogutsky house in Warsaw, Anatoly's Moscow flat, and the cell phones of everybody involved, then calling him every few hours with updates. There weren't any, beyond the initial confirmation that Natalya had arrived home safely and that Gustaw's letter had been received in California and filed.

No one had heard anything from the missing men—four of them now, by James's count, as neither Anatoly nor Marko had checked in anywhere.

A generous wire transfer from home had placed him in the good graces of the hotel concierge, who moved swiftly to launder his single set of clothes and supplement his wardrobe with decent and serviceable, though not luxurious, new garments. In a matter of hours, he had fresh clothes, pajamas, toiletries, and a suitcase to pack them in, as well as a new leather wallet and a modest supply of local currency. The hotel regretted that smartphones were not so easy to procure in Mariupol. Perhaps the gentleman would care to have a refurbished Android phone shipped to him from Kyiv?

He declined the offer, not telling the solicitous functionary that he intended to depart the next day. He hadn't told his assistant that either, though he would surely need someone's help arranging transit out of the city.

He was finding that the better equipped he was to navigate this unfamiliar place, the less he wanted to leave the confines of the hotel, which felt safe despite its aesthetic drawbacks. Three of his four missing friends (Was Stepan a friend? Was Marko?) had started from this very spot and disappeared out there in the city somewhere. Under the circumstances, optimal lighting and décor were the least of his worries.

In the end, though, James didn't have to do anything to arrange his departure. Nina, the armed and ready UkraineLaw receptionist, appeared at his hotel room door the next morning.

"Pack your things, Mr. Jensen," she instructed without preamble, looking as somber and unyielding as a secret service agent. "We return to Kyiv in ten minutes."

When and why she herself had come to Mariupol was left unexplained as she melted out of the entryway, leaving behind an aura of expectation and urgency as he closed the door. He didn't have a better plan, and he did want to leave this place, he told himself. Nina had proven to be a capable security detail in the past, so it made sense to go with her. It wasn't the same as following orders.

He packed his new things into his new bag and headed to the lobby. By the time he got there, she had fallen into step beside him, though he couldn't quite pinpoint the moment she had reappeared.

The car she directed him to on a side street looked exactly like the one he and Marko had driven here from Kyiv. As he slid into the passenger seat, he noticed three identical cardboard boxes lined up on the back seat.

"What's in the boxes?" he asked as he fastened his seatbelt.

She ignored the question and started the engine.

"Really, though, what are you doing here? Have you heard from Marko? Or Stepan?"

"No, but I've spoken to your office several times—and your wife. I'm getting you out of here before I return to look for them."

"Is that really wise when no one who has gone looking has come back?"

"Perhaps not, but it is my job. Maybe one of them left some clue about his progress." She indicated the boxes in the back seat with a quick nod of her head.

"What's in there?"

"Their things."

"What things?"

"From their hotel rooms."

"Have you looked through them yet?"

"Later. When we're well away from here."

"Wouldn't it be better to look right away, before the trail gets cold?"

She turned on the radio to a volume just a little too loud for conversation. James wasn't accustomed to having his opinions dismissed so easily, but he needed her to navigate this unfamiliar, apparently dangerous place. Worse, he felt judged, like he was somehow responsible for all these disappearances, with his international networking and retainer fees for detectives and naïve plan to open another Ukrainian business. So far, everything he had done to try to improve things here seemed to have compounded the disaster.

Now that he understood what they were, the nondescript boxes behind him made the hair on the back of his neck stand up, as if they were transporting not mundane possessions but the missing men themselves, reduced to their final essence. Their very uniformity underscored the horror, as if each man's individuality had been bled into insignificance with his disappearance. And James's suitcase rode comfortably alongside them, containing a small subset of the material possessions that would be rendered useless by his own disappearance. He shuddered and tried to think of something else.

Like what he was going to tell Natalya about the ransom payment that went awry. Was it his fault? Had he botched the money drop? Or were the kidnappers never planning to release Gustaw anyway? He would like to have returned to the park to see if the cash was still there somehow, but he didn't know where it was or the name of it. Anatoly had been the one to give directions to the taxi driver, and the original instructions must still be in the misplaced flophouse with his phone, laptop, and luggage. Maybe the police would find it—James had insisted that the concierge file a report with local authorities when he realized his passport had also been left there—but he hadn't stayed in town long enough to find out.

And if the police did make it to the park, what were the odds that a bag stuffed with American dollars had gone unnoticed there for two days? Or that the officers who found it wouldn't simply pocket the funds and claim to have found nothing? No. The money, like his friends, was gone. His one consolation was that, in keeping with a lifelong principle, he hadn't overextended himself. Yes, it was a lot of money to throw away, but he and his family would not go without because of its loss. He'd made bad investments before.

Then there was UkraineLaw. What would become of the company, already apparently in its death throes, if Marko never returned? Did Nina or someone else at the business have the connections to keep it limping along, hoping for the country's economy to improve? Polish Academic Publishing management had been itching to unravel the joint venture for years. That outcome seemed almost inevitable now.

And what of Polish Academic Publishing, James's own passionate project to restore free thought to the Soviet bloc? Now that its managers had resorted to self-censorship to keep the current government happy, was that dream dead, too? The company brought in impressive revenues and a modest profit, certainly, but had it lost its way? And if so, why was he, who didn't need the money and had plenty of other irons in the fire, still in Poland? Because without those chats with Gustaw to mull over world events, future travel to Warsaw would be a desert.

After twenty-five years, maybe it was time to turn Poland's cultural treasure back over to the Poles. For the right price, of course. Regardless of its difficulties in earlier years, today the publishing house would be an attractive acquisition for some enterprising investor.

And if that new owner chose to follow the Law and Justice Party's lead in deciding what to publish, well, the country had had a quarter century to decide what model of government and society it preferred. James would share Gustaw's disappointment if that preference took an authoritarian turn, but lately, he had started to wonder himself if democratic institutions were all that he'd once believed them to be.

Because the world certainly had not turned out the way he assumed it would when he was forty and the Soviet Union was dying a well-earned death, leaving its inhabitants to pick up the pieces under a new paradigm where capital and innovation could flow generously into the vacuum. International institutions, unhandcuffed now that the Cold War had ended, were supposed to mediate disputes and create a level playing field between countries—a community of nations that could discourage antisocial behavior from imperialism to trade tariffs among its members. And the benefits of those freedoms and alliances would stream across and within borders until the whole human race acknowledged with one voice the obvious advantages of liberties economic and political.

What the hell had happened?

Quite a bit, obviously, starting with China, a place where his investors' modest infusion of funds years ago had grown many times faster than their Polish stake. As proud as James was of getting in early, growing the company, and sticking it out through the IPO, though, he couldn't pretend that his and his partners' business skills had been the only factor in their Chinese company's success.

The Chinese government had been putting its thumb on the scales of its own economy for decades. It wasn't just the currency manipulation or protectionist trade policies for which Western politicians scolded the rising world power. Some domestic companies got a little more help than others, and theirs had been one of the fortunate ones. James didn't approve, of course, but he hadn't done anything to court that favor, either. His business partners and their connections were responsible for that effort, and he had had no part of it.

And if he had profited handsomely from what he couldn't refuse to call corruption, well, he had suffered for it, too. Because when that New York Stock Exchange IPO had finally taken place a few years earlier, he and his investors had to threaten legal action to get those government-favored partners to pay up. If they had chosen a stock exchange in China instead, they might never have seen their share at all, and those same official forces that had pushed the business forward might have blocked its foreign investors from seeking any legal remedy for the theft.

So, James had seen the risks and rewards of an unfair system first-hand, but those experiences did not negate his awe and appreciation of the double-digit annual growth that China had achieved in recent decades. If a little centralized oversight and protectionism could produce those results, well, it shouldn't be dismissed so easily. The living standards of hundreds of millions of people had been raised in the process.

Of course, it didn't work for the government to make *all* the economic decisions. The disaster of the Soviet economy had shown that well enough, with raw materials failing to make it to the factories, which failed to produce the planned number of goods. And the products they did make were of abysmal quality. Meanwhile, the only thriving market was the black market, and the only shops with anything decent available to buy sold Western imports reserved for upper-level Communist Party members.

But free market democracies had their own inefficiencies to answer for. There were the usual suspects—labor unions demanding higher pay and benefits than a truly free market would have delivered; public schoolteachers failing to educate the next generation of workers and citizens; and pandering politicians promising voters the moon while borrowing their countries into a debt hole from which their economies might never re-emerge.

Nor was his own class immune from criticism. Collusion between business leaders fettered markets, as did the capture of government policymaking by self-interested industries intent on negotiating themselves a sweetheart deal.

Similar drawbacks were evident in all those multilateral institutions that had seemed to hold such promise a few years ago—the European Union, NATO, the International Monetary Fund. They were all bogged down in bureaucracy, more intent on dictating to their members than on serving their interests. No wonder the formerly enthusiastic new recruits to democracy were disillusioned by the results.

And now Gustaw had discovered that the freedom of everyday people was being traded away in secret by world leaders with their own hidden agendas. How might already-disaffected citizens across the globe react to that news? If they ever learned of it, of course.

James was deep in these musings when Nina suddenly pulled off the road at what looked like a farmhouse surrounded by green fields and set well back from the highway. He guessed they'd been traveling for at least an hour. She drove up the winding, packed-dirt driveway past the main house and around to the back, where a few steps led to a wraparound porch.

James felt his heart skitter out of rhythm as he glanced over at Nina in panic. What was this place, and why had she brought him here? The last few days suddenly shifted into focus: an elaborate ruse orchestrated by Marko and his people to get Gustaw and Anatoly out of the way and James isolated so they could . . . what? Extort him for money? Hold *him* for ransom?

"Could you give me a hand getting these boxes inside?" she asked, already out of the car. From the covered porch, two fit young men dressed in black descended the steps to greet her. "No, leave that," she clarified when one of them reached for James's suitcase. "We won't be here long."

James hadn't moved from his seat, unsure whether to make a run for it now or look for another chance when their guard was down. Nina paused on her way to the house and turned toward him for a more thorough appraisal.

"Are you alright, James? You look unwell." She walked back and approached his door with a concerned frown. "Let's get you inside. Can you walk?"

He nodded and took a few slow, deep breaths before easing himself to his feet. His legs were shaking as he made his way up the porch steps, right arm wrapped around Nina's shoulder for support.

They got him settled in the kitchen, where three more men were milling around drinking coffee. One of them fastened a blood pressure cuff to James's arm, shined a light in his eyes, and listened to his heart and lungs with a stethoscope before allowing Nina to give him a glass of water.

"Everything seems normal to me," the man said. "Do you have any medical conditions?"

At his age, who didn't? He considered telling them about his heart but shied away from that intimacy. The atrial fibrillation seemed to have corrected itself anyway.

"I feel okay now." He tried to smile at the man who'd taken care of him. "It's been a very stressful few days."

"Would you like to lie down for a while? There's a bedroom upstairs where you could relax."

James shook his head. Resting seemed to be all he had been doing lately, and it hadn't helped so far. He took another sip of water.

"Where are we?" he asked, glancing around. The room was stocked and functional, if sparse on decorations and homey touches. There was no clutter of unread mail on the counter, no appointment reminder cards or children's artwork attached to the refrigerator with magnets. Even the wall clock was a bland, functional item—black Arabic numerals in a circle on a plain white face. Despite its pastoral surroundings, the inside of the house had all the charm of a military barracks.

"A friend's place," was all the medic offered.

By then, the two of them were alone in the kitchen. Becoming aware of activity in the next room, James realized that Nina and the rest of her team were disassembling the cartons of the missing men's belongings that they'd brought with them from Mariupol.

"Spread out," she cautioned. "I don't want anything getting mixed up."

James was once again puzzled to realize that they were communicating in English. Were these mercenaries not all Ukrainian? Nina chuckled when he stepped through the doorway and asked.

"They are, but they all speak English as well. They work for a company that provides private security to foreign visitors, among other things. I thought it would be easier not to have to translate everything for you."

"Thank you." After his moments of suspicion and panic in the driveway, he was humbled by this courtesy. "You didn't tell me we were stopping on the way to Kyiv."

"Didn't I? I apologize for the oversight. I was most concerned with getting you away from that place while we still knew where you were."

"Nothing from Marko yet?"

"No, but it's too soon to give up."

She did not explain herself further, returning her attention to the perusal of possessions going on around them.

James moved between the three pairs of cataloguers, looking over their shoulders and trying to believe that something in the modest piles in front of them held higher meaning. He had seen a movie once where a man suffering from amnesia was able to restore his memories and save the world using an envelope of mundane objects that he had left himself as clues. But in this case, there were no momentous discoveries.

Surely Stepan and Marko had taken notes as they retraced the steps of their respective quarry. Even Gustaw must have recorded somewhere the names and contact information of the job candidates he had pursued. Had every one of their laptops, cell phones, and notepads disappeared with them? Was there no cryptic phrase scrawled on hotel stationery that could point them in some direction?

Apparently not. The teams examined their boxes, consulted with each other, then switched places, hoping one pair would see what another had not. They took photos and used flashlights to inspect clothing inch by inch to look for stains, fibers, and blemishes that might indicate where the wearer had been. For all James knew, there was a full-scale crime lab set up in the barn to run fingerprints and identify chemical compounds.

It was into this diligent but fruitless process that he thought to inject Gustaw's letter, forgotten in his luggage since its transmission home. He brought it from the car and read its contents aloud.

The commandos paused in their sorting and stood around listening. They were quiet at first, respectful of the missing man's words, perhaps cognizant, as James had been, that they might be Gustaw's last communication. Solemnity gave way to excitement, however, as they parsed the letter for clues.

"So, he was taken in an industrial area," someone broke in when Gustaw described his abduction.

"A front for organized crime," noted another.

"Someplace with high-end internet connectivity," Nina added.

"But that was days ago," James pointed out. "How does that help us find him now?"

She gave him a look of exaggerated patience. "It depends on whether the people who took him are still using that space. When we find and question them, we will learn where they took him, who they gave him to."

When, not *if*. James liked the certainty in her words, with their undertones of coercion. Was that wrong? He recalled that bound prisoner back at UkraineLaw now as an example not of vigilantism but of ruthless competence.

"We're talking about mobsters, the kind with powerful friends, from the sound of this," he pointed out, giving the letter a shake.

"We do have some resources of our own," she said.

And why is that? he wondered. How could Marko, with his dying company, afford a premium security operation such as this? Who was paying them and how? And was it a good idea to ask? Maybe he should just be grateful that there were assets on their side (he hoped) that were not his.

"What's the end game here?" he blurted out. "If you do find them, how will you get them back? I already tried paying them off. You see how well that worked. Are you planning to go in with guns blazing and take on the entire Russian Army, if that's who we're up against?"

"It's too soon to say," Nina answered. "After we find them, we can decide how to retrieve them. Until then, it doesn't matter what we think is possible or practical. But to address your question directly, I'm not ruling out physical force. Or negotiation, if there's an opportunity for that."

"You sound pretty confident you *can* find them."

She leveled her gaze at him, and for a moment the iron will and efficiency of the security chief flickered into lip-quivering desolation. "I don't see another option. I should never have let him go alone."

Then she realized her slip, and the devastated little girl was gone, replaced once more by the energetic professional. "We'll find them."

They hung a paper map of the Mariupol region on the living room wall and started narrowing down the search area, supplementing their limited knowledge of the city with Google Earth images. It was obviously going to be a tedious process, but whatever skepticism the team members might be feeling, they were smart enough not to express it out loud.

They had been at the farmhouse for hours when Nina looked over at James, eyes widening at the apparent realization that she still hadn't taken him back to Kyiv as promised. Darkness showed through the curtained windows, and in the kitchen, a couple of her mercenaries were preparing food for the evening meal.

"Forget it," he said before she had a chance to speak. "I'm not leaving, and you're obviously needed here. If you want me in that car, you're going to have to drag me there."

He had no doubt she was capable of exactly that—even indulged himself by imagining it for a moment—but instead of calling his bluff, she chuckled and shrugged her shoulders. "I suppose you're safe enough here. Perhaps you'd like to call and update Mrs. Jensen on your circumstances?"

She had a satellite phone, which she dialed for him after a five-minute lecture about not revealing the details of their plans and location to Anna. No danger of that, of course, since he didn't know where they were and had no insight into the plans they hadn't yet made.

"We're well outside the city, and we've stopped for the night," James explained to Anna carefully. "It's safer to travel in daylight."

"No, no, we're nowhere near the war zone here," he tried to reassure her. "It's just to avoid traffic."

"Well, I'll certainly feel better when you're out of that country altogether." Anna harrumphed a little, but he could tell he was in the clear with her. "Please be safe and get home as soon as you can. And James, I am sorry about Gustaw. I prayed things would go more smoothly."

Dinner was a hearty combination of meat-and-rice-filled cabbage leaves, potato pancakes, and fried sausages seasoned with unfamiliar spices. The food was flavorful, and there was plenty of it, but James longed for a green salad or some steamed vegetables to balance out the meal. His younger companions wolfed it down.

They chased their food with small tumblers of vodka. Then Nina confiscated the bottle before it could be passed around for refills.

"Gentlemen, we have a long night ahead of us," she cautioned. "I want to have clear search parameters and a list of potential abduction points by dawn. Mr. Jensen, let me show you someplace where you can get some sleep."

It wasn't a request. He would've preferred a bracing cup of espresso with an antacid chaser followed by an after-dinner stroll to settle the heavy meal, but he didn't want them to decide he was too much trouble to keep around. So, he followed her obligingly upstairs to a room with two sets of bunkbeds. Someone had brought in his suitcase, which was sitting on the desk against the far wall, along with a neatly folded towel and a bar of soap. Nina pointed him toward the bathroom down the hall and walked out, closing the door behind her. He held his breath as he heard it latch, half expecting the telltale click of a lock turning to trap him inside.

James sat down on the lower mattress nearest the door, ducking his head to avoid banging it on the upper bunk. He reasoned that the fit young commandos downstairs could take on any ladder climbing that needed doing. He didn't want to exit an unfamiliar bed in the middle of the night and find himself dropping from five feet in the air. Besides, he had a feeling his companions wouldn't be allowed much shuteye anyway.

Personally, he was exhausted, emotionally drained, and uncertain about what was happening next. Relieved to be out of a city where people kept disappearing, he also feared being left behind when the team downstairs returned to it. He imagined waking to an empty house, perhaps descending to the kitchen and finding a note posted on the refrigerator.

If he stayed awake, he could keep an eye on things. However, as fit and healthy a sexagenarian as he knew himself to be, that probably wouldn't work, and it certainly wouldn't do his heart or his digestion any favors. Since he'd already allowed himself to be sent to bed, he decided to try to get some sleep so he could deal with whatever he found when he woke in the morning. He dug his new pajamas and toothbrush out of the suitcase and headed down the hall.

14

Anatoly

Kyiv, Ukraine

"I tried to warn him not to go through with it, but it was too late. They'd already found the original, rolled into a wad and tucked under the back edge of his mattress, where only a fool who had never seen a single prison movie would try to hide something.

"But they fell for it anyway, waving the crumpled pages in my face in outrage, as if I'd personally taken advantage of their good nature. 'You saw me bringing him paper,' I told them. 'Did you think he was going to use it to draw pictures? I thought you wanted to find out what he knew.'

"What they really wanted, of course, was James's cash, but I couldn't let that happen, not after it became clear that they weren't going to let him go after all.

"'No one will believe it,' I tried to explain to them. 'Look, there's not enough information here to convince anyone of anything. The whole idea sounds ludicrous.'

"But the same idiocy that got him taken in the first place was back in play. They wouldn't even let me in to see him again, so it was fortunate he'd slipped me the copy at our last meeting. I suppose I was lucky to get out of there myself after that.

"So, yes, I took the money. Why wouldn't I? It wasn't going to do Gustaw any good, and James won't miss it, but in my life, it could have made a big difference. Oh, I know it wouldn't have made me rich. It's a pittance compared to what I once had. But it was enough to get away on—slip across a few borders, bribe people who need bribing. I'd have been broke wherever I ended up, but at least it wouldn't be Russia."

"Your rescue plan fell apart, so you stole your friend's money?" The questioner's tone was contemptuous.

"You can call me a thief. You aren't the first. They were saying that when my home was still the Soviet Union, accusing me of siphoning money from my own company, as if that wasn't the way our system had worked since the beginning. Why should I have been the first one to start doing things differently?" Anatoly's chin jutted out in defiance as he spoke.

"And then you abandoned him in Mariupol to find his own way home?" The black-clad man inhaled sharply and shook his head.

"Call me a coward, too, for not staying to tell James the truth about his friend. I'll admit I didn't want to have to face him with the news," he said, lowering his eyes and his voice simultaneously. "I know James was in a difficult spot, but he'll come through it alright. He always does. And I did leave Gustaw's letter where James or his Ukrainian friends should find it. That's all Gustaw seemed to care about anyway.

"As much as I wanted to help a fellow revolutionary and prove to our mutual friend that I still had some influence, I couldn't save Gustaw. With James's money, though, I could have saved myself. Maybe I am old and tired and out of friends, but in a new place with new opportunities, I could still make it work. One thing I've never been short on is ideas."

15

James

A farmhouse, eastern Ukraine

It wasn't dawn yet when he woke, though he felt surprisingly well-rested. From where he lay, he could see that the bunk opposite was untouched, and he sensed that he was alone in the room.

There was plenty of activity elsewhere in the house, however. James's first thought was that Nina and the others were preparing to leave for their return to Mariupol. He rushed downstairs in his pajamas to try to intercept them, regretting his lack of slippers when his feet hit the cold, wood floor.

The security detail had grown overnight, with at least eight people now milling around the kitchen and living room. Breakfast was underway—scrambled eggs, ham, and toast heaped in dishes on the counter next to a large drip coffee maker that seemed to be continually brewing a new pot. The identically dressed men in black stood or sat with their plates and cups, trying to speak softly but somehow making more noise with their clinking and murmuring than if they hadn't been trying so hard to let him sleep.

"What's going on?" James addressed the room at normal volume, then raised his voice slightly and repeated himself. All conversations stopped, and sixteen or more eyes turned toward him in surprise.

"Good morning, James." Nina emerged from the pack of men to greet him. "Help yourself to some food while you can. This is a hungry bunch."

"What time is it? Did you guys get any sleep?"

"Almost five-thirty." Somehow, she made that sound like a relatively late hour of the morning. "And no. But we have had a productive night."

She did not elaborate, a trend he was becoming accustomed to. He shrugged it off and began looking around for a clean coffee mug. Impatient with waiting for the latest brewing to complete, he removed the half-full pot with one hand while sliding his cup in with the other, filling it directly from the stream of fresh coffee. There was a slight sizzle as a few drops landed on the hot base of the machine before he could get the pot reseated. He dumped some white liquid he hoped was cream into the cup and headed into the living room to look for a seat.

The map on the wall now bloomed with color—entire neighborhoods outlined in contrasting hues of highlighter pen, ink-laden Post-it notes fluttering from dozens of locations. A pad of butcher paper on an easel had been placed next to it, as if for a briefing or brainstorming session. Most of the hand-written bullet points contained unfamiliar foreign words spelled out in Cyrillic letters—place names, perhaps. Or maybe the team had abandoned their English-only rule once he went to bed. The one word among all of it that meant something to him was *Anatoly*.

"What does this say?" he asked the man seated next to him. Startled, the man tried to swallow a large bite of toast too quickly, then coughed for several seconds before he could answer.

"'Review Anatoly's statement,'" he read obligingly. "I think it's to do with the one who went to Romania. The other team brought him back overnight."

"Back? Anatoly is here?"

"No, no, of course not," the man laughed. "Kyiv, at headquarters. Why would they drag him all the way here? They'll let us know what they find out, though. Don't worry."

How could he not? He was already pushing his way back into the kitchen to find Nina.

"What are you doing to Anatoly?" he demanded. "Is he alright?"

"Doing to him?" She raised her eyebrows at him over the rim of her coffee cup. "We're talking to him, James, and he's in perfect health, if that's your question."

He had a sudden flashback to his conversation with Marko in the darkened offices of UkraineLaw. Was Anatoly in for similar treatment?

"But before you get too anxious about his welfare," she continued, "you should know that he had most of your cash with him when my team found him."

"My cash? But I left that in the . . ." he stopped, suddenly seeing the setup. Anatoly always needed money these days, didn't he? Why not take advantage of the fact that James was looking for his missing friend in the next country over to get some?

"So, the whole ransom story was a lie, then? He never knew where Gustaw was?"

"We're not sure yet. We don't know if he had anything to do with the others disappearing either," she said. "We will find out, obviously—as politely as possible."

He suspected those last words were meant to be reassuring, but they came out ominous. He knew he would be outraged once the weight of Anatoly's duplicity settled in. He didn't feel it yet, though. In his heart, the Russian was still one of the missing, and his return was a gift.

"I'd like to talk to him."

Nina considered for a moment. "That might be useful, eventually. For now, though, I think I'll let my people see what they can find out. We still have three other men to locate."

And Gustaw was one of them. At the very least, Anatoly's deception had cost them days of valuable search time. James felt the first stirrings of fury at his old friend. "Did you figure out anything that could help?"

She led him back into the living room and gestured toward the map on the wall. "Some neighborhoods are better prospects than others, obviously. Mrs. Bogutsky got Feliks to give her the address of his employers, but of course we expect it to be cleaned out by now. What we really need is to figure out where they moved it. They wouldn't have simply closed down the operation, not with a whole new agenda to push."

James shook his head in confusion. "Wait a minute. Feliks? The one those thugs were looking for in Kyiv? What does Natalya know about him?"

"Marko really didn't tell you anything, did he? He must've suspected Anatoly couldn't be trusted."

"At the time, it seemed more the other way around," James admitted, then added at her frown, "Anatoly said he didn't know if we should trust Marko. But Natalya?"

Nina filled him in on the relocation to Warsaw of the young man Gustaw had considered hiring.

"Well, why didn't he just tell Marko everything before we left for Mariupol? Wouldn't that have saved everyone some time?"

"I'm sure he did, but Marko didn't tell me much." Nina bit her lip. "I guess he decided the fewer people who knew, the better, at least until Feliks and Natalya were safely out of the country."

"And are they safe now?"

"Safer, I suppose. Borders aren't armor, James. Remember, Anatoly made it across a border, too."

"How did you find him?"

"He had your laptop with him."

Well, that was an affront of a very personal, if financially petty, nature—a drop in the bucket compared to the cash he had stolen, but something that belonged to James, that he had brought with him with no intention of abandoning. And while he was waiting for his friends' return and worrying about what had become of them, Anatoly had picked it up and left the country.

"So, what are you going to do now?" James gestured at the bleary-eyed crowd shoveling fried potatoes and coffee into their mouths. "You can't go storming into Mariupol on no sleep."

Nina paused as if that were exactly what she intended, but instead of arguing, she nodded. "Evening is the best time to search for the tech operation. Meanwhile, we'll sleep in shifts, so we can keep working and narrowing down leads. If you're ready to return to Kyiv, I'll have one of the others drive you."

Anatoly was supposedly in Kyiv, and James would certainly be ready to have a few words with him by the time he arrived. But he hadn't yet done what he came to Ukraine to do. With Nina and her team on board, the hopelessness he'd felt in Mariupol was receding. She was obviously most concerned about finding Marko. If he stayed, maybe he could make sure she kept her focus on all of the missing.

"I'll stay here with you for now," he said. "I know I wouldn't be much good at storming gangsters' lairs, but I'll help however I can."

She shrugged and nodded her head. "Okay. If I think of something, I'll let you know."

Feeling dismissed, he retreated to a chair and finished his coffee. Some of the mercenaries drifted upstairs, presumably to sleep. Whatever scheduling or division of labor they needed to do must have already happened, as there were no gatherings in the living room to discuss tasks for the day.

He returned to the kitchen to fill a plate from the half-congealed platters on the counter, then warmed it in the microwave and sat down at the table to eat, looking around in vain for half a grapefruit or some cantaloupe to supplement the heavy fried food. He received friendly-enough nods and greetings from his companions, but there was no attempt to engage him in conversation.

Normally, James would've been the one to initiate the small talk that would lead to a more penetrating discussion, but he was feeling unmoored by the strange surroundings and circumstances and the news of Anatoly's betrayal. As anger and embarrassment coursed through him at having misjudged his old friend so dramatically, he had to remind himself that Anatoly had not kidnapped Gustaw. If he had, there would have been no reason not to let him go. No, the Russian had only exploited a situation that James had naively brought him into. He wondered how long it would take the interrogators in Kyiv to get the whole story from him.

Would Nina even tell him what she found out? Sudden doubt made him want to extract that promise from her. Looking around the room, though, he didn't see her. Nor was she visible in the living room area.

He decided to see if she'd gone outside. It wouldn't hurt to stretch his legs a little, either.

After putting on his clothes, James approached the back door. Conversation in the two rooms had stopped, and he felt everyone's eyes swivel toward him. He reached for the handle anyway. No one intervened as he opened the door and stepped out.

The dawn air was chilly. He should've worn his jacket but didn't want to face the gauntlet of stares inside again. The car they'd arrived in was still sitting where they had left it, the hood misty with dew. Beside it was a black cargo van without a drop of moisture on it. The "other team," whoever they were, must have arrived recently.

A barn on the far side of the parking area was his only logical destination without either leaving the property or getting his shoes wet in the grass. The only visible entrance to it was a standard person-sized door. He assumed that a larger opening on the other side gave better access to the adjoining land, if this were still a farm or had been in recent memory. He could imagine a tractor or combine rolling out into a verdant sun-drenched field, ready to cultivate the breadbasket of Europe. Instead, when he poked his head through the door, he saw only darkness where he imagined the egress should be.

He stood motionless in the doorway and allowed his eyes to adjust to the dark, which was not as complete as he'd first thought. Off to his left, a dim light shone under a door. As he walked toward it, his hands raised slightly in front of him to ward off unseen obstacles, he could hear a soft murmuring. Was someone being interrogated behind that door? Perhaps Anatoly was here after all.

Pausing outside the room to listen, James realized there was only one voice—a distinctly female voice—though he could not make out what she was saying.

He raised his fist and knocked on the door. The murmuring broke off abruptly, and a moment later, he heard a brisk, "Come in."

Nina showed no surprise or annoyance at his interruption or his unapologetic perusal of the table where she was sitting. Before her, an open notebook was saturated with scrawling he couldn't decipher, while scattered papers surrounded it in various stages of marking or dissection. Some had been cut into pieces, others highlighted in a rainbow of colors, still more flagged with stick-on tags. Upon closer inspection, he recognized Gustaw's own handwriting on the pages. A moment later, he understood that he was looking at photocopies—several, by the look of it—of the letter Gustaw had written him.

"What are you doing?" he asked, recalling the extensive—to his ears—brainstorming session the previous night. "How much more do you expect to get out of that letter?"

"Nothing yet," she said. "But we have to keep trying."

"Trying what? Why are you alone out here?"

"Well, it *was* quieter than inside," she said with a wry smile. "I've been doing some basic cryptanalysis on the letter—every third word, first word of every paragraph. I know your friend Gustaw was in the underground, so I thought he might've included something more to help us. Did the two of you ever communicate using a code?"

"A secret code? No, of course not." What was this, middle school?

"Do you know if he had any formal training in cryptography?"

"Not that I know of. His wife might know more. Or she could contact some of his friends from the underground and ask. I doubt it, though."

"Why?"

Because it was all just too much. Gustaw missing, kidnapped, held for ransom—or maybe not. Anatoly conning James with a fanciful story about a ransom demand—which he had fallen for without hesitation. Menacing thugs in Kyiv, armed mercenaries led by the obvious mistress of his longtime business partner—himself shamelessly picking the joint venture's pocket, if Gustaw's suspicions were correct—and not one but two conceivable international conspiracies against democracy and self-determination?

"Just a gut feeling," he answered. "How do you know so much about code breaking?"

"Army training," Nina said, as if there could be no other answer. He gave her a critical look, trying to decide if she was old enough to have enlisted under Communism. Did Ukraine have mandatory conscription back then?

"What is a skilled cryptologist and bodyguard doing working as a receptionist at a publishing company?" he demanded, expelling his mounting exasperation with that single bewildered question.

One side of her mouth turned upward, approximating mild humor. "You still don't understand, do you?"

"That you're sleeping with Marko, sure." Fatigue and frustration made him blunt to the point of coarseness. "How he can afford an operation like yours given the state of UkraineLaw, no. That makes no sense to me."

"He can afford it because it's his company. Our company."

"What? Since when?"

"Since Crimea. You must have some idea what it's been like here since the Russians invaded. At first it was a side business, the odd contract for personal security. We would get referrals from his police friends and call up trained people we knew who were available for a few days of work. Pretty soon, we had enough regular customers to bring on full-time employees. UkraineLaw would never have held out this long without our rent money keeping expenses down."

"You mean you've been operating from the same building?"

"Of course. That's where you met me, remember?"

How could Gustaw have missed that, with his quarterly visits to Kyiv? Or maybe he hadn't. Maybe that's where he suspected the joint venture funds were going.

"It must have been challenging for Marko to focus on running two companies at once," he said, sounding more bitter than he intended. Nina looked ruffled for the first time in the conversation.

"I manage most of the security business myself," she explained softly. "But you should know, he hasn't taken a salary from UkraineLaw in almost a year."

The information gave James pause. On one hand, it suggested that Marko had forgone his own paycheck to prolong the company's survival.

Then again, he might have used his non-salary as justification for putting most of his attention into this security business. Not that any of that mattered much right now.

"By the way, James, there is a question that I'd like to ask you since we're alone." Nina hesitated, as if giving him time to object, before she continued. "If Gustaw thought this letter was his last chance to pass a message along, why do you suppose he addressed it to you?"

"Well, Anatoly was *my* friend, and he must have been the one who smuggled the letter out, so perhaps Gustaw figured he knew how to get it to me."

"Of course. But if you were imprisoned somewhere and thought you might never be released, is this the kind of letter you would write?"

James paused to think about it. The letter would go to his wife, probably including a section to his children. It would be a final expression of love and gratitude for their presence in his life. Gustaw was an old friend and a dear one, but James wouldn't squander his final missive to the world on him.

"I suppose that Gustaw wasn't thinking about a final goodbye so much as how to let people know about what he had learned," he said. "He and I have spent a lot of time over the years talking about the way the world was evolving. He probably thought I was more likely to appreciate the significance of the information he had uncovered."

Nina nodded but said nothing.

"And, of course, he would have known from Anatoly that I was in Ukraine looking for him."

"You're a good friend to come so far."

"Thank you."

An unwelcome image flashed through his mind: a distraught Gustaw, puffy eyes red with sleeplessness, pleading, "Support me, James, please. It's the only way I'll get through this."

James had tried to be a good friend, even then, but he also had a responsibility to his investors, who had entrusted him with their money. The bankers were right about management overspending, and so Gustaw needed to be replaced for the good of the company. James had swallowed hard, looked directly into his friend's desperate eyes, and told him so.

"Can I help you with what you're doing here?" he asked Nina now, swinging his arm over the scattered papers like a benediction.

At first, she seemed poised to refuse him. Then she shrugged and handed him a clean copy of the letter, a few blank sheets of paper, and a ballpoint pen.

"Try circling the first letter of each word and see what you come up with," she suggested, waving him toward a stool in the corner.

He didn't have his reading glasses with him, so he held the paper at arm's length against the rough wooden wall of the building and, half-squinting, began to do as she asked, but it was evident almost immediately that that tactic produced only gibberish. He would have reread the entire letter, driving himself mad looking for new clues, but the eye strain in that dim space prevented him. Instead, he sat quietly for a few minutes, listening to Nina's pen scratching as she talked herself through another theory, then deposited his pages on the table and slipped out of the room.

He could see the larger area outside her workspace more clearly now, and it was no museum to Ukraine's halcyon days as an agricultural powerhouse. There were a few vehicles stored here—not farm machinery or decaying antique cars, but the kind of sleek black SUVs favored by convoys of dignitaries. The security company must have regular business shepherding people in and out of this part of Ukraine. He wondered if Russian clients ever made use of their services.

The far wall was lined with tall metal cabinets that might hold office supplies. When he approached one and attempted to turn the door handle, however, he discovered that it was locked. In the corner, heavy-duty plastic tubs were stacked to a height of eight or nine feet. They appeared to be labeled in Ukrainian.

So, this was the sort of place mercenaries hung out when they were planning their next move. Which would be what, exactly? A raid on some industrial building in Mariupol or Donetsk? If by some miracle they found out where their friends were being held and they were all in the same place, what were the chances of even an elite force getting everyone out safely?

He turned and paced back toward the room where Nina was working. He should leave her alone to think, but he didn't want to go back to the house. There, the well-fed but sleep-deprived commandos eyed him suspiciously, wondering what he was doing in the middle of their operation. He couldn't just take off walking down the highway, either.

Maybe he would stay here in the barn for a while. If only there were a soft pile of hay in an old horse stall where he could curl up and take refuge from events he could neither control nor, from the feel of it, effectively participate in.

He was staring at the nearest SUV wondering if it would be unlocked, its back seat suitable for private napping, when one of the men threw open the door and strode toward Nina's little office. Sensing a momentous development, James followed him.

The man hesitated at his presence, but Nina's clipped "Go ahead" dismissed his doubt about speaking in front of the American.

"The Russian has given us a few names," he explained in English. "His old contacts who put him in touch with the people holding the Pole. I assume you'll want us to question them directly?"

"Of course. You know where to find them?"

"We have some addresses to start with."

"Then gear up your team and go. Report back as soon as you know something."

He was out the door and Nina had turned back toward her hideaway before James could get a word in.

"But what about Anatoly?"

"What about him? If they learn anything more from him, they'll let us know."

"When can I see him?"

"Anytime you're ready to go back to Kyiv."

"No." He didn't hesitate. As restless and useless as he felt where he was, he wanted to stay at what seemed like the epicenter of the search for his friend.

She nodded, making no attempt to dissuade him. "You may as well make yourself comfortable, then. It could be another day or two before we have anything to go on."

16

James

A farmhouse, eastern Ukraine

Three days later, Nina woke him at dawn. "Pack your things and get dressed," she told him. "There's coffee and food downstairs if you can move quickly. We leave in twenty minutes."

Still groggy, James put it together in his head. The remaining team was about to leave the farmhouse. "Why?" he asked finally.

"We have a location to look for the missing men. Of course, it might be the wrong place entirely," she cautioned, and James had been in business long enough to recognize when someone was trying to manage a client's expectations.

The team that went to hunt for Anatoly's friends had not returned, but James assumed they were the source of this information. He'd feared Nina's plan was to leave him behind, isolated without news in the farmhouse, perhaps with a minder or two to watch him. In seconds, he was wide awake.

James had had one other conversation with Nina since refusing to return to Kyiv, approaching her in her corner office in the barn to ask again about Anatoly and his present circumstances. He was still furious at his onetime friend's manipulation of his own plea for help, but James's ire had cooled somewhat when he learned that Anatoly really had sought out—and apparently found—Gustaw and his captors. Clearly something had gone wrong with the plan to free him, and Anatoly had opportunistically taken the cash James provided for that purpose.

Obviously, he could never trust the Russian again, but no one at the farmhouse had given him a satisfactory explanation of why the ransom plan failed in the first place. They just said the captors had changed their minds about letting Gustaw go. He would like to have heard it from Anatoly directly, but Nina made it clear that that would only happen when he got to Kyiv.

"Surely I could speak to him on the telephone?"

"Too dangerous," she insisted. "What if our communications are being monitored? Do you want to alert the kidnappers that we have Anatoly?"

As far-fetched as that concern sounded, as with everything else in this improbable situation, he couldn't rule out its legitimacy.

"Was there something else you needed?"

"If you won't let me talk to Anatoly, could you at least tell me where he is and what you're doing with him?"

She frowned with the hesitation of someone unused to being second-guessed.

"He is still our guest in Kyiv, if that's what you're wondering. My people continue to question him, but he has cooperated with our inquiry and these interviews have remained . . ." she paused before finishing the sentence ". . . cordial."

"And how long do you expect he will remain your . . ." he inserted a similar break in his own sentence ". . . guest?"

"Until we find and recover our missing men or until we are confident he can't help us any further." She appraised him and let her expression soften. "I can see you are still worrying about him, which is more than he did for you when he stole your money and abandoned you in Mariupol. You needn't. All his needs are being met. But he knows people who know the people who took Gustaw. Maybe the same ones responsible for Marko and Stepan disappearing. We may need his help to contact these people. I can't release him and risk him leaving town again." She paused, allowing her logic to penetrate through his unspoken objections until he reluctantly nodded.

So, he turned to small talk, hoping to smooth the awkwardness of her refusing what had seemed a simple request.

"What is this place, anyway, a farm?" he asked. "Where are the farmers?"

"This was my grandparents' place, in their later years, anyway," she explained. "A big agricultural company leases the land now to grow sunflowers, along with most of the neighbors' plots, but the house makes a convenient secondary office."

Office indeed, James thought, considering the full range of room, board, privacy, and storage options offered by the location. Meetings seemed to take place in the living room, and the only desk he had seen was the one in his bedroom, unless you counted the table in the barn where Nina did her solitary thinking. And he had a feeling those metal cabinets on the far wall were not storing file folders.

James seemed to recall seeing rolling fields of sunflowers on his long-ago visits to Ukraine, but only in passing, from the window of a moving car or train. Apparently, it was too early in the year for the plants around Nina's farm to be mature and blooming.

"So, you would visit your grandparents here when you were a child?"

"A teenager. It took some time for the government to figure out a system for giving the land back and deciding who was going to get which plot. It's not far from where their parents were driven from their farms during collectivization. And the house and barn were already here to be renovated and made livable again."

"What a lovely inheritance. It must be beautiful in the summer," he said, wanting to imagine her as a little girl in a white eyelet dress playing hide-and-seek among the sunflowers. "And how nice that you've been able to repurpose it. I'm sure a lot of people would have been tempted to sell the place, living so far away."

"Sell my grandparents' farm?" She half-laughed and shook her head at the thought. "Anyway, it wouldn't be possible, you know. Ukrainian farmland can't really be sold."

"What do you mean?" It had been decades since the Soviet Union collapsed. Could there still be land restrictions of that kind on the books?

"It's because of the Holodomor," she said, invoking the Stalin-era famine that killed millions of Ukrainians after they were forced into collective farming. "After Communism ended, the farm workers were all given a plot of land so that they would always have a place to grow food. The government didn't want big foreign companies coming in and buying it away from them for a pittance, so they made it illegal to sell land to corporations or foreigners. I'm sure the laws will change someday, but for now, this land can only be leased."

He shook his head at the poor logic and inefficiency of that system. Between endemic corruption and its undeclared war with Russia and its own separatists, Ukraine had enough challenges. Why handicap the industry that had made Ukraine the breadbasket of the Soviet Union? Nina didn't look like she regretted the restriction, however. He wondered how these buildings had been used before she and Marko started their security business.

"Well, it's a nice, peaceful part of the country," James said. "Thank you for letting me stay here with your team. If not for our missing friends, I'm sure it would be very relaxing."

"Maybe I'll turn it into a little hotel someday," she suggested lightly before her expression hardened again.

"By the way, I have something that might help you occupy your time while we wait for word."

She reached into a backpack sitting on the floor next to her chair and withdrew his laptop. James took the device, thanked her, and retreated, reading her suggestion as a request not to bother her again until she came to him with news. He had been given no updates since.

James stumbled out the back door eighteen and a half minutes after Nina woke him, suitcase handle in one hand, a mug of coffee and two slices of toast wrapped in a napkin wedged in the other. Two of the sinister black SUVs from the barn were lined up in the driveway, engines idling. The modest compact car in which he and Nina had arrived sat neglected where she'd parked it upon arrival.

James wheeled his carry-on to the back of one of the vehicles and handed it over to a commando loading tactical gear and hard-sided black cases into the cargo area. The man accepted and stowed it without comment.

"Where are we headed?" he asked, but the man ignored the question and James moved aside to drink his coffee and eat his half-smashed toast.

Nina came out of the barn, noticed him, and nodded in acknowledgment. He smiled and waved her over, but she didn't approach to explain any more about their plans. James turned away to lick the melted butter from the side of his hand like blood from a wound.

In five minutes, they were piling into the SUVs. James headed for the one where his suitcase was stowed, and no one moved to correct him. He was already inside with his seatbelt buckled when he noticed that Nina was climbing behind the wheel of the other vehicle.

They moved forward on the gravel driveway, turned right onto the highway, and accelerated in the gray morning light, a high-speed convoy of two sleek, heavy conveyances packed with armed, trained mercenaries on a mission no one had explained to him. He wished there had been time for a shower.

As the kilometers rolled by outside, James rested his head against the cool window glass and tried to doze, kicking himself for not keeping his laptop accessible to pass the time. His fellow travelers stared impassively forward or played hand-held videogames. For some reason they were not wielding iPhones, as Americans their age—James's children included—certainly would have been. Perhaps cell reception was poor in this part of Ukraine.

He assumed their trip would be short—the same hour or so he and Nina traversed to leave Mariupol. But they were still driving seemingly hours later, when the vehicles pulled into a public park for a much-needed restroom break.

He emerged from the men's room and looked around for Nina, who had her team organized in a small semicircle around her. They were no longer speaking in English. He hovered on the edge of the group until they finished, then rushed to intercept her.

"Where are we going?" he asked. "What's the plan?"

Nina gave him a sober look, reached up to touch his right shoulder, and ushered him behind one of the vehicles, a little away from the group of mercenaries.

"We're about to cross into rebel-held eastern Ukraine, James. That's where we think the men have been taken. If you don't want to join us, I'll have someone come get you and drive you to Kyiv. This is your last chance to turn back."

"Okay. I understand," he said slowly, waiting for his mind to process her words. "But what do you intend to do when you get there? Do you have their location? A contact for the kidnappers? Do you know how many there are? Are all three men together?"

She waited for his outpouring of questions to subside before speaking.

"A couple of our guys are already there, and they're reasonably confident that they've found the right place. It's not well-guarded, so we're just going to go in and get them. We don't want to lose the element of surprise."

He had told Anna he wasn't going to eastern Ukraine. Matt Larson, too, when James had called his old fraternity brother from the airport a seeming lifetime ago. *What sane person intentionally travels into a war zone?* was the question he'd been asking himself throughout this entire ordeal.

"If I go with you, is there something I can do to help get our friends back?" Why in the world wouldn't she have left him at the farmhouse otherwise?

"If everything goes as planned, you'll sit in the car while we go in and get them. Then we'll all slip back across the front line and head for Kyiv."

All his life, he had done his best to understand the potential downside of a decision before going forward. "And if things don't go as planned?"

Nina hesitated. She avoided making eye contact at first. Finally, she shrugged. "Well, it wouldn't hurt to have an American of means around. Your disappearance would be a much higher-profile affair than mine or Gustaw's. Your family and friends would make a lot of noise. You would be international news. Even the Russian government couldn't shrug that off."

So, he was to be a human shield? How discouraged would the men holding Gustaw be, though, given the enormity of the conspiracy they thought they were protecting? And how much faith should he have in Nina's plan, given her desperation to recover her boyfriend Marko? Was she thinking clearly? Assessing risk appropriately?

But what were his options if he refused to go with them? Would she really abandon him in this park until one of her underlings could come and retrieve him? How would that be a safer choice?

And, in the end, where did he want to be when they found Gustaw? Maybe Nina wasn't giving him a real choice, but he hadn't left himself much of one either.

"Please understand," she said as if reading his mind again, "I have no intention of putting you in any danger, but I know you want to recover Gustaw and Marko as much as I do."

James nodded at that. "Of course I'm going with you."

17

Natalya

Warsaw, Poland

I stood in the kitchen, not moving, after Feliks left, thinking about the groceries needed to restock the refrigerator after being away. Should I be shopping for one person or two? It seemed disloyal to buy only the things that I like—as if my husband's disappearance were some kind of personal holiday for me. But I could picture myself, days later, discarding the wasted items I got in an unpardonable moment of optimism or denial.

What was that young man doing in our office for three hours? I sat in the desk chair, opened an internet browser window, and looked for his search history. Erased, as I knew it must be. I glanced around the desk and rummaged through the wastepaper basket, scrutinizing the room inch by inch for some bread crumb he might have left for me, but there was nothing extra, nothing disturbed, no sign the young man was ever there. I should at least have taken a closer look at the taxi that drove him away.

So, after months of not seeing eye-to-eye with him, I realized I would have to start thinking like Gustaw. If I were to believe Feliks, and I thought I did, then he was following my husband's instructions to try to get sensitive information to a public that had no reason to expect it. Who might he contact? A journalist, probably. We know several of those. Would it matter if I reached out to the wrong one? Surely the Law and

Justice sympathizers had all revealed themselves already. But did those loyalties even matter, in this case, when the potential victims of the plot crossed geographic and political boundaries in ways we wouldn't be able to imagine until it was too late?

I'm sure my mother never guessed when she married my father that she would end up raising her children alone. His Jewish heritage wasn't supposed to matter anymore by then, a generation after Communism had come to Poland to erase such arbitrary, bourgeois distinctions. But it was always there, a footnote in a file somewhere, ready to be discovered when the government needed a reason to rid itself of one more agitator.

My mother never said an unkind word about him, even when she had to whisper in our ears so no one would overhear her praising an exiled traitor. I was too young when he left to remember him much, but to me Father was like a war hero, only instead of being dead and buried on a battlefield somewhere, he was off in Western Europe fighting for the cause of a free Poland. At the time, Western Europe seemed about as remote as heaven anyway.

Meanwhile, Mother worked day and night, stretching her single salary as far as she could, then staying up late and rising early so we would have a clean home, well-mended clothes, and nutritious food. When the cancer came, her body was too worn down to fight it. So, she didn't live to see the freedom he had supposedly left us to achieve. Or learn about the other family he had started as soon as he got to Switzerland.

When I started dating Gustaw, my big sister rolled her eyes and muttered something about "Daddy issues," but I ignored her. How could I be accused of missing someone I didn't even remember? Anyway, my future husband's activist days were supposed to be long past then, no more relevant to our marriage than the guilt he might have felt about letting his first wife manage alone with their young children all those years ago.

Gustaw believed I was indifferent to his causes, his struggles, his will to shape history in a healthy direction. He was wrong about that. But what was the benefit of furthering societal freedom if he himself became a slave to its pursuit? I wanted to be able to enjoy an open and just Poland *with* my husband in our remaining years, whether few or many.

Or, perhaps, none left at all. I shouldn't have been so angry with him so often. Perhaps if I had let him talk to me about what he was doing, we would have had more to go on in looking for him.

One evening about a week before Gustaw went to Kyiv, he arrived home and came into the living room where I was reading a book in my armchair. It was after dinnertime, of course, though we were already past the point where we wanted to linger in each other's company every night. He strode in looking excited, purposeful, and he glanced over at me as he set his briefcase down inside the door. I got the impression he wanted to tell me all about whatever meeting he'd just come from—something he hadn't done in a while. And to be honest, it had been a while since I'd have wanted to hear about it.

I'm sure I didn't look very welcoming that night either. I'd had another phone call with my son in London earlier that day and learned that he and the kids wouldn't be visiting this summer after all. They'd decided on an Italian holiday instead. Well, who could blame them? Of course, I'm glad that they are doing well. They have laptop computers and nice clothes and television sets and can take for granted the kind of travel we never even dreamed of when I was growing up.

But they didn't come for Christmas last year either, and I couldn't help thinking that if he had been able to find a decent job in Poland, I'd at least get to watch my grandchildren grow up. Is that the best that European Union membership has to offer us—prosperity with estrangement? But I know better than to say that sort of thing in front of Gustaw.

So, when he came in, I didn't smile and ask him about his day, as I might have a year ago. He opened his mouth as if to try anyway, and then he stopped, shook his head, and kept walking into the bedroom.

I can't say for sure, but I felt at the time that he had noticed the book I was reading and that was what changed his mind. It was a popular novel, nothing too trashy, but I imagined that he had seen me relaxing in a cozy chair, reading purely for pleasure, and been irritated by it. There I was indulging in frivolous fiction when there were so many weighty matters that needed attention—his attention and that of other serious-minded patriots, of course.

There was a time when I might have followed him into that bedroom and confronted him for judging me, which he would probably have denied doing. On that particular evening, though, discouraged by my son's news, I was too tired to bother. I'd been thinking maybe Gustaw and I could travel to Italy ourselves and join the kids for part of their vacation, if I could drag him away from his efforts to save Poland from the Law and Justice Party for a few days. And then I'd been thinking about how difficult it was going to be to persuade him to go. Without a word spoken between us on the matter, I'd all but convinced myself that I would have to take the trip without him.

Sometimes, when we argued about the time Gustaw spent on what he had lately referred to as his "work," the all-consuming passion with which he followed political and social developments, breathlessly conferring with friends and former colleagues with the fervor of a football fan in World Cup season, I could see the ghosts of my predecessors in his eyes. It's such a cliché, I know, the neglected wife resenting her husband's career, but it didn't change what I felt. Neither did reminding myself that, like those other wives, I had my own work, friends, interests—plenty to occupy myself, if necessary, in the coming years of solitude.

But I should not have let Feliks walk out my front door without knowing where he was going or how to get in touch with him. How will I know if he succeeds in the task my husband set for him? How much difference would it make if he did? If there is one thing we all should have learned in recent years, it is how little the firmly held understanding of one person may interest, let alone convince, another.

18

James

A sport-utility vehicle, eastern Ukraine

He noticed the change first in the air around him. Electricity—anticipation—replaced the casual absorption with which his companions had cradled their tablets and video games. His eyes had been on the scenery, but it was only with the increased alertness in the SUV that he reassessed their progress from smooth open highway to a narrow asphalt road lined with increasingly dense trees. Personally, he would not have smelled danger there. The sun shone cheerfully overhead. He heard no gunfire, saw no plume of smoke in the distance.

"Where are we?" James asked as the driver pulled off the road and bumped down the side of a deep ditch lined with high grass.

"We walk now," someone said as the occupants of both vehicles piled out and began rummaging through the equipment stored in the back. When James got out, however, Nina waved him back inside.

"You will stay here," she explained unequivocally. "We are three kilometers from our destination. You are safer remaining hidden, and we are safer without an untrained companion."

"But what if you don't come back?" he asked, already seated again. "How long should I wait? Whom should I call?"

"We'll be back," she assured him, slinging a short-handled rifle over her shoulder. "No more than three hours, but probably much sooner. Do not worry, Mr. Jensen. We know what we are doing."

She handed him a bottle of room temperature water and a foil-wrapped rectangle that he assumed was a protein bar, shut the car door, and waved her team into formation behind her. They crept out of the ditch on the side opposite the road and migrated slowly out of sight, a crouching herd of black-clad hunters evaporating into the shadows of the trees.

Did they even leave me a set of keys? was James's first thought. He didn't see any in the ignition or center console. He placed the snacks on the seat beside him, checked his watch, and turned around to shuffle through the items in the back until he found a paperback novel he'd picked up at the farmhouse. He flipped it open, hoping to distract himself from Gustaw and the people who were trying to save him.

A few minutes later, ashamed, he closed the book and turned his thoughts firmly toward the commandos and their mission. He reached out to the universe, visualizing a successful, violence-free extraction, willing a good outcome. He was unsure whether this process should be called prayer, meditation, or the power of positive thinking, but it was something he could do during his interminable wait. Throughout his life, he'd always felt better when he knew that others were doing the same for him.

Notwithstanding Matt Larson's taunt during that airport phone call before he left California, James had weighed his Catholic conversion very seriously before taking the plunge twenty years earlier. But it didn't mean to him quite what the Pope might have expected. His own views on such issues as birth control, the death penalty, and a celibate, male-only clergy did not factor into the decision. He did not sign on to a body of rigid dogma so much as a formal belonging in the houses of worship that made him feel most at home. Open day and night, smelling of incense, and architected to reinforce a lofty worldview, Catholic churches had always nurtured his spiritual inclinations, elevated his thoughts, and helped him to believe that some external presence had his back.

An SUV parked in an overgrown drainage ditch in Ukraine wasn't ideal for summoning those sentiments—he preferred his annual retreats to an isolated monastery in the French Alps—but it would have to do. "Please bring Gustaw home safely—and the others, too," he beseeched that presence on a silent loop. "Please bring Gustaw home."

When the litany became intolerably monotonous, he looked at his watch again. It had been barely twenty minutes since the commandos left. How was he to endure another two and a half hours? The protein bar looked inviting—they'd taken no lunch break—but it seemed wiser to save it in case the team's mission took longer than expected. Now that he was alone, he refused to entertain the notion that they might not succeed.

Perhaps he could nap a while to pass the time? Despite the drama soon to be underway down the road, it seemed possible. He'd had an early morning, and his recent activities had been emotionally, if not physically, draining. He turned sideways to lean against one car door and stretched his long legs across the seat toward its opposite, trying to rest his head against the window glass. He closed his eyes, slowed his breathing, and invited lethargy to flow through him.

A moment later—surely no more than that—his eyes popped open. He needed to answer the call of nature. From what Nina said, he was two miles from wherever she and the guys were headed. No harm in getting out and walking into the trees for a little privacy.

A light wind greeted him as he exited the vehicle, but he did not turn back for his jacket. Walking would warm him, and this was a quick errand. He ducked into the trees, looking for a dense patch of shrubs to use as a screen.

He was just zipping up when the low rumble of distant voices reached him. The commandos returning? He glanced at his watch. It had been almost an hour. He must have dozed a little after all.

He couldn't hear the voices well enough to make out what language they were speaking, let alone what they might be saying. Hesitating to reveal himself, he hovered in the brush, squinting toward the SUVs as they approached. He could see only four figures—too few to be Nina's team returning, unless they had split up. Or worse.

The voices grew silent, but James could picture the figures entering the ditch where the vehicles sat as clearly as if his view were unobstructed.

He crouched down, hoping to get a better look, and cringed as his shoulder grazed a branch, setting off a rustling that sounded to his ears like an avalanche. He froze for a moment, but nothing happened, so he expelled the breath he was holding and listened to his heart pound as it squeezed oxygen through his deprived bloodstream.

If it was Nina's team, they would notice his absence and call for him. Then he could emerge from hiding. Otherwise, he was safest waiting until the intruders had gone.

A car door opened and closed, accompanied by animated cursing. The voices conferred—there was no attempt at quiet now—and boots came stomping through the trees.

He knew they would find him, as near as he was to the vehicles, themselves poorly hidden in the ditch, probably advertised by a telltale trail of flattened grass. Nina must have assumed they were far enough away to avoid casual detection.

James shivered as a chilly gust of wind raised goose bumps on his arms. He looked around frantically, hoping to spot some escape route. He didn't see anyone coming to save him, though, and it was too late to run, even if he had known which way to go.

Besides, Nina had brought him along as insurance in case she and the others were captured. Perhaps becoming a fellow captive was the only thing he could do now to help Gustaw or the rest of them.

He didn't want to be discovered cowering behind a bush, however, so he stood up straight and raised his hands with his palms out to show he was unarmed.

Their eyes turned his way.

His captors were not Russian soldiers. That much was evident even though James had never encountered Russian soldiers, in or out of uniform, except on television. These men were older, heavyset, semi-shaven and slovenly, their automatic weapons hanging slack against their sides. Pro-Russia militiamen, he assumed. They communicated with a series of grunts and menacing gestures that worked reasonably well to inform him that he was to go with them and not try any funny business.

They guided him back to the SUVs, which two of them were searching, and directed a lot of what he took to be pointed questions at him. His mind reeled with the awareness that he was their prisoner now, but he managed to shrug and shake his head in response to their questioning, hoping to convey confusion rather than defiance.

Fortunately, Nina's team seemed to have taken all the weapons, but it was obvious from the foam voids lining the cases exactly what had been transported in them. He gestured toward his own body, pointing out his lack of tactical gear, inviting a more thorough search, which they did not bother to perform. Clearly, he was not part of the strike team. Proximity was the only thing to link him with the vehicles.

Then someone found his book and began to address him in thickly accented English.

"What is your name, sir?" The grizzled man blurted out the honorific, which sounded less like a courtesy than a reversion to rudimentary foreign language training, as if, somewhere in this man's mind, "I am going to the library" and "Where is the bus station?" awaited their moment to cross his lips. James grinned to himself at the thought, eliciting angry looks from the paramilitaries. His smile fell.

"My name is James," he answered, articulating carefully. "What is yours?"

His questioner nodded, satisfied, but ignored the query. "What you do here?"

"I am looking for my friend." He couldn't think fast enough to make up a lie.

"Your friend come here?" The man pointed to the SUV.

"No. He came before." James gestured behind himself, indicating the past.

The man's forehead crinkled as he tried to puzzle out this message. Finally, he shook his head.

"Not here," he insisted. "No English here."

"No," James agreed. "Not English. Polish. From Poland. Warsaw." He would save his own nationality as a trump card, just in case. He hoped it would prove to be the bargaining chip Nina had anticipated.

The men chattered to each other for a few minutes while James pondered what exactly he had just done. There was no way to know if these men had come looking for him because Nina had been captured and revealed his location or if it was just rotten luck that their patrol came this way. For all he knew, they were only looking for a quiet place to eat their lunch.

The men seemed to have reached a consensus, but they did not try to explain it to him.

"You come with us," his interlocutor insisted, gesturing off into the trees in what may or may not have been the direction Nina's team took.

James reluctantly joined their march, regretting his left-behind jacket and provisions but preferring not to underscore his association with the vehicles by laying claim to what was inside them.

The ground was uneven and his captors' pace brisk, but James managed to keep up, and they were patient when he slowed or stumbled. They seemed confident he would obey them and not attempt to escape.

Nor did he intend to try. The moment for such heroics, if there had ever been one, had passed. Back in the thicket, he had chosen a dignified surrender rather than a frantic and probably futile, if not lethal, retreat. So, he did his best to retain the dignity he had bought with his last moments of free will. There was nothing in the trees they passed to tell him whether he was a hero or a fool.

He hadn't been bound or blindfolded, he reminded himself, containing the panic that threatened to rise through him as he focused on the next step, then the next. The men had been civil, and he could only hope to keep their interactions on that level as long as possible.

While he dodged hanging branches and watched for exposed tree roots, James recalled Gustaw's letter and the story of his friend's abduction. What would happen to him when they reached their destination? Some kind of interview or interrogation, of course, about what he was doing in the woods and his connection to the empty SUVs.

What could he tell them but the truth—enough of it to seem plausible anyway? He was looking for his missing friend and hired a private firm to help him look. As to why they were looking here or why they brought heavy tactical gear along, well, he was only their client, and they had not shared their intelligence or reasoning with him. Perhaps that would be sufficient explanation. He wondered if they had found copies of Gustaw's letter in the vehicles.

Anna would have been furious to see him in this position. "All you had to do was come home!" he imagined her shouting at him, although Anna never shouted. Surely his being taken prisoner, after all the chances he had to turn back, warranted an exception.

He was certain these men or their superiors would confine him somehow and wondered if they would restrain or hurt him as well. Gustaw had avoided writing about what his jailers had done to him, leaving it up to James's imagination to invent the indignities and torments his friend had suffered. It had not been a pleasant exercise. Now, with his own skin on the line, those earlier mental pictures returned in high-definition, complete with surround sound audio of his agonized screams. He hoped he would be as brave as his friend. He prayed, with enough reverence to fill a soaring cathedral, that he wouldn't have to be.

19

James

Evening, a forest in eastern Ukraine

Booms echoed off the labyrinthine halls as James ran, stumbling, through pale yellow corridors, feet slapping the cold tile. Was he barefoot? He leaned on Marko—where had he come from? He felt something wet on the publisher's shirt, but the Ukrainian's grip on his arm was firm and steady, guiding him around corners and through doorways as if he knew where they were going.

Gray surrounded them now. A cold wind told James they were outdoors, and the ground became uneven. The noises, too, ceased their echoing but continued unabated as they ran, other footsteps tramping around them punctuated by sharp shots, each a new explosion of light inside his head.

He'd always been a good runner, did it every day, loved his jogs along the beach at daybreak back in California. The ground had some give to it there, for sure, not like this root-riddled clay tripping him up, slicing into his soles. Sometimes the dogs ran with him.

No, that wasn't right. The dogs were at La Mancha, his vacation house on Spain's Costa del Sol with its pristine teal-blue water, schools of dolphins so close you could see them from the shore. He liked to stop and watch them frolic for a few minutes at the end of his workouts. It was his reward for the early morning hour and exertion, for putting his health and fitness first when people decades younger—his own children—were still asleep, unconcerned about following in their late grandfather's path: that fatal, chest-clenching bolt from the blue on poker night that left the forty-two-year-old James stunned and adrift. La Mancha, home to impossible dreams and naïve fools, had been his father's legacy to the family.

He craned his head into the distance, hoping for a glimpse of those dolphins playing in the surf, but everything around him was trees—clumps of pine and oak, not the palms and bamboo his cousin Greg might have dodged on his last march through the Vietnamese jungle.

James shivered and tasted metal. Then the painful brightness in his head plunged into his chest, a roller coaster on its big descent, and he was careening down with it, Marko's slick fingers grasping frantically at his arm as he teetered.

"I think it's his heart," said a voice from far away, and that made sense to James: weak-hearted American capitalist heartsick at the disappearance of his friend loses heart in the middle of a Ukrainian forest during a firefight at dusk. That vital organ so rich in metaphor, indifferent to his years of careful attention, had finally broken.

Gentle hands supported him as he was lowered to the ground, a soft bed of pine needles with one persistent tree root poking into his spine, its sharpness spiking up through his chest no matter how much he tried to wriggle away. Until it stopped.

Now he communed with the dolphins, their smooth, cool skin sliding past him as he floated, luxuriating in the warm, salty Mediterranean water. The dogs watched him from the shore, even their tails motionless, anticipating their master's return. But he was comfortable here, like an infant in the womb, a being of pure sensation.

20

Natalya

Warsaw, Poland

I phoned UkraineLaw and told Nina everything Feliks had said about his plans with Gustaw and about his disappearance into the night. She reciprocated by letting me know that she had found James in Mariupol and removed him from the city. I was assured that the search for my husband would continue. With no new information to exchange, soon my calls to Kyiv dwindled and petered out.

When Gustaw's friends in the Polish press learned that he was missing, I was the recipient of fancy meals, enveloping hugs, and countless offers to exert pressure by making his disappearance public. I declined them all, afraid that if Gustaw were still alive, publicity might tempt his captors to permanently dispose of all evidence that they ever had him.

Instead, I probed for news of Feliks or confirmation of the unholy alliance between Russia, China, and the Republican candidate for U.S. president. I could see that these journalists and publishers understood the stakes, but there was no recognition in their eyes when I mentioned the conspiracy. Soon they were placating me with the improbability of such an arrangement, the unlikelihood that the third conspirator would ever be in power anyway. In meeting after meeting, warm greetings gave way to cold comforts. I was faced with the consensus that my husband had disappeared over a farce.

When I finally ran out of people to call for news, I began the notifications, starting with Gustaw's ex-wives and children, his sister's family, his colleagues and cohorts. Then the information spread on its own, organically, until everyone who should know did. Some called, others wrote, a few even brought food to the house, but we would not have the finality of a funeral or memorial service, even a legal declaration that he would not be returning to us, for some time to come.

I opened his mail, canceled his appointments, packed up his things, and tried to tidy away a life that may or may not ever be resumed. They were quiet tasks, echoing in the new silence of our home. My frustrating, headstrong husband and everything he had been and was ever likely to become remains persistently absent.

Marko wrote me a heartfelt remembrance of Gustaw, with recollections dating back twenty years to Polish Academic Publishing's original investment in UkraineLaw. It was only after reading it that I understood that Marko and his detective friend had both returned to Kyiv and their former lives.

So, what became of Feliks and his mission to pass along the supposed proof he hand-carried all the way across Ukraine to Poland? Why did no one sound the alarm? Marko, my only link to the young man, claims to know nothing of his fate, and it is a mystery I lack the energy to pursue further. I have followed my husband's obsession far enough, and now that I understand what he had been doing and why, I choose not to become its next casualty.

21

James

It wasn't discomfort that dragged him from the peaceful sea, though there was plenty of that. A persistent beeping penetrated his calm, and he opened his eyes to the harsh industrial light of what he knew immediately must be a hospital room.

He couldn't lift his head or turn it. He wanted to ask a nurse to make the beeping stop, but when he tried to lick his lips, his tongue found hard plastic and he gagged a little in the empty room.

Only his eyes moved, and they could not peer far enough to read the data on the monitors, which were surely tracking his heartbeat, blood pressure, oxygen level. He'd been through the procedure to correct heart arrhythmia three times in the past, and each had ended in just such a recovery room. This time felt different, somehow. He wondered if the attempt had been successful, but there was no one around to tell him, so he allowed the metronomic beeping to lull him back to sleep.

When he heard the beeping again, it was accompanied by soft voices. He parted his lids slowly, squinting in anticipation of the sharp fluorescents overhead.

"You're awake," said a man, his voice crisp, businesslike. Marko?

Through the veil of fog in his head, James recalled being taken prisoner by the men searching the SUVs. Then he was fleeing through the woods, gunshots all around, and somehow the Ukrainian publisher was next to him. Had Nina rescued the missing men?

Then that would mean . . . He tried to sit up and see who else was in the room, but his body ignored his efforts.

"You're in a hospital in Kyiv," Marko explained slowly, standing over the bed, making eye contact, perhaps waiting for some kind of response. "You've had a serious heart attack, but the doctors say you are stable now. Your wife is flying in tomorrow."

Anna. She would know what to do about the harsh light and his body that wouldn't obey him.

Meanwhile, he wanted answers. He willed the questions into his unblinking eyes and stared back at Marko, who looked as clean-pressed and unruffled as ever, although his left arm dangled in a sling. With his right, he pulled a chair up next to the bed and sat down with a sigh.

"Gustaw is still missing," he said. "He wasn't being held with Stepan and me. I don't know, maybe he *was* there, but then they moved him. Stepan seems to think so—said he talked to him through the wall in his cell. In any case, Nina's team didn't find him before the Russians realized what was going on and started shooting. Then it was all we could do to get ourselves out of there. One of our guys was shot in the abdomen, so we had to leave quickly. He's still in surgery."

Of the time between being taken prisoner and running through the forest, James remembered nothing at all. How was that possible? Had he hit his head? Been drugged by his captors? It couldn't have been more than a few hours, though, if Nina and the commandos were still around to rescue him. He wondered what Nina's men might have done to the paramilitaries, who had treated him decently enough, considering. Were they dead? Shot? Unconscious and tied up in the woods? Better them than him, of course, but still.

"Nina said you were brought to the same place we were. That they were questioning you when our team went by the room," Marko said. "We were lucky the door was open, and they were able to just walk in and take you. When you feel better, you can tell us about your conversation."

James could only look up at Marko, unable to communicate that he had no idea what he might have told his captors. Had he revealed that Nina and her team were coming to rescue their friends? That he—and they—knew about the international conspiracy Gustaw had uncovered? Could they all still be in danger?

"It was the Russian Army who had us, you know," Marko mused, almost to himself. "Oh, they didn't wear insignia, but it's easy to recognize when you're dealing with official powers. The chain of command is more disciplined, less thuggish. The soldiers obey because they're trained to, not because their mobster boss will shoot them in the head otherwise. Of course, I don't mean to imply the Russian officers wouldn't do that, too. People are capable of so much more than most of them ever have a chance to learn, thank God."

He shook his head, and James wondered what dark memories Marko was banishing with that gesture. He had always thought of people pushing their limits as a positive thing—developing new skills, overcoming fears, spreading their wings. His time in Ukraine had hinted at the opposite point: that people pushed far enough could succumb to the stress with violence and abuse. Perhaps his paramilitary captors had been middle school art teachers or prize rose gardeners before conflict came to their neighborhoods. Perhaps they would be again someday.

"I'd like to have stayed a publisher," Marko went on matter-of-factly, his statement melding perfectly into James's train of thought. "Not much chance of that anymore. Polish Academic Publishing didn't want anything to do with UkraineLaw even before Gustaw disappeared here. I guess I'm in the security business full-time now." He added a shrug.

"Whatever you think of my management decisions, though, we did keep the publishing house going years longer than our competition, and when historical change made it impossible to continue, I adapted. Isn't that what you always used to say we should be doing—anticipating the future so we could move forward to meet it?"

James had said that, yes. It was his argument for digitizing content at UkraineLaw, for making the move to e-books at Polish Academic

Publishing, for founding the company to sell books online in China when Amazon was just becoming a household name at home.

"Surely the rising nationalism in Hungary and Poland and even America today is just such an evolution," Marko was saying. "Gustaw could have chosen to ride it out rather than fighting against it. What has his grand gesture accomplished, after all?"

Marko left the question hanging, his conversation partner unable to accept or refute the logic of his argument aloud. But James never meant that people should just give up when things got challenging.

"All that upheaval at the end of Soviet Communism thrust so many of us into the swirling cauldron of history," Marko continued with unexpected lyricism. "We touched lives we never would have connected with otherwise, changing them, changing ourselves. Unlike Gustaw, I had not sought those changes. Unlike you, they did not confirm my long-held philosophical beliefs."

James was stunned by these analytical reflections from an associate he would have dismissed with a few unflattering descriptors: institutionalist, self-dealer, whatever the opposite of "visionary" was. All these years that he'd been bouncing ideas off of Gustaw, maybe they should have included Marko in the conversations.

Was the Ukrainian—a Communist government insider turned private company manager under capitalism turned security company owner in a time of conflict—the great adapter that James himself had always aspired to be? He'd never considered before how adaptation and opportunism could be two sides of the same coin.

"We *will* keep looking for him." Marko waited for his promise to sink in, searching James's eyes again for something like acknowledgment.

But disappointment dragged James back inside himself, drifting off again, and soon he was peacefully in the past, privatizing a publishing house, printing an uncensored encyclopedia, bringing capitalism and free thought to the once-Communist masses with Gustaw at his side.

"Jimmy, are you awake?" Anna asked in a tone loud enough to leave no doubt. This was fortunate, because his eyes were still the only part of his body he had any control over.

His nurses had been resorting to the "blink once for 'yes,' twice for 'no'" method of communication and, truthfully, he was relieved when he could muster the energy to make that work.

He was very sick, that much was clear. How soon he would get better was something no one had thought to explain to him. Now that his wife had arrived, though, everything would start to get sorted out.

"I talked to the insurance company, and we're going to have you flown to Germany," she was saying. "Dr. Erickson is sending all your records."

Marko was standing behind her shoulder. Was he the other part of the "we" she'd spoken of?

"You'll get good care there," he said. "They have heart specialists, the best equipment."

James wanted to go home, to sleep in his own bed for a while, but no one presented that as an option. He must not be well enough for the longer trip.

A recurring half-stupor settled him into unconsciousness, providing blessed relief from the jostling, ambient noise, and airplane pressurization that punctuated his transit. He'd never slept so much in his life.

He came to in a different bed with different machines but the same bright lights and monotonous beeping. Anna was there, and a stream of doctors and nurses and lab techs paraded through his room in scrubs and white coats injecting or removing fluids, rustling through his chart, and peering at the machines before wandering out again.

Then one day an oddly familiar voice boomed at him as he opened his eyes.

"James!" Matt Larson peered down at him from the bedside, addressing him with oratorical style and volume. "How are you feeling?" The question created the odd impression that his old fraternity brother was the one overseeing his care.

They had removed the tube from James's throat, but his prior attempts to speak had emerged as unpredictable croaks. When he moved his lips now, a nurse stepped forward to moisten his mouth with a tiny sponge on a lollipop stick.

"That's alright, old boy, don't try to talk," Matt urged, patting him on the arm. "Thank you, my dear. I can look after him for a bit."

He dismissed the nurse with a smile and pulled the bedside chair around to where James could see him when he sat down. The metal feet gave an unnerving squeal as they scraped across the tile floor.

"Just press the call button if you need anything. I'll be back with his medication in a little while," the nurse promised as she left, pulling the curtain closed around them.

"There, now. Just the two of us," Matt declared. "I sent Anna back to her hotel to rest. Poor woman looked like she hadn't left your side in days."

Days? How long had he been here? And what was Matt doing in Germany?

"I had a conference to attend in London," his friend was saying, as if he'd spoken his question aloud. "When I heard what happened to you, I decided to take an extra day and come visit.

"It's a real shame, how things went in Ukraine. If only you'd stayed out of the war zone . . ."

Matt let the what-if trail away, shaking his head ruefully, leaving James to reach the silent conclusion that he had done this to himself—as if he needed anyone to tell him that.

"At least you're alive," Matt observed, like that should be some consolation.

James didn't understand his prognosis. They kept telling him he was stable, that he might be able to fly back to California in a week or two. There was talk of physical therapy, of round-the-clock, at-home care. But when he would be able to sit, stand, walk, run along the beach with his dogs again . . . No one was talking about that, and with his erratic, froggy voice and boundless exhaustion, it was more than he could manage to ask the question.

Somewhere back in Ukraine or Russia, Gustaw was a prisoner—or worse—his freedom gone, as James's had been when he stood up out of that thicket and allowed the paramilitaries to capture him. James's body had been rescued, but his freedom was still gone. He hadn't been able to make a single decision for himself since that moment. Lately, it was hard to feel that he ever would again.

Matt was watching him closely, perhaps trying to intuit the direction of his thoughts. James sensed a wiliness in his gaze, like the master spy was calculating or plotting something. His gaze sharpened even more when he realized James was staring back at him.

"I have no idea what's become of your friend, James. I want to be very clear about that. And I didn't lift a finger against his young messenger, either. Quite the opposite. I offered him my help."

James's lack of response did not dissuade him from continuing to speak.

"Not with his mission, of course, spreading some crackpot theory to undermine American democracy. And I can't believe you would've gotten caught up in such clumsy, liberal nonsense either. No, I offered to assist him with relocation, university applications, housing—a fresh start in a Western country far from the thugs he worked for, who were probably the same people who put him up to telling these tall tales in the first place. I am not a callous person."

Matt leaned in closer, licking his lips while he let the claim sink in.

"But he refused my offer, doubling down on his story, getting all flushed and waving his arms, demanding that I believe him with all the fury of idealistic youth. I have taught university students for thirty-five years, James. His naïve passion was not new to me.

"I did take away his flash drive before contacting security to escort him from the building, though. He raised quite a fuss about that, calling me a thief and a liar. But who were they going to believe, some screaming, skinny kid with an accent you could cut with a knife or one of their own senior fellows, standing unruffled in his office doorway with an air of long-suffering patience? I've practiced that look in the mirror, James. It always closes the deal."

It took James some time to sort out who Matt was talking about and what he meant by "crackpot theory" and "liberal nonsense." When he did, he couldn't tell if Matt was bragging about or confessing to his unexpected role in whatever had gone awry with Gustaw's plans. In any case, Matt's monologue hadn't paused.

". . . Gustaw and the kid must've figured an American think tank could disseminate their propaganda more effectively than an Eastern European newspaper. They knew I knew you, so I was the perfect mark. But why would I take their word for such an improbable story? Russia is one thing, but Donald Trump has spent his entire—albeit short—political campaign railing against China. Did Gustaw really imagine they would be joining forces in the unlikely event he ever took office?

"The young man kept insisting: 'I'm not just a messenger, I'm a witness. I was there. You can interview me. I saw everything.'

"Well, after I looked at the flash drive, I could see why he needed to make that argument. Documents anyone could've forged and low-resolution videos of people sitting around a board table were not going to change the course of a city council campaign, let alone an alleged international plot, even if they were in a language people could understand, which these were not."

Matt shook his head in a facsimile of sadness or disappointment.

"It's hard for me to believe I took the only existing copy of his 'evidence,' weak as it was. But if he kept up that *'I'm a witness—I know everything'* routine wherever he went next? That could explain why no one knows where he is now. It's truly unfortunate if he's had a misadventure of some kind, but it's none of my doing. He was in league with shady individuals of dubious character before I ever met him."

James tried to croak out an objection, though he wasn't sure why he felt called on to defend some young man he didn't know. In any case, the sound emerged weak and inarticulate from his throat.

Matt paused politely, giving him a chance to try again, but the effort had exhausted him. He collapsed back into his pillow, defeated.

"Frankly, James, I have no idea how the kid even made it across the international borders to find me, but it shows that he's resourceful and maybe had some high-level help.

"Just between you and me, though, imagine if I *did* share that story with someone who could dig into the truth of it. Just the act of looking into such an allegation would bolster its credibility. It takes so little for people to believe wild accusations these days."

James would have begged his friend to do just that, for Gustaw's sake, but he could see it was a non-starter, for Matt as well as for his own powers of speech.

"Don't worry, though," the analyst said, back to consoling him. "That guy'll never be elected anyway. All the polls say as much. So even if the conspiracy were real—which of course it's not—there's no chance anything would ever come of it. I'm afraid you and your friends went through all of this for nothing."

Matt paused, shaking his head, and it seemed he was going to leave the thought there, on that depressing, if sympathetic note. But then he looked up to meet James's eyes, and there was the sudden sheen of excitement in his own.

"If he did win, though . . . Well, wouldn't that be something? There is so much good someone like him could do for the country—tax reform, deregulation, judicial appointments that would finally put a brake on left-wing activist judges. And that doesn't even touch on where single-party rule could take us in foreign policy—getting the Iranians under control or the Palestinians back to the negotiating table for a more secure Israel."

Matt held up his hands before continuing. He added a confident smile.

"No, James. I'm sorry about your friend, but I'm afraid things turned out exactly as they should have with this one. Anna will see that you get the best care, and I'm sure you'll be past this little blip in no time. What lasting harm could there possibly be?"

Afterword/Acknowledgments

Underground Man is a work of fiction. The 2016-era events of the story are products of my imagination.

However, the characters of James Jensen and Gustaw Bogutsky and the backstory of their friendship were inspired by historical events. The end of Communist rule in Poland, and the subsequent privatization of its state-owned enterprises, did indeed bring together a Polish underground publisher and an American entrepreneur who worked together to lead one of those companies.

Grzegorz Boguta and James Jameson met in 1989 as the Iron Curtain was crumbling. At that time, Jameson led an international organization of company executives and was hoping to launch a new chapter of that organization in Poland. Boguta was looking for technical assistance to help the underground publishing company he had founded as an anti-Communist activist evolve into a profitable free-market business. Neither man found quite what he was looking for in that first encounter.

A short time later, Boguta was hired to run PWN, Poland's prestigious technical and scientific publishing house. At his invitation, Jameson organized a group of Western investors to buy into the endeavor, and the Polish government accepted their bid for half of the company. This professional collaboration lasted for several years, but the friendship it sparked has endured decades longer.

My own interest in their story—and the plot of *Underground Man*—sprang from the question of how two aging characters might respond at seeing the brave new world they had built as ambitious young men start to fall apart as they neared the end of their careers.

When *Underground Man* was conceived, the war in eastern Ukraine was considered a historical footnote to many in the West. Some doubted that American readers would be interested in a tale set in an out-of-the-way place like Eastern Europe.

With Russia's 2022 invasion, however, Ukraine displaced the COVID pandemic as the center of geopolitical attention. Within a few months, Europe's first land war in decades helped shift global political alliances, disrupted the international flow of energy and grain, and raised questions about the future of self-determination and stable national borders, all amid the seemingly renewed threat of nuclear war.

One person who did predict this situation well ahead of time was Grzegorz Boguta, the real-life inspiration for the *Underground Man* of the title. His gloomy predictions about Vladimir Putin's aggressive expansionism and the rising popularity of autocracy in Western Europe seem to be coming more-or-less true years after he first uttered them during our conversations in 2015 and 2016.

I am grateful for James Jameson's patronage of this project and to both men for generously sharing the details of their stories. I would also like to thank Steve Anderson and Deborah Murrell for their editing skills, as well as all the others who read and provided feedback on various drafts of this endeavor, including Kimi Canete, Sarah Johnson, Divina Infusino, Jaime McCloskey, and Sara Rupp.

Christina Murray
Vista, California
August 2024

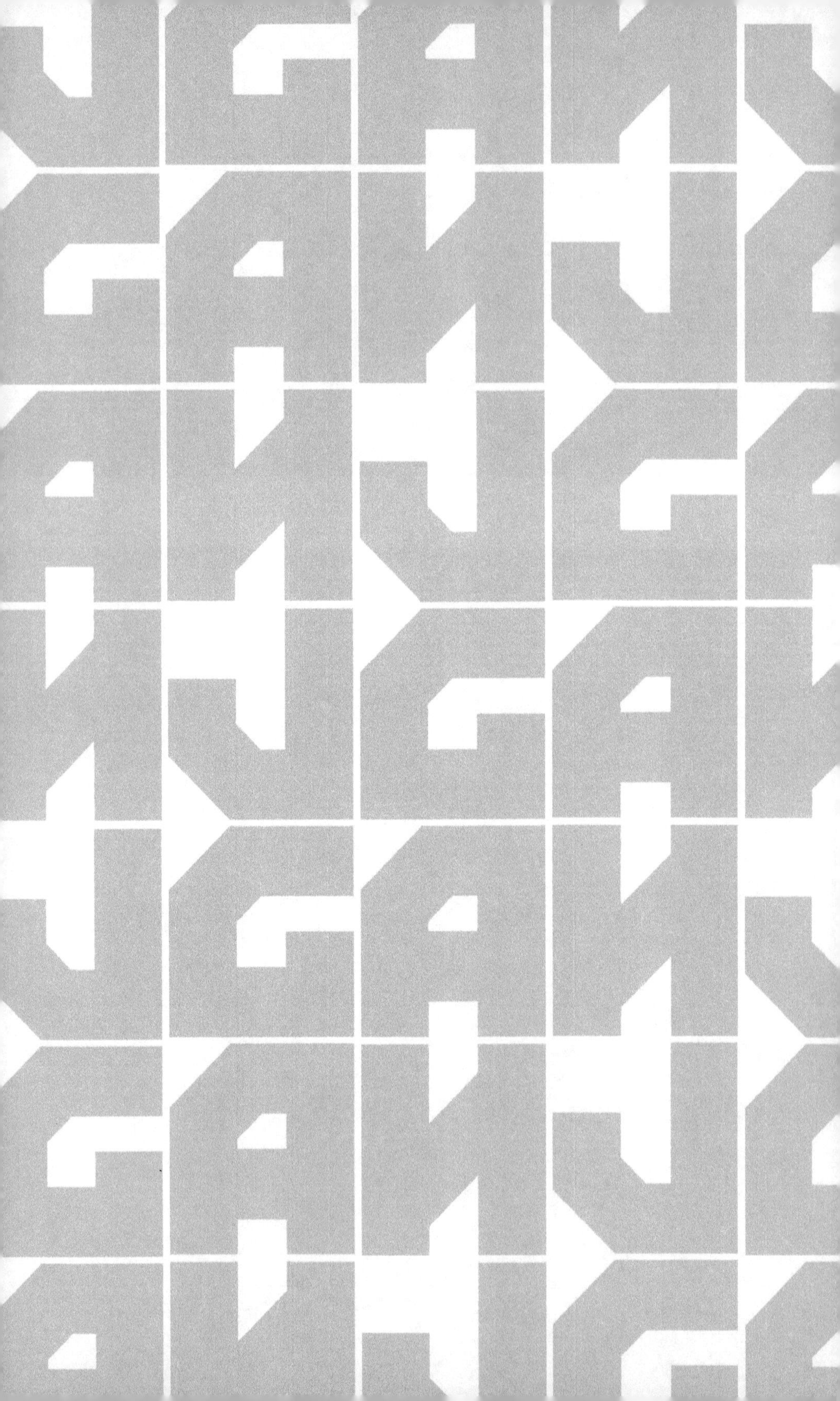

www.ingramcontent.com/pod-product-compliance
Lightning Source LLC
Chambersburg PA
CBHW020501310726
48979CB00016B/2748/J

9798990305021